PRINTOUT OF A SCAM

CONFIDENTIAL TO PRINCIPALS. FBI/TREASURY

PRELIMINARY OBSERVATIONS FOR THE PURPOSE OF EFFECTING A SOLUTION TO THEFT OR EMBEZZLEMENT BY A PERSON OR PERSONS UNKNOWN.

THIS OFFICE CONSIDERS IT OF URGENT CONCERN THAT THE METHOD(S) USED TO EFFECT UNAUTHORIZED MONEY TRANSFERS BY ELECTRONIC MEANS IS/ARE AT PRESENT UNKNOWN.

THE COMPUTER DEPARTMENTS OF IBM, CHASE MANHATTAN BANK, TEXACO, LOCKHEED, GM, AND THE U.S. TREASURY ARE UNABLE TO OFFER A TECHNICAL EXPLANATION OF HOW THE CRIMES WERE EXECUTED.

TO DATE 10.2 MILLION DOLLARS ARE MISSING.

EXTREME CAUTION IS ADVISED.

THE TERMINAL TRANSFER

TREVOR MARTIN

Created by the producers of
Wagons West, The Australians, and
The Kent Family Chronicles.

Chairman of the Board: Lyle Kenyon Engel

AVON
PUBLISHERS OF BARD, CAMELOT, DISCUS AND FLARE BOOKS

THE TERMINAL TRANSFER is an original publication of Avon Books. This work has never before appeared in book form.

AVON BOOKS
A division of
The Hearst Corporation
1790 Broadway
New York, New York 10019

Published by arrangement with the author
Library of Congress Catalog Card Number: 84-91098
ISBN: 0-380-88450-X

First Avon Printing, August, 1984

Printed in the U. S. A.

WFH 10 9 8 7 6 5 4 3 2 1

AUTHOR'S NOTE

The individual characters who appear in this book are wholly fictional. No character bears any resemblance to any person, alive or dead, whom I have ever known. Any apparent resemblance of a character to any person alive or dead is entirely coincidental.

On the other hand, names of actual corporations have been employed in order to add a desirable air of realism to the story that I am telling. However, I should add that I personally know of no one who is employed at any of these companies and banks or who has been so employed. Further, so far as I know, none of the events that is described in the book has occurred at any of these businesses.

PART ONE

CHAPTER ONE

Jordan Freeling sat in the window seat, his nose glued to the Plexiglas as the Boeing flew into a rapidly advancing dawn. Since the first light had lifted the blanket of darkness outside, changing it to the visible order of heaven and earth, he could see little but ocean, empty in all directions. Now and then a solitary ship would appear, distinguishable at first more by its wake than its substance and almost motionless on the slate gray panorama six miles below. Soon the gray of the ocean was exchanged for emerald green, surprisingly brilliant in the morning sun, and the long Atlantic crossing was over. The Boeing banked gently toward the south, and Jordan removed his nose from the window. "We're over Ireland," he announced.

"How do you know that?" His mother, in the next seat, was still deep in her magazine.

"Ireland's the first place we hit. I saw the route on an airline map. We just turned right, so we must be headed for London now."

"That's very clever of you, darling."

"I don't recall much about London." Jordan dug into a bag of cookies and bit into one. "Unusual for me. I usually seem to remember everything."

Virginia Freeling gave up trying to read. "It's a long time since we were there, Jordan. Let's see, it must be eleven years ago. You were only four . . . or was it five? Of course you don't remember."

"I can remember clearly when I was five."

"Perhaps it's because there really wasn't much for you to remember. We were in London only a couple of weeks, passing through. We hardly left the hotel. Mostly just to visit the embassy with your father a couple of times."

"Is it fixed now, for Dad to be stationed in London?"

"It seems to be. It's a semipermanent position, and important to your father's career. So it looks as if we'll be living in London for a few years." She looked closely at her son. "Will you miss Washington, Jordan? I mean, your school and your friends there?"

"No, they're nothing that special."

"We must arrange for your schooling as soon as possible. They have opportunities in London for the children of embassy staff. There's an American school with a high academic reputation. . . ."

"Couldn't I go to a British school?"

"Why would you want that? I'd think you'd prefer to be among American children."

"I'm not a child anymore."

"I know. But I wondered if you might feel uncomfortable among British boys. Their whole outlook will be different."

"They're not so different," Jordan countered. "We had a couple of English kids in class in Washington. I got along okay with them." He was silent a moment. "One day I'd like to go to Manchester University."

"Oh. And what's so special about it?"

"It's where the computer was invented."

"Is that so?" Virginia feigned interest.

"They had just one large room, crammed with electronic equipment—old-fashioned thermionic tubes, all glowing with heat. Every time they switched on the equipment, it got so hot it all melted, until they realized it had to be kept cooled."

"Amazing."

"It was so sensitive to variations in electric current they could only operate at night when the trolley cars weren't running in the street outside."

"Where did you learn all this, Jordan—at school?"

"No. There's a new science magazine out. It has a section on computers."

"And you understand all this?"

"Sure I do," Jordan told her scornfully. "It's all based on math." He delved into a pocket and brought forth a miniature electronic calculator. "You see this? It's a more powerful computer than the whole roomful of equipment they had at Manchester."

"Fascinating. You're very clever, Jordan."

"You see why I'd like to go to Manchester? They experiment with new applications in math."

"Well, I'm not sure if your father will like the idea," Virginia said uncertainly.

"But I want to talk to him about it anyway."

"Yes, we can certainly discuss it."

"Okay." Jordan found the last dry cookie. "Where will we be living in London?"

"Your father expects to get an apartment in Knightsbridge. He says it's in a very good section. Apparently someone from the embassy has a lease, and we can make a deal with him."

"Maybe it's near a school."

"Jordan, with your interest in mathematics and all your chatter about computers, would you actually want to specialize in subjects like that? For a career of that kind? You've always seemed so uncertain before. You know that your father would like you to consider the diplomatic service?"

"Haven't thought about it that much."

"Well, this is a good time for you to start thinking seriously."

"If I had to pick now, I'd think most about being a mathematician. I want to know everything that can be learned in mathematics."

Virginia was uncertain how she should reply. Such discussions were more suited to Walter, and for a moment she wished he were there. She felt safe with saying, "I should think there'll always be something new to be learned, in mathematics or any subject. I'll ask your father to talk with you about this, first chance he gets."

It was a bright, dry morning, and Walter Freeling felt good as he strolled along Piccadilly. Conservative Mayfair's mellow environment suited his mood. His prestigious new appointment had restored his confidence and self-esteem. This morning he seemed to feel years falling away.

He realized now how tedious life had become in Washington. A static career outlook, added to the worries of Virginia's philandering had been carrying him toward a psychological precipice, with a far side that he couldn't even think about. All in all, the London appointment had come at a most convenient time, perhaps saving the remnants of their marriage. He knew himself well enough to recognize that he still felt a fondness for Virginia. Whether it was love, or even love's dross, he was uncertain. But he was invigorated, in any case, by the prospect of starting over. Pleased that he could again look the world in the eye, he unconsciously thrust his shoulders back and straightened his spine.

He crossed the road at Queen Street, defying the black taxis that slid by within inches of his nose. On the opposite sidewalk he resumed his pace, studying, as he walked, an imposing Edwardian house. Set back from the street, it could have been the Mayfair residence of a particularly well-connected aristocrat, but he knew Curzon House to be the secret headquarters of MI5, Britain's intelligence arm. He was not alone. It was a secret everyone knew, a local tobacconist had told him wryly.

At South Audley Street he turned toward the American Embassy, dominating the west side of Grosvenor Square. Here the street narrowed, and he passed a terrace of town houses, tall but otherwise unremarkable, relics of the Georgian period.

Jenny Handel, Walter's new secretary, reached for the telephone as soon as she saw him at the doorway. "A car for Mr. Freeling, please! Immediate, at the front entrance. It's a local trip."

"What's up?" Walter wanted to know.

"They've been calling from Regent's Park. The ambassador is waiting to see you." As she spoke, she was dialing another number. "This is Mr. Freeling's secretary. He's been located and is on his way." She replaced the receiver. "You usually have lunch in the cafeteria," she said reproachfully. "I've had people searching all over the building for you."

"It's such a nice day, I decided to take a stroll down to Piccadilly for a sandwich and a glass of beer. Do you know why the ambassador wants me, Jenny?"

"I believe he has someone with him he wants you to meet."

"I hadn't been told to expect anything. Well, I'd better get moving. . . ."

Ten minutes later, the limousine deposited Walter at

the American ambassador's residence. He was ushered into the library, and within moments Ambassador Hayes Fitzgerald entered with one of the most striking women Walter had ever seen.

She was tall and slim, her hair middle parted and combed back severely, Spanish style, over a high, intelligent forehead. Her luminous green eyes hypnotized Walter. He broke his gaze with some difficulty.

"Ah, Freeling," Ambassador Fitzgerald said. "I have a special assignment for you, one you'll find most agreeable." His cherubic face had a hint of subdued mischief around the sharp eyes. "First of all, Lady Bolsover, let me introduce Mr. Walter Freeling."

"My pleasure, ma'am," Walter said.

Her "How do you do?" was impersonal.

"Her Ladyship is helping us in a rather delicate matter," the ambassador went on, "and I'm assigning you as liaison for the embassy with her. Please see that Lady Bolsover receives whatever assistance she wishes from us."

"Certainly, Mr. Ambassador." Walter waited for Fitzgerald to elaborate.

"This concerns the projected American submarine base on Solway Firth. You know how important the base can be to NATO."

"Yes, indeed, sir."

"And you are aware, then, of the objections, here in Britain and elsewhere, to the prospect of another American base. We must regard it as a sensitive issue to be handled with great care. The base will be built regardless, of course, but we must try not to exacerbate relationships in the process."

Fitzgerald shook his head regretfully. "Among other things, construction work is delayed, hasn't even begun. The base is to be in a coastal area known as Cumberland Dale. It's something of a beauty spot, apparently, and a protest movement is growing among the residents. They've staged weekend marches—people sitting on the highway to delay traffic—so the media are taking an interest, as you might expect, and it's our objective to prevent a tide of anti-American sentiment. Do you follow me, Freeling?"

"I certainly do, sir," Walter replied.

"Lady Bolsover is acting at the suggestion of our English counterparts." The fleeting cherubic smile crossed his face. "I'll leave it to Her Ladyship to elaborate on how you may assist her."

"I'm sure Mr. Freeling and I will get along splendidly," Lady Bolsover put in easily.

Fitzgerald turned back to Walter. "I have dispatched a background file to your office. You will have direct access to me at any time, in the event of any unexpected problem."

"Thank you, Mr. Ambassador. I will do my very best, I assure you."

An aide knocked, put his head around the door, and reminded, "Your next appointment is in your office, sir. Shall I ask His Excellency to wait?"

"No, I'm almost through here. I must bid you good day, Lady Bolsover, and I anticipate hearing from you as your good efforts progress." Fitzgerald moved quickly to the door as parting amenities were concluded.

Walter cleared his throat. "Perhaps I should familiarize myself, Your Ladyship, with the contents of the ambassador's file before we begin discussions."

"As we're going to be working rather closely together," she said, "don't you think it might be well if we dispense with formalities?" The green of her eyes now seemed even lighter as she smiled. "Your name, I believe, is Walter? I'm known as Nina. A little less daunting than Lady Bolsover."

"Well, in that case . . ." Walter was flattered. "I'm honored, ma'am."

"Perhaps I can give you some idea of what we're up against, Walter," she said seriously. "You heard the ambassador's brief description of what is happening—that certain groups are resisting the proposed submarine base."

"Just who are these groups?"

"One includes residents who feel they have a genuine grievance—that the quality of rural life in Cumberland Dale will be gone forever and that a dairy-farming area with old, old traditions will be destroyed. Then you have the ecologists—the conservation lobby is a national movement. They are supported by a large and vocal group of naturalists who deplore the loss of a bird sanctuary in

Solway Firth. I happen to sympathize with them, for that matter."

"But these are minor interests. Don't such people understand that defense steps for the West must come first?" Walter interjected. "They'll be looking in the dictionary for Russian names for their birds and their cows if they prevent proper defense of their country."

Nina flashed him a rueful smile. "Pollution and the progressive erosion of the countryside by developers have become big issues, Walter. We're dealing with fears of provincial people here, and sometimes they get their priorities wrong. It just takes patience, that's all. There's also an element, politically motivated or otherwise, that instinctively resists an American project involving our participation. They take the position that Americans are turning this country into a target. It's a moot point, of course, and the result is constant debate."

Walter was puzzled by the apparent uncertainty in her tone. "You don't believe that yourself, do you?"

"So long as Britain remains a nuclear power, we have no alternative but to support the United States. In my opinion, we can't afford to have a partial defense. And that means that our interests coincide, even if it proves more than a little inconvenient at times."

"I'm not clear as to your function," Walter said politely.

"Oh, let me explain. My family's connections with the locality go back six hundred years. Bolsover Castle is in Cumberland Dale, and it's traditionally a focal point where controversial local issues are discussed. Obviously, I have certain influence in the area, and quite simply, the government hopes that by being known to support its plans, I can help counter resistance."

"I see." Walter digested this information. "And so how may I assist you?"

"Your purpose will be to advise on the American viewpoint, and that will help me formulate a response when I am questioned. I will have to attend some meetings and speak, and of course that means being cross-examined. You can help me back up my own statements with data or whatever information will strengthen the reply to the skeptics. There may be also an opportunity for you personally to put the case for the American government."

"I'll certainly do my best."

"I'm confident that you will. The ambassador recommends you most highly." She was consulting her watch. "I'm afraid that's all I will have time for today. I'll call you soon, after you've had a chance to study the file."

"I'll get right on it."

"Good-bye then, Walter." She gave him the benefit of a brilliant smile, turned, and walked quickly to the door.

Riding back to the embassy in the limousine, he found himself bemused at the prospect of being associated with this very self-possessed woman. It would certainly be a pleasant change from routine business.

When he reached his office, he asked his secretary, "Jenny, does the name Lady Nina Bolsover mean anything to you?"

"Oh, yes. That's a well-known name, Mr. Freeling."

"How come?"

"Well, it appears quite often in the society columns."

"Is that so? Do you, uh, know much about her?"

"Only that she's the widow of a war hero—Lord Alan Bolsover. He was one of the youngest officers to be awarded the Victoria Cross."

"The war?" Walter was puzzled. "You don't mean World War II, do you? That simply can't be. She's quite young. Late thirties, I should think, at most."

"Lord Bolsover was a lot older. They were distantly related, and the rumor is that they married to conserve the family fortunes. Probably a tax dodge. I think he left her a lot of property."

Jenny turned and picked up a package. "By the way, this envelope just arrived by messenger. It's marked urgent."

"Yes, I'm expecting it."

Walter took the thick file, sat at his desk, and began studying the problem of the Solway Firth submarine base. He found difficulty in concentrating on the facts and figures. A quite different figure kept drifting into his mind and disturbing his equanimity.

At breakfast Virginia said, "I'm so pleased you found this apartment, Walter. I was simply dreading having to traipse around looking for one."

"It was a lucky break." Walter gave a short laugh. "The last thing Henry Brooks expected was to be moved back to

Germany. He was planning on staying in London at least three years."

"Which park is this?" Virginia was gazing out the wide window.

"Hyde Park; and the street, it's Knightsbridge. We're in a very good section. Over there is the most famous lake in England. It's called the Serpentine—see it behind the trees? You'll find families and couples walking in the park."

Virginia turned her attention to the sparsely furnished room. It held little other than the table and chairs they were using.

"I'm glad Mr. Brooks sold his furniture," Virginia sighed. "We've lived with other people's furnishings too often in the past. Now we can choose our own." Walter started to comment on the cost and stopped himself. "One other thing I like," she went on. "We're among fine people in this building. I met some very interesting women in the lobby yesterday."

Jordan, who had been listening quietly, chipped in, "I was out early. I counted five Rolls-Royces down in the garage this morning. And a Bentley. That's neat, man."

Virginia cut in severely. "Jordan, I wish you would take the opportunity of learning to speak English properly. You won't find young English gentlemen saying 'That's neat, man.' "

"Heck, I'm no English gentleman," Jordan complained.

"Weren't you telling me how you'd like to go to an English school? Can you imagine what they'll think if you talk like that?"

Jordan grunted an unintelligible reply.

"I've been making some inquiries," Walter said. "There may be a chance for you to enter Saint Paul's School, if you want. It's near Westminster Abbey. Many British families in public life send their sons there to prepare for university."

"Sounds interesting."

"Unfortunately, there's one hitch. Saint Paul's won't accept new students midterm. Which means you'd have a three-month wait."

"That's out of the question," Virginia put in. "Wouldn't the American school take him immediately?"

"But I *would* like to go to an English school, Dad," Jordan objected.

"Yes, I understand," Walter said. "And I agree that you should take advantage of the opportunity. The experience will be good for you. Educationally nothing will be lost, to say the least. A good English school has extremely high academic standards."

"Did Mom mention Manchester University?"

"What about Manchester?" Virginia had not brought up the subject.

"Experimental mathematics. I've read about it."

"Well, university's some way off yet." Walter wasn't committing himself.

"In the meantime, I think he has to go to the American school," Virginia said. "A boy like Jordan can't just hang around wasting his time."

"I don't waste my time," Jordan rebutted, feeling aggrieved. "I study advanced math. And I'll have lots of things to try to see and do in the city."

"There may be one more prospect," Walter mentioned. "I've taken up the question of a school for Jordan with Lady Bolsover. She's making some inquiries for me. I should hear soon."

"Lady *who?*" Virginia immediately wanted to know.

"That's the woman I'm working with on the submarine-base project. I did mention her to you. She's very well connected, as you might expect. Any advice from her will be the best, you can be sure."

Curious now, Virginia said with a slight sneer in her voice, "Sounds as if you have been damn well impressed by this Lady Whatsit."

Walter looked at his watch and rose from the table. "I have to leave now, or I'll be late for my first appointment."

"I'm expecting to go to Harrods this morning," Virginia reminded him. "Are you sure you've made the necessary arrangements for a charge?"

"Yes, it's all okay. There's an envelope from Harrods on my night table. You'll find the credit authorization in it. Just remember to take it easy on the cost, won't you?"

She looked at him, annoyed. "You don't expect us to live like paupers for four years just to save a dollar or two, do you, Walter?"

"I didn't say that, Virginia! All I meant was please be a

little conservative and bear in mind I am only a government employee. Do try to keep within the relocation allowance."

"Well, if you prefer to live in squalor . . ."

Walter, frustrated, had no time to argue further. He gave his wife a quick peck on the cheek, ruffled Jordan's hair, and was on his way.

Walter was unprepared for the splendor of Nina's castle near the border of Scotland. "Marvelous! This is a truly lovely place. I would never have guessed." He gazed around the luxurious interior in appreciation.

"Do you really like it, Walter?" Nina was like a child showing off her doll's house. "This is my home—my real home. I have the town house in Belgravia, of course, but I don't think of that as home. Here I'm surrounded by the things I know and love."

They had retreated to her apartment in the castle's tower after a stormy session in the cavernous library, where a contentious throng of concerned local residents had demanded satisfaction—namely, that the United States and NATO get out of their backyard. The proposed submarine base had been bitterly attacked by speaker after speaker, whom Walter—officially representing his government—had been hard put to rebut effectively. Nina, as the grand lady of the region, had been treated somewhat more respectfully, but in the end she, too, had been shouted down by one particularly insulting hothead. Walter, at least, had been educated at first hand in the antagonisms of people in Cumberland Dale toward any development that would despoil their untouched corner of England. After that tense encounter, it was time to unwind, and Walter felt fully inclined to take advantage of the opportunity. He was reassured as Nina's smile emerged like a rainbow. "Pour yourself a drink, Walter, while I go and freshen up." She spun around and walked off.

Walter looked about him. The place was surprisingly spacious. He moved to gaze up and down the stairwell, where a wide, spiral staircase climbed the height of the turret, giving access to a completely round room at each level. Seen from inside, the archery slits were surprisingly tall, enough for a man to stand in the recesses they formed in the yard-deep granite. Inside the apartment the mildly dank atmosphere pervading the rest of the castle was banished. He could hear an air conditioner hissing quietly in the background, and the room was at a comfortable temperature and dry. They were on the second level, in a living room that was a tribute to the skills of a talented interior designer. It was all in white, from the deep shag rugs to the wide leather banquette ringing its circumference.

When Nina returned, she had changed into a soft green wool sheath. Covering her from neck to toes, it had no shape other than hers and clung to every line of her body. Walter could see, for the first time, the perfection of her figure.

The color enhanced the green of her eyes so that they appeared wider, the pupils darker and more mysterious. Or perhaps it was her hair—the artificial light seemed to reflect blue highlights in her jet black hair, now combed out full and free so that, unfettered, it fell to her shoulders.

She was also shorter now, and he guessed she had discarded her high heels, along with her usual air of polite detachment. He began to feel even taller than usual and squared his shoulders like a preening bird.

"Did you take a drink, Walter?"

"Not yet. I've been admiring your home."

"It's not to everyone's taste, I know, but then it was intended to please only me." She smiled. "What will you have? Is scotch all right?"

"Scotch will be fine."

She poured two shots from a bottle of Chivas Regal, filled a small silver bucket with ice cubes from within the nickelodeon bar, and brought them so she could sit on the white leather near him.

Nina sipped her whiskey. "Now that you've seen our opposition in action, you know how easy it is to whip up anti-American feeling."

"Yes. But thank goodness your neighbors aren't fools. We'll make them see the wisdom of this submarine base."

Their arrangement was to return to London immediately after the meeting, and it was a long drive back. He glanced at the white clock. "When are you planning on leaving, Nina?"

"Do we have to—tonight, I mean? I really don't feel like driving all that way in the dark. We should have flown up,

I suppose, but then I do illogical things now and then—reminds me I'm a woman." She was girlish again, charming him with her enchanting smile. "Walter, would it be inconvenient to stay here tonight? There's a comfortable guest room upstairs, even a shaver in the bathroom. If you have something important on tomorrow, we could start back early in the morning."

"I've nothing special on my calendar for the morning," Walter said amiably.

"It's agreed then?" Her look was one of anticipation.

"By all means. I'd just like to call home, if I may."

"That's marvelous, Walter! Thank you! The telephone's over there."

On a white instrument he put in a call to Virginia, telling her with appropriate regrets that he was delayed overnight on business. When he had said a forlorn-sounding good-night, he turned, but Nina had left the room. He poured another scotch. When she had not returned two drinks later, a euphoric mood was creeping over him. Good whiskey easily could do that. He knew he was out of commission until the morning, and the notion struck him that he, Walter Freeling, diplomat, husband, father, wet nurse to a female British aristocrat, had been switched off, like a clockwork toy. Now the question was: Would Walter Freeling the man emerge to take his place?

When Nina returned, he pulled himself together. "Nina, shall we go out to dinner? Let me call for reservations at some place that you favor." When he used stilted expressions like that, he knew he was on the edge of drinking too much.

"Thank you, Walter, but we'll be eating here. Nanny's arranging dinner right now."

"Nanny?"

She laughed. "English children grow up with a nanny. Most are dearly loved, and mine stayed on in the family. She has looked after me since I was a tot. Nanny doesn't see me a lot these days, and she's getting on a bit. I can't deny her the pleasure of fussing around me."

"How charming."

The dining room was on the next level above, where, under the watchful eye of a pleasantly plump nanny, an elegant dinner was served by a butler obviously terrified by her. They sat close together at one end of a long, glistening table, beneath a vast crystal chandelier. Nanny lit a triple candelabra and placed a small bowl of wildflowers by it. Walter was intrigued as the chandelier dimmed, and he was amused by the glances the old woman sent his way. Nina, it seemed, had failed to explain their business relationship, and Nanny was sizing him up as a prospective suitor.

"You must excuse Nanny," Nina observed. "She's a little overanxious for me."

Afterwards, she escorted Walter into the living room, where she insisted that he try a fine Napoleon brandy. Now he was feeling mellow and relaxed. Somewhere at the back of his mind a fantastic notion had started up, but he dismissed it. Ridiculous! It would be totally out of character for him to . . . and yet, was he mistaken or was she encouraging him, challenging him?

"Actually, I can understand Nanny's concern," he said. "It is a hell of a waste."

"What do you mean?"

He took a deep breath. "You—a beautiful, intelligent woman in the prime of life. Keeping yourself apart. Holding yourself aloof. Nina, you draw a rigid line, and nobody dares step across it."

She took so long to reply he thought he had blundered over that very line and ruined a friendship he was just beginning to enjoy.

"I'm terribly vulnerable, Walter," she said at last, "and a woman in my position must be careful. It's difficult for me to know a man's motivation, when the unfortunate fact is simply that most are fortune hunters." Her voice had dropped so low it was almost inaudible. "But I'm a normal woman, believe me. And sometimes it's a little unfair. . . ."

It struck him only then. The intimate dinner, the candlelight, Nanny's solicitude for her lifelong charge. The older woman was in on it, too, he felt sure. It had all been neatly planned, and he was nominated to be the partner in exorcising Lady Bolsover's sexual hang-ups. Why him?

Because he was safe, and they knew it. This duty was more suited to a younger, more virile man. But then a stud might not have a diplomat's discretion.

Knowing he was irretrievably drawn into Nina's scheme, he saw no point in embarrassing her. Walter put down his glass and rose to his full height, looking down at her. "I think maybe this is my lucky day," he said easily. He smiled and reached out for her.

"Oh, Walter!" She uncurled, to rise into his arms. Just before they kissed, she held his gaze for an instant, her magically green, hazel-flecked eyes seeking mockery. She saw none, then the green was gone behind closed lids, and she blended to him.

Feeling his rapidly increasing tumescence, she emitted a moan. Walter could hear his voice grow husky. "Where in God's name is your room?"

She led him by the hand up the circular stairs to the level above the dining room. He had little interest in her massive Queen Anne four-poster, set in silks and satins. Turning her around, he struggled to find the zipper on her wool sheath, then slid it down from her neck to her waist. She stepped out, wearing nothing.

It all held a quality of fantasy. The whole thing was nothing but an indulgent, erotic dream that would end suddenly with his rejection and dismissal, he was sure. But now the sight of her perfect shape sent the blood coursing through his veins anew, and he knew it was all for real. Her body was that of a young, unspoiled girl, her skin milky white.

She was warm and tightly moist, and he penetrated with a hardness that to him was a long-forgotten wonder.

CHAPTER TWO

The three boys eyed each other curiously. It was new to them: Wynchgate School's institutional aroma of carbolic soap, the woodwork scarred by scions of ages past who had yielded to the compulsion to carve initials in the long-suffering oak. Now the room as ever stood ready to shelter another batch of young males growing rapidly toward manhood who would share their innermost secrets with its walls.

On arrival at Wynchgate on the strength of Lady Bolsover's recommendation, Jordan had been introduced to the other two. Piers Ledermain was French, with a faintly arrogant air and a general contempt for the entire proceedings. He appeared an unwilling participant. Prince Hakim El Morro Sa'ud was related to the ruling family of Saudi Arabia. His dark eyes swung rapidly from Jordan to Piers and back again. All three appeared uncomfortable in stiff new serge blazers.

When Piers spoke, his English, with an attractive American-Gallic accent, was precise and perfect. "I don't know about you two," he said, "but for me all this is an utter waste of time. I have no intention whatsoever of cramming for entrance to some stupid English university. I intend to have a good time during my residence."

"Then why are you here?" Jordan stopped unpacking his case to turn toward him.

"*Alors,* it is my father's wish. Since my mother died, he insists on visiting me every weekend, wherever I am. He feels he must demonstrate that a succession of girlfriends does not absorb his entire affection. All that means I must be conveniently nearby."

"Nearby where?" Jordan inquired.

"Wherever he is creating a new branch of his merchant bank. Because of the Common Market, he has ambitions to grow big in Britain. So we'll be here for some time, I think."

"And you, Hakim?" Jordan turned to the Arab boy.

"This is my first time at school," Hakim responded unhappily. "I do not think I will find it very congenial."

"You've never been to school before?" Jordan and Piers stared, incredulous.

"I have had only private tutors, you see. Back in Riyadh it is not seemly for a prince to go to school. My uncle persuaded them that I should have an English university education. Because he went to Sandhurst, he is something of an Anglophile—"

"A what?" Piers grunted.

"He admires the English and their philosophies," Hakim explained.

"*Sacrebleu,* they are savages, the English. The man must be a maniac," Piers said.

"Because of him I am here." Hakim looked around the room with the air of a man in the condemned cell.

"Entrance to Oxford is tough," Jordan said, "and they're very selective."

"Oh, not so tough," Piers said nonchalantly. "Not for us, I think."

"What do you mean?"

"Don't you know? Graduates of Wynchgate get preference. Why else do you think we have to serve a couple of years in this sanitarium?"

"I didn't know that." Jordan returned to his unpacking, feeling a sense of annoyance. He would prefer to get through on merit. This way, the challenge was taken out of it. "Personally, I can do without Oxford, anyway. I'd rather go to Manchester," he said.

"Why would any person in his right mind wish to go to Manchester?" Piers sneered.

"I'd like to specialize in math," Jordan explained. "Manchester's a good place for that."

"You're good at mathematics?"

Jordan nodded cautiously.

"That's excellent. You can help me; I'm terrible." He turned to the Saudi prince. "What are you good at, Hakim?"

"I can most certainly beat you in a race with camels," Hakim assured him mournfully.

"Is that it?"

"As I am prince, my tutors always obey my orders. I usually send them away."

"Hmm, this could be less boring than I expected!" With an impish look on his face, Piers set about his own unpacking.

When Walter had explained to Lady Bolsover that his son wanted to attend a good English school, she explored her connections. The result was Jordan's prompt admission to Wynchgate. In nearly four hundred years, Wynchgate had seen thousands of boys arrive as raw adolescents and depart young gentlemen, their heads filled with the classics and, more important, modes of behavior appropriate to a narrow, privileged sector of English society of their various generations.

At first Jordan balked at the notion of boarding school. He acceded, however, when his father pointed out that this was the best path to choosing a university.

Almost in unison the three boys jumped when the door opened abruptly. A thin man with a stoop, dressed in academic cap and gown, entered. "I am Mr. Hutton," he said. "I'm your housemaster." He turned to Hakim. "You are Prince Hakim El Morro Sa'ud, I assume?"

"Yes, sir." The Arab stood at attention.

"This is not the army. Titles are not used at Wynchgate, nor are prefixes. You will be known as Mr. Morro for the duration of your stay."

"Thank you, sir."

"Which of you two is Freeling?"

"That's me, sir," Jordan said.

"I've been looking at your academic record, Freeling. Patchy, to say the least, and I can't say I properly understand American grades. You'll need to explain them to me."

"I think I can do that, sir," Jordan began. "At my last school, in Washington—"

"Not now, Freeling. Tomorrow." Hutton cut him off liverishly and turned to Piers. "And you're Ledermain, of course." Piers said nothing. "I can't make head or tail of your reports either, Ledermain. Have you actually completed a course in anything?"

"Pas du tout," Piers said.

"Oh, my God—don't you speak English?"

"Yes, sir, I do," Piers said airily. "I find it easier to speak in my native tongue. I am a Frenchman, after all."

"Not here, you're not, Ledermain." Hutton responded to Piers's challenge immediately. "Here at Wynchgate you are neither French nor a man. You will speak only English within the walls of the school, and if I hear one word of French other than in a language class, you will be on report. The significance of being on report will be revealed to you in good time. Do you understand that, Mr. Ledermain?"

Piers muttered, "Yes, *sir!*"

Hutton addressed them all. "During the next few days you will be taking tests. The purpose of these tests is to establish what standards, if any, you have achieved in general education and how far behind you are in subjects that are part of the Wynchgate educational profile. Far behind you will be, I assure you. I shall prepare the test papers personally, and from the results I shall attempt to formulate a curriculum that will bring you forward to university entrance standard. Whether or not I will succeed, considering the unorthodox educational backgrounds of you three, remains to be seen."

He turned and went to the door. "Dinner is in thirty minutes. When you hear the gong, proceed to the dining hall and look for me. I will arrange for your places at the table." He went out, closing the door with a precise fussiness.

Walter was angry. "This can't be right," he said through pursed lips. "Virginia, I specifically *asked* you to go through these accounts and verify that the charges are correct. There has to be an error somewhere."

"I've been through them, but I don't see anything wrong." Virginia's response was offhand, unconcerned.

"Surely that can't be—it means you've overspent by thousands of dollars. Are you *crazy,* Virginia? Where in *hell* do you think the money's coming from? Just because it's pounds sterling doesn't mean it's play money, you know!" He stared dismayed at the bills before him.

"I only spent what was necessary. We've been putting a home together, haven't we? That doesn't cost peanuts in any currency. Look around you and you'll see where the money's gone."

"Can't you understand there's a limit to what we can afford? You've gone way over the top."

"Oh, come on, Walter. Things aren't that bad." Virginia giggled appeasingly. The best response to complaints about her excessive spending was a show of good-natured submission. Somehow he had always found the money to pay the bills. "You're a senior diplomat, after all. And you're not down to your last nickel yet."

"Oh, no?" He thrust some papers at her. "Have you seen these? They're the bills for one term at Jordan's school. The incidentals practically double the amount I expected to have to find. Then there's that damned value added tax they pile onto everything. I had forgotten to take that into account."

"Well, nobody asked you to put him in such an expensive school. Jordan could have gone to the American school and lived at home."

"The school is necessary if he's to go on to a good English university. We can't deny him the opportunity of a suitable education. It's been tough enough for him as it is, shunted around from country to country. It's the least we can do for him."

"I'm sure there must be less expensive schools than Whichgate."

"Wynchgate," Walter said, irritated. "That may be so, but I don't think you appreciate how fortunate he is. Because he's sponsored by Lady Bolsover, he'll be directed into the right channels, meet the right people. Things like that count here."

"That woman seems to be taking quite an interest in your private life." Virginia spit it out quickly, unexpectedly, a crease appearing in her forehead.

"I asked her for advice, Virginia. She's influential. I'm grateful she offered to help."

"That doesn't answer the question, does it?"

"What's the question?"

"Why is she so interested in you?"

Walter hesitated. "When I'm working closely with someone, he—or she—is bound to become aware of certain personal matters. It's only to be expected, surely."

He had used his diplomatic voice, and it was too pat an

answer. An entirely new thought struck Virginia, one she dismissed at first as ludicrous. *Walter having an affair?* Reliable, constant old Walter? Impossible! He'd never given her cause for a moment's jealousy. And yet the nagging doubt would not be stilled.

"She's not getting too personal with you, Walter, is she—Her *Ladyship?*" She said it half-seriously and with little humor.

"Now what makes you say a thing like that, Virginia? A woman of Lady Bolsover's standing can find something better to do than chase a middle-aged man who's having trouble keeping up with the cost of living. I should think that's obvious."

He said it in what he hoped was an offhand manner. But because he was so predictable, she guessed something was amiss. Ordinarily, Walter would have responded with a monosyllable. The less importance he gave to her statements, the shorter his answers. Now he had protested too much. And, she had noticed, he had looked away to blink a couple of times—a sure sign that he was bothered; it made him look devious. *"You bastard! You're having an affair with that woman!"*

"What? I—I—how can you say that?" He was blustering and had gone pale.

"I don't believe it!" Virginia yelled. "All the hard times you've given me—all the bad times because maybe I flirted once in a while. And here you are, probably doing worse than what you accuse me of, you damned sanctimonious hypocrite!"

"Let me explain, Virginia, will you? . . ."

"Explain what? How you've been screwing some high-class whore? While you're complaining that I spend too much, trying to make do on the pittance you allow me?"

"But it's not like that at all."

Virginia's face twisted into ugliness. Swooping away, she snatched up her handbag. She was already dressed for a visit to a new hairdresser she had found in Sloane Street.

With as much aplomb as he could muster, Walter said, "Don't you think you should stay and discuss this, Virginia?"

"There's nothing to talk about! You've had your fling, and now it's my turn. I have news for you: You're not much of a lover, old boy. Oh, you may be able to give that bitch a thrill, but I need a real man to satisfy me. I've never told you, Walter, that you're not man enough for me. Got the picture?"

Virginia slammed out of the apartment.

Walter, left alone in the sudden, welcome stillness, turned to the big window nearby and gazed out across the park. He stood motionless except for a deep sigh that racked his frame, but his thoughts were in turmoil. Everything that he had hoped for and tried to achieve in his marriage was proving to be futile. Virginia's spendthrift ways, her nasty irascibility, her eternal annoyance with him, the philandering that she excused as "flirting once in a while," the frequent recourse to alcohol ending in the occasional binge—it was too much. Thinking against his will of Nina's ladylike beauty and charm, he recoiled from complete recognition of the bitter contrast. But he knew nonetheless that time and reason dictated that their uncomfortable marriage had, at last, reached its end point.

CHAPTER THREE

The endless maelstrom of traffic battled its way around Hyde Park Corner. Walter drove warily, keeping an eye on the ubiquitous taxis charging up from the direction of Victoria Station. He didn't relax until he reached Park Lane, where the northbound flow of traffic smoothed out.

"I just don't understand, Dad. What's happened, anyway?" Jordan sat beside him, gazing out of the window on his side.

"We will be divorced one day. Your mother and I have agreed. I'm telling you now so that you can get used to the idea. We'll part eventually. In the meantime, neither of us has anywhere else to go. There's a great shortage of accommodations here in London, and we're sharing the apartment for a while until we can make some other arrangements. It's a big enough place so we needn't be under each other's feet."

"When you split up, who will I be living with—you or her?"

"We have no agreement yet, Jordan. I hope we'll be parting as friends, and I presume you'll want to spend time with each of us."

"Will I have to leave Wynchgate?"

"No! This won't affect your education one bit."

Walter stole a glance at his son. The boy gave little sign of any reaction to the breakup of his parents' marriage. "Look, it's your birthday soon, Jordan. I would like to give you a special present. Kind of compensate for the tacky news."

"That's not necessary," Jordan said dully.

"It would make me feel better, and I'm sure that's true

of your mother. Is there something you want? Name it and it's yours."

"Thanks, Dad, but there's really nothing I need."

"This is a never-to-be-repeated offer. You'd better make the most of it." For the first time that day, Walter smiled.

Jordan sat quietly, and Walter waited. "Well, there is something I'd like, but I can't expect it."

"What is that?"

"An Apple."

"An apple?"

"It's a minicomputer. Apple is the brand name."

"Oh, a computer. Sounds . . . different."

"It's expensive for a present, maybe," Jordan said uncertainly.

"Now, you just let me worry about that side of things, son." A moment later, "Uh—how expensive?"

"A couple of thousand dollars, I think. Maybe as much as three."

"That so—two or three thousand bucks?" Walter moved uncomfortably in the driving seat.

"There may be others that cost less. But I really don't know about them. Heck, I wish I knew a computer expert," he added wistfully.

As Walter swung into the parking area of the embassy, a new thought struck. "We have people here who are computer specialists."

"We do?" Jordan sat up.

"The engineer who heads up electronics research for our international communications network is based in the building. A man named Hugh Auchterlonie."

"Hugh Auch—" Quizzically, Jordan tried repeating the name.

"He's a young Scot who's apparently an electronics wizard. As I understand it, he originated a mathematical concept that enabled us to jump years ahead in satellite communications."

"Mathematics?" Jordan became instantly alert.

"I'm sure Hugh can find a few moments to give you some advice."

"Hey, Dad, do you think he would show me around the communications section? I've been wondering what goes on down there."

"I'm not sure, Jordan. It's all top security, and they

don't allow anyone near . . ." Walter stopped the car and killed the engine. "Hell, I guess I can talk them into letting my own son take a peek."

"Wow!" Delight shone from Jordan's face.

From his office, Walter made a couple of persuasive telephone calls. A short while later, Jordan was being led through the labyrinth of tunnels beneath the embassy.

Dr. Hugh Auchterlonie looked even younger than his twenty-eight years. His black tightly curled hair crowned a high forehead. His modulated voice betrayed just a hint of his native brogue. Lean and wiry, Hugh was smaller than the fast-growing Jordan, who had to break into an occasional trot in order to keep up with him.

As he led the way, Hugh turned his head. "You say you're interested in computers, lad?"

"Yes, sir!" Jordan panted along.

"And with which machines are you familiar?"

"None, sir. I'm hoping to learn."

"How old are you?"

"I'll be sixteen."

"Sixteen!" He stopped to turn and speak sternly. "You're beginning awfully late. Many a laddie's made a start at eight, or ten, and has a good grasp of the subject by the time he's in his teens. You'll have a lot of ground to make up."

"I can learn fast, sir."

"Understand something—it's unlikely you'll ever learn fast enough to know all about computers. Do you know why that is?"

"No." Jordan was baffled.

"Because the damned things are developing so quickly, they're out of date before they get into service. By the time you've got the hang of the last one, somebody has thought of an improvement. The industry is still in its infancy, and standards haven't been set."

"Well, doesn't that problem apply to everyone, sir, and not just me?"

"Aye, it does. And stop calling me sir, will you? The name's Hugh. I'm twenty-eight years of age. Does that hold any significance for you?"

"Ah, no," Jordan said cautiously.

"It will. It means I'm ancient. In the world of computers you don't find many people over thirty. God alone knows what happens to computer people after thirty—they evaporate, or something. Often they can't stand the pace and crack up. Now do you appreciate why it's necessary to make an early start?" Without waiting for a reply, he turned and resumed his rapid walking. Jordan followed dutifully.

"How's your math?" Hugh threw it back over his shoulder.

"Oh . . . okay, I guess," Jordan said modestly.

"Don't be reticent with me, lad. Math is the principal consideration in the computer business. If you're no good at it, you might as well forget the whole idea—"

"I'm very good!" It came out forcefully as he exhaled sharply and sounded boastful even in his own ears. "I mean, I'm top of my class, sir—Hugh." It was difficult conducting a conversation on the run.

"Always have been?"

"As long as I can remember. It's always been my favorite subject."

"Nobody can touch you at math, huh?" Jordan missed the knowing smile that flitted across his face; without realizing it, Jordan had passed his first test. "Well, we'll see about that."

They had reached twin doors forming the entrance to the communications section. Beyond was a sensitive security area, and two burly armed guards examined the identification pinned to Jordan's lapel and checked it against their list. "For God's sake, he's only a kid! And he's with me," Hugh complained impatiently.

"You know the rules, Dr. Auchterlonie. Everyone gets the treatment. That means everyone."

Following Hugh, Jordan thrust his feet into a machine that vacuumed dust off his shoes. When the twin doors opened with a hydraulic sigh, they entered a fairyland of whirring equipment and blinking lights. Jordan, his eyes popping, stepped into the air-conditioned, humidity-stabilized computer room, subtly lit by hidden fluorescents so that even the walls seemed aglow. They passed between two banks of computers that spasmodically spun tape wheels, flashed, or clacked softly, motivated by some unseen, seemingly mystic force. Then they were stepping out into a circular zone surrounded by work stations that reminded Jordan of cinematic versions of spacecraft control rooms. Several operators, intent on their tasks, sat at consoles monitoring visual display units.

At a vacant station, Jordan paused to study an endless stream of integers scrolling up on a video display unit. When he looked up from the VDU, his eyes alight with curiosity, he realized that everything here cried out its complexity and, therefore, its dependence on mathematics. It was a life-directing instant.

"Come on, lad; my office is over here." Hugh's voice broke Jordan's fascination with his surroundings, and he followed across the spotless floor to a small untidy room, formed by the angles of a corner in the manner of an afterthought and totally out of character with the rest of the department. The ceiling was so low that exposed heating pipes crossing it bore the legend Mind Your Head! scrawled in marker ink. The door of the room had been removed, apparently because it would open inward and steal space. An entire wall was fitted with bolted steel shelving hurriedly put together, now packed and groaning under a weight of computer-operating manuals and data libraries. On the floor and resting against the walls were stacks of computer printout that appeared ready to cascade forward. In spaces between the stacks, several computer control boards, masses of delicate colored wires and intricate connections, stood propped up. On a simple desk in the middle of the room a computer terminal's screen was blinking lazily. A matrix cable feeding it snaked across the floor to disappear into a hole through the rear wall. The only other furniture consisted of two steel tubular chairs with vinyl panels.

"Before I show you around, let's discuss one or two points, " Hugh said. "First, I take it you're familiar with binary arithmetic?" When Jordan nodded warily, he added, "You've heard of Boolean algebra?"

"Well . . ."

"Okay, we'll start at rock bottom. Boolean algebra is the theory of digital circuits—something you'll begin in your junior year at university, if you're taking computer science."

Jordan was discomforted by Hugh's assumption that he would be making computers a career. "I expect to go to Oxford next year," Jordan informed him.

"Oxford? What in hell's name are you going there for if you want to learn about computers?"

"My father arranged it."

"You poor bastard. All you'll learn at Oxford is dead languages and how to argue socialist platitudes in an elitist British accent." Hugh's brogue had broadened.

"I beg your pardon, sir?"

"Oh, never mind," Hugh grunted. Then, after a moment, "You could teach yourself, lad, if you're determined enough."

"I can do it." Jordan sat forward on the edge of the chair.

"I'll bet you can." For a silent moment Hugh studied the youth seated across his desk, the back arched in readiness, fervor shining from clear eyes. He sighed quietly. He was still near enough to his own youth to recognize the symptoms. Sensing he was facing a kindred soul, he resumed. "You're aware of how conventional algebra establishes a working relationship between numbers? Then fix this in your mind: Boolean algebra does the same for statements. It's fundamentally a system of logic." He located a slim volume among those stacked on the metal shelves. He slid it to Jordan. "I'll come back to the algebra later. For the moment you can begin with this. It's BASIC, a kind of language you'll need so that you can communicate with your computer."

"I've already started it," Jordan announced proudly.

"Good! And when you've got the hang of BASIC, we'll give you other languages to get your teeth into. FORTRAN, COBOL, PASCAL . . . They all have different applications. You're going to have to sweat, if you want my help."

Jordan had expected only initial advice. The last thing he'd anticipated was that this important technician would undertake to teach him. Yet the man seemed to accept as his responsibility Jordan's introduction to the mysterious, fascinating world of computers. Delight rose in him. "I'm very grateful to you, sir."

Hugh studied the determination in the young eyes. "Of course, you're going to need your own minicomputer to run programs—"

"I'll be getting an Apple, I hope," Jordan cut in hastily.

"Not if it's my help you want!" Hugh snorted. You 'll not be throwing away your father's money on such luxuries, my lad. What you'll do is buy a kit and build one for yourself at a tenth of the price. Don't look for soft options around me." Hugh reached behind him and extracted a copy of a magazine from a pile. He leafed through *Computer Weekly* until he found the advertisement he wanted. Jabbing a finger at the page, he pushed the magazine across the desk. "This is a suitable kit, one that will enable you to expand with peripherals later. It comes with all the instructions you'll need. If you get into problems in constructing it, I'll help you."

"You will? Gee!" Jordan's gaze devoured the advertisement.

"Come on." Hugh scraped back his chair and rose. "It's time for the grand tour. The technicalities won't mean a thing to you, but you'll like the pretty flashing lights and things, so just try to look intelligent, will you?" For a moment he looked into the eager gaze level with his own. "What I'm going to do is blow on the little spark that's glowing under you. With a little luck it will grow into a burning bush. Or even a great forest fire, if you're equal to the challenge. That's the excitement of it, I suppose. You don't know what the hell I'm talking about, do you?"

"No, sir."

"Don't worry about it, laddie. Just follow me."

CHAPTER FOUR

The housemaster was busy at his desk when Hakim knocked and entered the study. He glanced up for an instant, then continued his work. "You wanted to see me, Morro?"

"Yes, sir." Hakim stood before the desk.

"Well, go on."

"I am considerably bothered by the lack of servants in the school, sir."

"What's that?" Hutton's pen stopped midway across the paper.

"Had I known of the shortage, I could have arranged for some to be sent from my father's palace. We have plenty to spare."

"Is that so?" Hutton dropped his pen and sat back, gazing stonily at Hakim.

"Yes, sir. I do not think it appropriate to have to make up my own bed. If my friends in Riyadh knew of this, I would be a laughingstock."

"You feel it is beneath you to have to make your own bed?"

"It is not a dignified activity for a member of the royal family. Similarly, the washing of dishes. I have come to ask that I be excused from kitchen duty."

"On the grounds that it is beneath you?"

"I will send for servants who will wash the dishes better than I can."

"You are not allowed to bring servants into the school."

"I do not understand, sir. Why not? If there is a shortage of servants here in England and I have some to spare, surely—"

"You are missing the point, Morro. The idea is for you to become self-sufficient," Hutton said in a controlled voice.

"Are you saying that the making of beds and the washing of dishes are part of my education?"

"You could put it that way, yes."

"I do not see how I will ever have a use for such aptitudes." Hakim looked genuinely surprised. "However, I will accept your superior wisdom in these matters, naturally." His manner was magnanimous.

"Good for you! When is your day for kitchen duty, Morro?"

"Tuesday, sir."

"From now on you will also wash dishes for an hour on Mondays. And Wednesdays, Thursdays, and Fridays, too. Until I tell you otherwise. That's all, Morro."

Hakim's face dropped as he realized he was being admonished. "Yes, sir. Thank you, sir," he said with restraint.

He had reached the door before his dejected attitude made Hutton think again. "Ah, just a moment."

Hakim turned.

"Was it your own idea, this servant thing?"

"It seemed obvious to me."

"Have you talked this over with your roommates?"

"Yes, I have. They suggested that I tell you my thoughts on the matter. That the school might be glad to receive extra servants."

"I see." Expressionlessly, Hutton said, "In that case, they can both join you in the kitchen for an hour every day until further notice. Present that information to Freeling and Ledermain with my compliments, will you?"

Hutton returned to his papers and Hakim crept out of the study.

Hakim did not return to the room immediately. When he arrived, he was in time to catch the French boy howling and waving a piece of paper. "What are they trying to do—bore us to death?"

"What is it, Piers?"

"Hutton has finally made up his mind about our curriculum," Piers said. "*Mon Dieu,* just look at this: in classics we are to study the influence on Greek cultural development of Oedipus and Jocasta."

"Who in hell were they?" Jordan asked, mystified.

"Probably a couple of—how do you say in English—a couple of Greek queers."

"What else?"

"For European history we are to specialize in the Norman conquest of Britain."

Jordan grimaced. "Is there any change in the math syllabus?"

"Not as far as I can see. That continues as scheduled. But just look at this—oh, this one's a lulu. In economics we study the integration of trade unions within the British rail system. Only a twisted mind could have dredged up that one."

"What we have to remember," Jordan said soberly, "is that the object is to ensure we get into Oxford. Hutton must have worked out that these subjects will give us the best chance. We have to assume he knows what he's doing. Just as he assumes that of course we would prefer to go there."

"If this is a sample of what we'll be studying at Oxford, I don't want to go," Piers exclaimed irritably.

"Once we're in the university, we'll have some options," Jordan suggested. "It doesn't much matter how we get into the university, does it?"

"And then you will go on to a diplomatic career, I expect?"

"I'm not certain that I'm interested in diplomacy." Jordan looked at him shrewdly. "What gave you that idea, anyway, Hakim?"

"I happened to see it in Hutton's confidential file. He left it in class one day last week." Hakim grinned.

"Hand me that voltmeter, will you, Jordan?" Hugh asked. "Okay. Now while I run the leads across these terminals, you watch the monitor. When the menu appears on the screen, we'll have located the fault."

Jordan's eyes were glued to the cathode-ray tube. It flickered a few times, but no menu appeared. After a few minutes he reported, "Nothing's happening."

"Keep watching. It'll come." Hugh was confident. "There's nearly a thousand connections on this board. It takes time to run through them."

Momentarily the screen had sprung to life, then faded. "I saw something. I think you just hit it!" Jordan sang out.

"Okay. I'll go back slowly."

"Got it. That's the one."

"Right." Hugh straightened. "That's one more problem solved. Did you get the hang of the procedure with the sensitive voltmeter?"

"Yes, I was watching you."

"Think you can handle it yourself?"

"Yes," Jordan said with assurance.

"Just yes—not maybe?" Jordan said nothing. "If you're so sure, then you can try running through that little lot." Hugh pointed to a complex mechanism joined by wires to a mushroom patch of transistors. "I already know what's wrong in there, but for you it will be a good exercise. You can do it after we've had a cup of tea. Let's take a stroll to the cafeteria. I need to stretch my legs." As they walked along, Hugh asked, "Do you understand fully what's happening? How the NAND and AND gates are motivated by impulses? How the functions relate to the Boolean concept?"

"Not completely," Jordan admitted, "but I'm studying it."

"You will know well enough when you've grasped it. Your mind will be illuminated as though the sun has come out from behind a cloud."

"Is that how it happened with you, Hugh?"

"Something like that."

They sat sipping tea in Hugh's office when Jordan announced, "I won't be in tomorrow. I have to prepare for school on Monday."

"Has it been a whole week?"

"I've been here two weeks. I get two weeks at midyear."

"Pity you're going back. I've kind of become used to having you around." The suspicion of a smile hovered around Hugh's lips. "Have your parents objected to your spending all your time down here?"

"No, they're not concerned."

Hugh thought he caught an inflection in Jordan's tone, but let it pass. "When will I be seeing you again?"

"Oh, I'll still be coming in weekends, the same as before. I'll come up to London every Friday evening."

"Do the other boys go home on weekends?"

"A few," Jordan replied quietly. "It's the exception."

"Tell me something. Would you be coming to London on

the weekends if it weren't to spend your time here with me?"

"I don't really know." He added truthfully, "No, I guess not."

"And what gives you the idea that I like spending seven days a week here in this dungeon just so that you can learn about computers?"

Jordan looked startled. "I didn't realize. Is it because of me you're spending all your weekends here at work?"

But Hugh was chuckling. "Don't let it bother you," he said genially. "I honestly don't remember the last time I took a day off. I'm one of those fools who imagines the place won't function without him. Fortunately, I've got no wife or other distractions of that nature. If you want to be unkind, you could say I'm married to my work." Then he was back to his usual gruff self. "That school of yours—you say they haven't caught up with computers yet?"

"No. I did suggest to Mr. Hutton—he's our housemaster—that it might be a good idea for Wynchgate to offer a computer science course."

"Of course it would."

"He said it doesn't fit our educational profile. If any Wynchgate alumnus ever decides he has need of a computer, he probably could afford to employ someone to operate it."

"That's one way to look at it. Money speaks its own language. It's a lesson you'd better learn mighty quick." He smiled at the boy. "Let's get back to work."

"Okay, Jordan, now I'm going to teach you assembly language—how to communicate with your computer so that it will understand your instructions. After all, the person who designed it, maybe he spoke only Swahili. How in hell are you going to talk to the machine in Swahili, eh, Jordan?" He thought about it and added, "Don't take me literally. I only say that to illustrate my point."

"I've been reading up on assembly language," Jordan began.

"Just listen, will you?" Hugh said, somewhat irritated. "You're interrupting my train of thought."

Jordan bit his lip.

Hugh went on. "First, I will show you how assembly language instructions are applied when they're fed straight into the circuits of the machine. That was how it used to be, with each instruction governing a specific function directly. A machine of that type is known as hardwired. I want you to learn how that is done so that you'll better understand the next stage. Because of complexity, designs have moved on—don't ever be afraid of complexity in a computer, lad; the damn thing thrives on it. Complexity demands a more facile method, and so assembly language in computers goes through a process that changes it into another language with greater capacity and flexibility. That is known as *microcode,* and it is microcode and microprograms that you'll be specializing in. Doing it that way, you'll be able to run rings around your everyday computer programmer."

Jordan waited a respectful moment. "Can I speak now?"

"Of course you can. I'm not holding your tongue, am I?" Hugh said perversely.

"Do you think I'll be able to design a computer myself one day, Hugh? When I'm proficient in microcode?"

Hugh nearly smiled. "Better than that, lad. With your ability, before I've finished with you, you'll be able to make a computer get up and dance and sing for you, if that's what you want."

It was the first real compliment Hugh had ever paid him. Jordan felt great happiness and a glow that reached right down to his toes.

Avoiding Walter, Virginia holed up in the apartment, often staring at TV. She liked to watch "Coronation Street," a twice-weekly soap opera. She had chosen it because she was finding concentration difficult. Her thoughts were inclined to wander back to her predicament and what were turning out to be her limited options. She realized now that she had expected Walter to relent. Despite his declaration of independence, she'd believed that he would soften and return to her, forgiving her wayward behavior just as he always had in the past. But as time went on and it hadn't happened, she began to realize that with another woman involved she was in a very different ball game. In the past Walter had been predictable. She always had pushed him, testing his patience. She realized now it was a miracle their marriage hadn't collapsed long ago, not that she would have known what to do if it had.

Over the years none of her admirers had expressed a desire for marriage or even for living together. She had been too easy, too quick to seek physical satisfaction.

Virginia realized that she was no longer watching the television program. Where in hell had she left the bottle of gin? She got up, walked into the kitchen, and found it. Pouring a stiff shot, she tinted the liquor with a little vermouth, threw in ice, and returned to her seat. She tried to concentrate on the screen. It worked for a few moments, then her thoughts strayed again.

Where was he tonight? she found herself wondering. Walter was rarely in the apartment in the evenings anymore. Sometimes he would come home after a day's work to drop his briefcase and attend to correspondence. He rarely ate at home. What was more, the number of nights his bed remained unslept in was growing. Without question, he was away sleeping with that high-toned bitch, she told herself. In sudden anger she downed the half tumbler of gin.

Virginia started to rise, intending to pour herself another drink. She noticed absently that "Coronation Street" had given way to a news report on a ceremonial dinner and notables were being shown arriving at the Guildhall. Mention of "Lady Nina Bolsover" caused her gaze to fly to the screen, in time to catch the item that "Her Ladyship is attended for this historic occasion by Mr. Walter Freeling, an American Embassy officer." Then there they were, stepping out of a limousine, Walter in a monkey suit solicitously rearranging the flowing cape of a tall, handsome, dark-haired woman.

The camera had moved on, but the picture remained, burning itself into Virginia's mind. In other times she would have been up there on Walter's arm, and the knowledge wrenched at her heart. She let the glass fall to the floor and subsided into the seat, desolate. For the first time she knew without a shadow of doubt that in her marriage to Walter she could expect no tomorrow.

CHAPTER FIVE

"You're looking tired, lad. Are you getting enough sleep?" Hugh was eyeing Jordan sideways.

"Me? Sure."

"Maybe you should take a real break. It's months now that you've been cramming on computers. That's bound to be a strain on top of your schoolwork. Take my advice and put this aside for a few weeks."

"I don't want to stop. Honestly, Hugh, I'm okay." A hint of alarm had crossed Jordan's features. The very thought that he should even briefly turn from computer technology when he was getting a firm grasp on the subject was enough to induce panic. He recognized forcefully just how deeply involved he had become in this ideal subject. Because of it he could almost feel his mind expanding at times. He no longer deemed it a joke when Hugh threatened to fit sockets above his ears so that he could plug straight into an IBM 370—he found himself wishing it were possible.

"Well, you'll have to take next weekend off, at least," Hugh was saying. "I won't be here for a week."

"You won't?" Jordan's surprise was mirrored on his face.

"I'm not exactly a plumbing fixture here," Hugh went on with a short laugh. "At times I have to attend to my private affairs, too, you know."

"Are you taking a vacation?"

"Not exactly. I'll be making a trip to Scotland to see my parents. It's been so long they may have forgotten what I look like."

"Gee—Scotland. I'd sure like to go there." It slipped out of Jordan, a desire evoked by Hugh's frequent graphic descriptions of beautiful snow-tipped mountains, the dark lochs nestling deep in the valleys. It sounded very much like Switzerland, to which Jordan had taken an instant liking during the family's itinerant life. "Say, Hugh, is there any chance I could come with you? I'd like to see Scotland."

"No, that's not possible, I'm afraid, Jordan." Good-naturedly he ruffled Jordan's flaxen hair.

"Oh." Jordan was crestfallen. "I'm sorry; I shouldn't have asked."

"No reason to apologize. In any case, you have enough to do without taking time off from school to go gallivanting around."

"I haven't had any time off yet. Most of the boys manage a few days here and there." He had not intended to press the subject, but one more try couldn't hurt. "I could pack in a flash. Besides, my passport's in order."

"It's about time you learned to take no for an answer, my lad. And something else," Hugh added, snorting with laughter. "You don't need a passport to get into Scotland, you jackass. It's part of the United Kingdom."

"Right," sighed Jordan, resigning himself to rejection. "Oh, well, another time. Who knows—maybe Dad's next assignment will be Scotland!"

"You've certainly been around for a lad. Your passport must be in tatters."

"Just about. I've always had my very own passport, you know," Jordan explained. "It usually turns out that Mom and I travel separately from Dad; otherwise, I could have been on his. Mine looks ordinary, but it's not. The number is a special one, and the letters show that it's issued to a dependent of someone in the diplomatic corps."

"Does it give you privileges?"

"It can be helpful, I guess. If there's trouble in a country, a diplomatic passport can prevent your getting grabbed at the border. There's a special identity code. The digits are mostly dates of birth, expiration, and so on. It's information no forger can get hold of easily."

"I wonder if forgery of passports is a big problem."

"Not forgery, but fraudulent passports are an industry."

"How come you know about it?"

"My father worked on it at one time. He used to talk to me about it—showed me how it was done."

"Isn't that classified information?"

"It's been in the newspapers, I think. And of course the criminals know about it anyway."

"I thought that a passport got issued only after careful investigation. They don't go around handing them out indiscriminately."

"Applicants are examined as carefully as possible, I think."

"Aren't we talking about forgeries, then?"

"No; the passports are authentic. They're fraudulent because they're not issued to the people who are identified in them."

"That doesn't make sense, Jordan. It's not hard to check up on information. They must have heard of computers."

"They use computers, sure. What they can't control is the information that goes to them. It's the volume of business that defeats them. Millions of passports are issued every year, and out of those, maybe sixty thousand are issued to people using names other than their own. It's not difficult if you're determined. You can get a birth certificate for almost anyone simply by applying. If you don't want to apply for someone's birth certificate yourself, you can buy one in an assumed name for a couple of hundred bucks. With that you can get a secondary document, like a driver's license. Or you can use the name of a friend—he'll probably never know the difference—or take the identity of someone who has died. That'll cost you maybe twenty-five dollars. And you're in business."

"Good Lord! You certainly know a lot about this, Jordan. Have you ever thought of taking up passport forgery yourself?"

They both laughed.

Suddenly Hugh turned serious. "Speaking of crime, has it occurred to you, Jordan, that computers have created a new environment for breaking the law?"

"How's that?"

"Bank robberies often net about ten thousand dollars, but embezzlement, monetary fraud, sums missing from banks—that kind of crime comes to about twice as much. And the average amount stolen through computer manipulation is nearly half a million."

"Gosh, that's incredible!" Jordan's eyes widened.

"But that's only part of the story. As you might assume,

a lot of computer crime goes unreported, or even undetected. And often the amounts taken are never known. So it looks like the true figure from computer theft is a million, or even more. A million dollars a hit! Who said crime doesn't pay?"

"There must be lots of computer experts in prison," Jordan observed wryly.

"That's what is so striking. Just like your passport criminals, many of them get away with it. First, because it's white-collar crime, nobody gets hurt—hit over the head, that is. So the courts are inclined to go easy: the crooks are often from respectable backgrounds, and it's usually their first offense."

"How do they steal the money, Hugh? I mean, I can understand how they can reprogram a computer, but how do they physically get hold of the money?"

"Well, say you're working in a bank; you could instruct the computer to credit your own account with a large sum and then go and draw it out. Or, if a computer were issuing checks, you could arrange for yourself to receive a nice fat one."

"Wouldn't that be found out?"

"In such a simple case, yes. People have done just that, then grabbed the money and disappeared. That's a little simpleminded, though, isn't it? The really interesting examples are the complex ones. A man who organized the checking accounts of a big New York bank programmed the computer to deduct a few cents from each of a large number of accounts by rounding off to whole numbers. Not regularly, just two or three times a year. For a while it wasn't questioned. No way an auditor would bother to call the bank and raise a query over a few cents. He'd just assume they got lost somewhere in the computation. And an individual with a private account would think the mistake is his own. The computer programmer had the money transferred to an account in his name at another branch of his bank, where he wasn't known. It was a long time before it came to light—something like three hundred thousand later. By that time he was far away."

"That's neat, man!" Jordan was smiling.

"Here's another dodge. People working for a credit card company acquire bogus cards, then program the computer so that they have bags of credit and go around buying anything they please."

"I'd like that, Hugh—to buy anything I want."

"I doubt if you'd like going to prison to pay for it."

"What else?"

"Oh, lots of examples." Hugh was looking at his watch. "But they'll wait. It's time to close up shop. Come along, laddie."

"Of course, you young men do not come to Wynchgate to learn about electrical equipment and mechanical devices. Technical colleges and places of similar ilk abound where you can learn how to replace a fuse. It is assumed that our students need not acquire such mundane skills in order to earn their livelihoods. We further assume that a Wynchgate student will have superior objectives motivated by a need to enhance the environment in which he will live, that he will wish to know the value of heritage, and that he will become well versed in spiritual, moral, and philosophical values; that we will succeed in implanting the understanding that his function in life is to lead, not to follow. It is no accident that a disproportionately high percentage of Wynchgate old boys occupy positions of authority in the political, judicial, and professional life of this country."

Hutton was addressing an informal gathering of the class, a slight sneer on his emaciated face. "However, we cannot ignore the march of technical progress entirely, and so, mainly at the instigation of one member of the class"—he looked at Jordan with a hint of reproval—"who apparently is fascinated by blinking lights and things that go click, the school has obtained a computer." He gestured disdainfully at the Apple on his desk.

"This is a computer," Hutton went on, unable to keep the scorn out of his voice. "I feel no shame in telling you that I personally have no idea how the contraption works or what it does, and furthermore, I have no intention of finding out. However, it seems, from what I am told, that these things are here to stay, and I wouldn't want it said that any Wynchgate student who wished to know about it was disadvantaged by being denied the opportunity. Accordingly, the *thing* will be installed in the science lab, and your science master no doubt will be able to instruct you in the mysteries of its operation. In the meantime"—he positively glared at Jordan—"our resident expert will interpret its applications to you in such a way that you will each prepare an essay, to be on my desk at eight tomorrow morning, describing the function of the apparatus. Freeling, you may step forward."

"But, sir, I'm not prepared—"

"In view of the enthusiasm you project, Freeling, and the understanding of the subject you thereby imply, I feel sure you will be willing to give us the benefit of an impromptu lecture."

"I've never given a lecture before."

"It's a good time to start. You may begin now, Freeling." He marched from the classroom.

As soon as Hutton was out of earshot, "You twit!"

"Yankee shithead!"

"It's sports night, for Christ's sake. . . ."

"I hate writing essays—and we've only got tonight."

"You'll pay for this, Freeling."

Back in his room, after he had attempted to explain the fundamentals of the Apple to his fellows, Jordan quickly wrote out a simple thesis on computer operations. And then he revised it twice over, at the glowering insistence of Piers and Hakim.

"Is it my imagination, perhaps, or is Mr. Hutton getting worse?" Hakim inquired.

"It's war, that's what it is," Piers declared grimly.

"It's about time something was done about Hutton."

"Like having him put down!" Jordan rarely expressed malevolence, but Hutton had put him in bad with his classmates.

Jordan, smiling, handed Hugh a newspaper folded open to an inside page. "There's a report in here of a wise guy who robbed a savings and loan of a million and a half."

"Oh, yes? How did he do it?"

"He was the chief teller, in charge of an IBM 1402, and took the money from big accounts, then had the computer cover up for him by shuffling around money from other accounts. When there was an audit, it took four days, and during that time, the teller would slip back into the office every night. He transferred money from the day's audited accounts onto the balance sheets for the next day and produced bogus printouts. After the auditors had completed a day's work, they didn't need to go back over the printouts they had finished with."

"What tripped him up?"

"That's the funny part. He never did make a mistake. What happened was the auditors thought it was fantastic that everything in the accounts was immaculate. So they sent the books to the head office as an example of how it should be done. That's when someone discovered that a million and a half was missing through his skimming."

"So what happened to him?"

"He was sent to prison for two years. Yet over here"—Jordan indicated another column in the newspaper—"is the story of someone who robbed a liquor store for ten thousand who went to prison for five years."

"Perhaps that robber was a habitual criminal. A number of factors can determine the length of a prison sentence," Hugh said. "Maybe the bank teller returned the money."

"Oh, I see. . . . You were going to tell me why it's difficult to prosecute computer criminals."

"Are you thinking of becoming one?"

"No, but it's interesting, the things people do with computers. And if they can't be prosecuted, that gives them a certain power, doesn't it?"

"Power?" Hugh looked quizzically at Jordan.

"Maybe that's not what I mean. Anyhow, do you have the time to talk about it?"

"I trust you're not considering a life of crime?"

"Oh, come on, Hugh."

"We'll have to make it quick. Now, let me see. . . . What we're talking about here mostly is embezzlement—misappropriation of funds in large institutions such as banks. It's vital for them to appear stable and safe—secure places for people to deposit their money. Rumors could do irreparable damage. When a computer crime in a bank is uncovered, at the same time it reveals that the bank's data-processing system is vulnerable. It implies that the bank is negligent in the handling of money, and people wonder what else is going on that the bank doesn't know about or is even trying to conceal."

"This is fascinating."

"There's one case where a bank computer programmer embezzled about a quarter of a million. When auditors took a close look, they realized that the bank had been losing another ten million through carelessness. The bank sent the thief quietly on his way with the quarter of a million. He had inadvertently exposed a situation that had been edging them toward bankruptcy."

"They could have prosecuted him."

"And lay themselves open to dozens, hundreds of suits for negligence in handling the bank's affairs?"

". . . Oh, I see."

"In fact, computer crime sometimes seems to be committed because the instigator is aware that exposure would embarrass the principals."

"So he got away with it?"

"Scot free—you should excuse the expression."

"Gee, that's incredible."

"I'm glad it amuses you. Now, do I have your permission to return to my work?"

Walter wondered if he were falling in love with Nina. Many of her attributes were those he admired in a woman, and he saw few of the faults. Most of all he liked her independence. She wore it like a badge, proud and sure of her ability to cope with the world—and proving it every day.

Their sex life had fallen into a pattern more suited to a virile younger man. Walter was surprised to find himself so sensual, reawakened to an awareness that matched Nina's hungry, sometimes ravenous, appetite. Before Nina, he had accepted the idea that his days of overt male performance were past, that his potency was on the decline. Now, discovering a new world, he was revitalized.

Up on Solway Firth, the predicament caused by objections to the new submarine base had finally resolved itself. Writs from residents and objectors, heard in court, were thrown out. Nina, by patiently organizing meetings and repeatedly explaining the necessity for the base, had managed to obtain the backing of several influential opinion makers. A TV discussion devoted to acceptance of such a base was warmly praised because of her rational presentation. Now bulldozers had moved into Cumberland Dale and work had begun in earnest.

"Hey, Dad, is it true—about that old guy in the cape who's been wandering around the embassy?"

"Yes, Jordan. His name is Professor Theodore Plutz. He's a Hungarian theatrical émigré and a master of disguise."

"Gee, imagine that. I thought Hugh was kidding me."

"Auchterlonie should keep his mouth shut. How did he come to know about the professor, anyway?"

"Oh, it's common knowledge in the building. And Hugh doesn't discuss things like that with most people. Only me. He knows I won't talk about it."

"You're talking now, aren't you?"

"Only with you, for Christ's sake—ah, what I mean, Dad—I don't tell things to outsiders. This Professor Plutz, I understand that he is teaching staff about disguise."

"Apparently you know the story," Walter conceded reluctantly. "Yes, it's true. He is to teach the art of disguise to some of the agents who occasionally come to the embassy from other offices."

"Any chance I can get to attend?" Jordan asked eagerly. "I'd like to know how to change my appearance. Will you see about the chances for me?"

"Yes, I'll ask. I don't suppose it would cause any harm. Now get out of here, will you? I have some work to do."

"I'll be with Hugh when you're ready to leave."

As he moved through the outer office on his way out, Jenny Handel, at her desk, gave him a slinky wink. He blushed self-consciously, wondering if she had observed him studying the swell of her breasts under her sweater as she typed while he'd been waiting for his father.

It worked out fine for Jordan. Because Professor Plutz had a commitment with an operatic company performing at Covent Garden, he scheduled his class for Saturday mornings at ten. Jordan found himself in company with a team of CIA men, slim hips and wide shoulders and Brooks Brothers suits, looking sideways at the young man with new hair on his upper lip. One of them, acquainted with Walter, had been requested to keep an eye on Jordan, and a quiet explanation from him satisfied the others.

In the embassy briefing room the agents sat waiting as ten o'clock came and went. Then impatience tinged the banter as the minute hand moved to ten minutes past.

"Where's the prof?"

"Hey, did we get the day wrong, or something?"

"No sign of him in the corridor."

"Maybe, with that cape he wears, he'll fly in through the window like Superman."

At that the door opened and an archetypical English military type with bowler and umbrella, bristling mustache and Abercrombie topcoat, stepped into the briefing room. "I say, you chaps, has anyone seen Professor Plutz? We had an appointment, but there's no sign of the blighter." His accent was pure BBC.

"No, sir." One of the agents had risen respectfully. "We're waiting for the professor ourselves."

"Damned poor show, what? If you don't mind, I'll wait here for him. He's bound to turn up soon."

The major seated himself rigidly, staring straight ahead, and said nothing more.

Conversation between the agents had become muted and sporadic. The minute hand of the wall clock moved on. When it reached twenty minutes past the hour, the major spoke. "Ah, the professor has arrived." The agents looked at one another, mystified. "Good morning, Professor," the major said, staring at the wall.

"Good morning, Major Finch," he answered himself—in the professor's voice.

Slowly the military posture of the major was relaxed. He removed his bowler, and the professor's unruly hair dropped free. He turned his face away from the rest to work on his features. When he turned back, the mustache was gone, the naturally bushy eyebrows had sprung back into place, and the blue eyes were again brown. He stood and slipped off his topcoat, which had been concealing his loose cape. As he faced the class, his appearance, with a few minor alterations, had returned to that of the untidy Professor Theodore Plutz.

He gave a small bow and, to a man, the agents stood and applauded.

"I hope that is a lesson to you, gentlemen," Professor Plutz said. "I might have been an enemy agent concealing a machine gun. I could easily have wiped out a number of valuable American agents and left without a problem. The lesson is: Don't trust the obvious!"

"Hell, Professor," one of the agents blurted out, "how can we protect ourselves against a disguise like that? I've never seen anything like it before. You were simply—a different person."

"It was a strong caricature. A personality already in your minds. I had only to suggest it, and you did the rest. If you had looked closely enough, clues would have told you that I could not possibly have been a British major."

"But I didn't see a damn thing out of place—" the agent began, but Professor Plutz stopped him.

"The very first thing is that the character was too overdrawn to be real. A parody of Colonel Blimp. A person could not be expected to conduct himself like that today."

"You sure fooled me," the agent said and sat down looking worried.

The professor, now of a perceptive gaze and mobile face, spoke with what sounded to Jordan like a German inflection. "We will be discussing two types of disguise in the beginning, " he began. "Later we will move on to refinements—speech, mannerisms, and habits. For the sake of simplicity, I'll call them coarse and fine. Coarse is for general use—to blend into a crowd in a city street, for example. The other is for close, intimate work. You may wish to convince your wife that you are a handsome movie star whom she admires. It is not impossible. Improbable, but not impossible." The agents laughed as if on cue.

"Could you make me good-looking?" one of them asked.

"Beauty is in the eye of the beholder," the professor responded. He was gazing keenly at two agents. "I note that you are above average in girth. That is a distinct disadvantage when one wishes to appear innocuous. We will therefore begin by considering clothes that, if they do not diminish your outline, will serve to blur the results of a surfeit of American fast food."

The reference helped to remind Jordan that he was feeling hunger pangs. He suppressed his stomach's complaints with willpower in order to concentrate on Professor Plutz's first lesson.

As the professor's explanation of visual deception continued, his youngest student clearly sensed the potential for the art. He promised himself that at the first opportunity he would make use of these intriguing instructions.

CHAPTER SIX

"I can't believe I finally made it! More important, that we are still together." Hakim gazed around the room they had been assigned at Oxford. With their belongings transferred en masse, it looked little different from the room they had occupied at Wynchgate. "My uncle the king will be most pleased that I managed to pass the university entrance examinations," Hakim added contentedly.

"You managed *what*?" Piers demanded cynically.

"I am here, am I not? What more do you want?" Hakim retorted with an attempt at dignity.

"Do you honestly imagine you would have passed those exams under your own steam?"

"Of course. That is, I would have."

"*Alors,* I do not believe it." Piers threw up his hands.

"Lay off the guy, Piers, will you?" Jordan interjected.

"He is mad. If it weren't for you, he would be heading back to the sand dunes by now. It's a good thing you took his math and physics exams for him. You got a hundred percent on both papers, and he probably still only managed to crawl in by an overall one percentage point in those courses."

"What's the difference? He made it, didn't he? That's all that matters."

"Piers is right." Hakim suddenly changed his mind. "It is dishonorable for me to take this attitude. I disgrace my forefathers by not admitting the truth. I am most grateful to you for your assistance, Jordan. Both I and my family are in your debt."

"Do you think Hutton suspected anything?" Piers wondered.

"Possibly. Who cares?" Jordan said airily.

"We'd never have succeeded if we hadn't come here to Oxford for the tests. And the timing, of course. You're a lucky bastard, Hakim, that Jordan was free both afternoons."

"I thank Allah for my good fortune," Hakim assured him piously.

"They think they're clever, splitting up those who arrive from the same school so that they have to sit different sessions. I wonder if anyone else has ever done that—substituting, I mean."

"Not much is new under the sun," Hakim observed.

"I guess it's been done before," Jordan murmured from the bed. He sat up to look out of the window. "Hey, some of these dames, they're not bad-looking."

"I mean the way you disguised yourself. That was incredible. When I saw you walking, I thought you were Hakim myself. Where'd you learn to do that, Jordan?"

"Oh . . ." He hesitated. "An old professor I know. He's an expert on makeup, and he showed me how. Hey, look at that one. Boy, that's real class. . . ."

For a moment all three of them studied the girl who had caught Jordan's attention.

"You know, I have one regret," Piers remarked. "Our departure from Wynchgate was an anticlimax. We will quickly be forgotten by Mr. Hutton and the rest."

"So what?"

"I did not leave my mark. We have a saying in French: Ships that pass in the night. That is how I feel."

"Forget it, Piers," Jordan told him.

"If I had your ability to change my appearance, I would disguise myself and go back and punch Hutton on the nose. I cannot stand that man."

"I can disguise you, if it means so much to you," Jordan said, half-jokingly.

"You can?" Piers came and sat on Jordan's bed. "Do you really mean it?" His eyes were round.

"Sure." Then, knowing how intent Piers could be, he had second thoughts. "Aw, forget it. What will that achieve—punching a master on the nose?"

"A great deal of satisfaction for me." He sensed Jordan's disinclination. "What's wrong?"

"It's not a good idea," Jordan decided. "You might be grabbed, and then there'd be hell to pay." They sat for a moment while Jordan studied the floor. "I have a better idea," he said. "I've been reading some newspaper reports about . . ." He stopped to lean back and study Piers. "Yeah. You're about the same size and shape as Hutton. We could get away with it."

"Get away with what?" Piers was impatient.

It was a two-hour drive back to Wynchgate. They made one stop, at a menswear store, to buy an off-white raglan raincoat and cap similar to those Hutton habitually wore. Piers put on the raincoat and cap. "What do you think?" Jordan asked Hakim.

"Turn around and walk, Piers," Hakim instructed. Piers walked away. "Bend your shoulders, the way Hutton does," he called.

At the far end of the store, the receding back had an uncanny resemblance to that of their old housemaster. "That's good," Jordan approved. "Okay, let's get going."

It was seven o'clock when they arrived at the service road behind the Wynchgate grounds. Forty-five minutes passed before Piers concealed himself in one of the arches leading onto the quadrangle. It was an area illuminated only by a few meager lights, and he could blend into the stonework. He waited. Everyone in the school knew that Dean Umberson dined at seven and that an hour later Mrs. Umberson took her dribbling little Pekingese for its nightly constitutional around the quadrangle. It was a routine she never varied.

True to form, Mrs. Umberson appeared on the stroke of eight, strolling slowly along the path that led toward Piers, her dog sniffing and piddling along behind her. Piers had calculated exactly where he wanted to be when she arrived at the arch.

As the dean's wife came level with the arch, he leaped out. Mrs. Umberson shrieked. Piers remembered to stand with his shoulders hunched in the housemaster's characteristic stoop.

"Oh, Mr. Hutton, you frightened me so!" The dean's wife held her hand to her chest. The Pekingese growled low.

It was then that Piers opened the raincoat to reveal his total nakedness. He pushed his pelvis forward in a primitive movement.

Mrs. Umberson stood gawking, too stupefied to move.

Piers snapped the coat shut and turned away. Puzzled

that Mrs. Umberson had not reacted, he changed his mind, turned back, and repeated the performance, embellishing it with suggestive gestures.

As Mrs. Umberson came to life, Piers disappeared into the darkness. He could hear her screaming, "Mr. Hutton, you filthy beast. I recognized you—don't think I didn't. The dean will know about this, Mr. Hutton. You're not a fit person to teach boys at this school. I'm going to call the police, Mr. Hutton, you little prick!"

"I've been reading up on computer crime," Jordan was saying. "I found a new book. Want to see it?"

"Not particularly," Hugh replied shortly, concentrating on the VDU before him.

"I'll bring it in next week."

"Why does the subject fascinate you so much, Jordan?"

Jordan peered at the display Hugh had produced on the screen. "It's a challenge, I guess. You know better than I that one of the biggest headaches computer manufacturers have is security. Almost no program can be devised that can't be unprogrammed."

"Computer crime often is committed by semiskilled operators. It's more a question of opportunity than skill."

"Oh, I'm not even interested in that. Those people are just thieves."

"And a skilled person isn't?" Hugh gave him a wry look.

"It's not the same thing when it's a challenge, is it? By the way, you crossed a loop."

"I did?" Hugh's gaze shot back to the screen.

"You can't use the same control variable if you haven't nested the other loop."

"I know that, dammit!" Hugh pressed some keys, vexed that his protégé had caught him up in a careless error. "Anyway, as I was about to say, security is improving all the time. Encryption's the thing now, using passwords."

"But encryption can never work properly as long as imperfections exist in the operating system. It's not so hard to find the flaws—just takes a little time. Then you can gain entry to the list of passwords, even ones you don't want. The more complex the system, the more the likelihood of flaws. It's a circle the designer can't beat." After Hugh thought that over, Jordan added, "Of course, there's the *other* way."

"Go on," Hugh urged quietly.

"Trapdoors! They're even better. You can use trapdoors that the audit system will never recognize."

Under his eyebrows Hugh peered at Jordan, surprised at the depth of understanding his pupil was displaying.

PART TWO

CHAPTER ONE

Over many months Virginia had settled into a way of life that now seemed as permanent as her alienation from Walter. Their married life together was slipping away into past memory. She still lived at the spacious Knightsbridge apartment, where she had made a separate nest for herself. Virginia no longer was imagining him in the bed of the noblewoman who had stolen her husband's affections. Surprisingly, he had done nothing to pursue a divorce, which caused Virginia to conclude that he did not expect to marry.

She would have returned to the States long ago had not Walter unexpectedly found her a job in the visa section of the consulate. Her aim, originally, was to occupy the empty days, but the work turned out to be interesting, and her newfound competence had restored some of her dignity. Usually she returned home at the end of her day, spending evenings with television for companionship. Jordan's weekend visits were all she had to look forward to.

Drinking alone was the hardest part at times. Occasionally she began conversations with herself she couldn't finish—times when she could have ended climbing up the wall if she stayed confined to the apartment any longer. At such moments she found solace in slipping out to the bar at the nearby Inn on the Park.

Tonight was one of those occasions when she felt impelled to be near people and their chatter, irreverence, and laughter. At the inn she could always find American tourists, mostly new to London, and often she struck up a conversation, discussing their European adventures.

She was early; few people were in the bar. Most of the hotel's residents would be still at dinner. She sat at a table, ordered a whiskey sour, and prepared to wait for company. At the next table a man sat alone—handsome, conservatively dressed, and perhaps forty years old. Definitely not an American, Virginia assumed, taking in a slightly square jaw and graying hair. A Pole or a Czech, perhaps. When he ordered a drink, he spoke English easily, with enough accent to suggest that he was German. He took a map from his pocket and opened it onto the table.

Virginia had already lost interest when she realized that he was looking toward her with an apologetic expression. "Execuse me, madame," he said carefully. "I wonder if I may ask a small favor of you? Unfortunately, I have left my glasses upstairs in my suite. I have a business appointment tomorrow at a place called Charing Cross. I am trying to locate it on the map, but the print is too small for me to read."

"Oh, certainly; bring it over," Virginia answered quickly. "Charing Cross, you say? Let's see, now. . . ." She consulted the listing. "Here it is, near Trafalgar Square."

"Yes, I see." He screwed up his eyes, standing politely over her. "That is not far from the hotel?"

"Three or four miles, maybe. Just give the taxi driver the address. London cabbies know every inch of the city."

"Yes, of course. You are American. Many Americans are here, I notice. It means that service is prompt and the bathrooms are clean. This is important for someone who travels as much as I do."

"You are German?"

"Austrian. Edward Branden, of Vienna." His head nodded mechanically in another small bow.

"I am Virginia Freeling, of nowhere."

"I do not understand. . . ."

"Oh, just a personal joke."

"Yes, I see." He clearly didn't and hesitated. "I wonder if I may ask . . . no, that would be presumptuous of me. You obviously are waiting for someone to join you."

"I'm not waiting for anyone." The abrupt truth came out spontaneously.

"In that case, I am wondering if I may ask to sit at your table. I assure you that I have no ulterior motive. I am a gregarious person, and I don't enjoy solitude. I shall be here in London for some time and relish the opportunity of discussion outside of business."

"Why, that would be very nice, Mr. Branden. Do bring over your drink."

"*Eddie*, please. And I am delighted to join you. May I order you another drink?"

"No, I'm fine, thanks." She was grateful that she didn't feel an immediate need for liquor. "What business are you in, Mr. Branden . . . Eddie?"

"I own a small engineering company on the outskirts of Vienna. Here is my card." It read *Obtek Engineering —Edward Branden, Director*. "And you? You are here in London on vacation?"

"No, I live here."

"At the hotel?"

"No, in Knightsbridge."

"You are married, of course? Oh, I am sorry—I did not mean to ask personal questions."

"That's all right. Yes, I'm married. My husband . . . my husband represents some American interests in London."

She didn't care to reveal a connection with the diplomatic scene and then to hear some cockeyed version of U.S. government transgressions. "He travels a lot, too. He's away at present."

"He is?" For a fleeting instant he seemed to frown. "Unfortunately, travel is a fact of business life these days. It plays havoc with one's homelife."

"It certainly does."

For an hour they talked of shows, music, climate, travel, small personal preferences. Virginia thought that Branden was perfectly impersonal while being attentive and polite. Finally he announced with evident regret that he would have to finish some paperwork before retiring quite early in order to be fresh for his early business meeting.

"I'm very grateful for your company, Virginia. Perhaps we can meet here again tomorrow."

"I don't come every night."

"What a pity. Well, I shall be staying at the hotel for some time. I'll be sure to look for you in case you feel like another little chat one evening."

"Okay, Eddie."

"*Auf Wiedersehen*, madam." Another of his little bows, and he was gone.

She stayed home the next evening to watch TV. She purposely did not pour herself a single drink and was bored by the endless, repetitious sitcom episodes.

The following night she left the set turned off. At the inn the bar was crowded. A big influx of tourists had arrived. She spotted Eddie Branden occupying a small booth at the back of the room. It was virtually the only empty seat. She walked toward him with a smile. "Hi! Mind if I join you?"

He rose, grinning broadly and clearly pleased to see her. "I've been hoping you would come. I seem to be the only one in the room who's not with someone."

She sat next to him. "I had the impression you make friends easily."

"I have a confession to make to you, Virginia," he said. "It was the first time in a long time that I have struck up an acquaintance with a lady."

She found something different, more pleasing about Eddie this evening. He had changed from his square-shouldered formal business suit to a blazer and open checkered shirt. He smelled of a good cologne, too, Virginia noticed.

A while later they could hardly hear themselves speak above the noisy chatter. "We seem to have hit a tourist party, " Eddie said, looking around.

"It's getting a little like a firemen's convention," Virginia said.

"May I make a suggestion? If you have the time, would you like to see the show at the Talk of the Town?"

"Tonight?"

"I don't know. Does it matter? I have a friend who is in that business—he will be able to arrange a table for us."

"But I'm not dressed for a night out—"

"Nor am I. We will go as we are."

Virginia brightened. "Okay, if you can fix it."

"I'll go make a phone call."

He was as good as his word. Barry Manilow was the featured star. Although she adored his voice, she would usually have resisted going to hear him in concert, where he'd be besieged by hordes of drooling girls. But from the comfort of an expensive table, she enjoyed the show immensely.

Eddie returned her to the Knightsbridge apartment in a taxi. When he kissed her hand, thanked her for the pleasure of her company, and then was gone, she was feeling almost like her old self.

The next evening, in response to his phone call, she had dinner with Eddie in the hotel. Afterward they sat in the bar and chatted. The riotous crowd of tourists had moved on, and the bar was back to normal. She returned home before it closed.

She was becoming pleasantly accustomed to Eddie's company, and though she didn't find him highly attractive, it was infinitely better than loneliness. She could sense familiar stirrings and the need to satisfy them.

Ten evenings passed before he asked her up to his room. She had already decided that if he made a pass, she wouldn't resist. She was soon pleased to discover that Eddie was as gentle and considerate a partner as she could recall. Unimaginative, yes, but she could supply exotic imagination. Eddie was eager to please and acquiesced rather clumsily to her excessive demands, patiently helping her to the heights of ecstasy and abandon she craved.

Their couplings became a habit, and Virginia was intent on making the most of Eddie's amorous attentions before his inevitable departure from London. She felt content to possess the satisfaction of each evening, putting out of her mind the boredom that was tomorrow's certain prospect.

And then he hit her with the bitter unbelievable truth of their nights. When she walked into his suite on a Saturday afternoon, he was wearing the business suit with square shoulders that reminded her of Poland. "Please sit down, Mrs. Freeling," he said formally.

"Mrs. Freeling?" She laughed but couldn't see the joke. Then she noticed the fixed, hard look on his face. His gaze was not meeting hers. Now he was a cold, calculating stranger, as if the intimacies they had shared were only illusions. A sudden thought shot through her—an awareness she had allowed to drown in self-pity. The shiver that flashed down her spine left her gasping, trembling.

"Eddie, what's wrong? Why are you behaving like this?" Even before she spoke, she knew her words would be futile. The only question was how bad it would be. A movie projector was propped on a chair and a sheet pinned to the opposite wall. Like an automaton, she took the chair that Eddie indicated with a curt gesture.

"I am going to show you some moving pictures of yourself, Mrs. Freeling," he said emotionlessly. "I will pull down the shade so that you can see better." He appeared not to notice how her body was vibrating uncontrollably. The room darkened. A click, a whirring, and there in color on the screen was an explicit record of the various ways in which she had satiated herself with an almost faceless bit player. The camera was merciless, and she realized that Eddie's ponderous actions had been an attempt to position her so that so far as possible, the concealed camera had an unimpaired view. Like a rabbit hypnotized in a beam of light, she could do nothing but watch, unaware of the barely human sounds she made watching her own prurient movements. The projector stopped; the shade was released and clattered noisily as it rolled up.

"You bastard! You filthy Russian bastard!" she hissed.

"I am not a Russian, Mrs. Freeling."

"Then what *are* you, for God's sake?"

"That is none of your concern." He spoke tonelessly.

"What do you want?" She choked on her words.

"I want information."

"I have no information to give you."

"It is information you will find easy to obtain. Facts about activities at the embassy—the numbers of people assigned to certain operations—a few names. Nothing you cannot obtain in casual conversations there. Or in pillow talk with your husband. I am sure you can find ways to distract him so that he will be unaware you are questioning him." A note of cynicism crept into his voice. "I will instruct you how it is to be done."

"And if I don't get this information?" Her own voice sounded like a stranger's.

"Then I very much regret I will be forced to send copies of this film to the American authorities and to the newspapers. Apart from the entertainment value it will provide, you will find it a considerable embarrassment when the pastime of a diplomatic wife is discussed in public. Your marriage may survive, but it is doubtful if your husband's career will."

Utterly defeated, Virginia sat in trembling silence until he added, "Is it agreed, then?"

"I can't do it."

"You are a foolish woman. The information I require is not highly classified material. Little more than gossip."

"I can't trust you."

"It is a business arrangement. No trust is necessary."

"You don't understand. I'm not close enough to my husband. We're getting a divorce and—"

"Now you are lying to me. That is very unwise, Mrs. Freeling. You live in the same apartment as your husband. Your son comes home—"

"Jordan!" A horrified gasp escaped her.

"Your son comes home from Oxford every weekend and spends his time at the embassy. I assume he is helping his father. All the signs are of a harmonious family life."

Virginia could think of nothing but Jordan. The shame he would endure if her exploits became public knowledge. She knew how it was possible for the shameless tabloids to publish suggestive pictures so that enough was concealed to avoid outright obscenity. But people knew, nevertheless. They guessed the rest. All the fight had gone out of her.

"Well, Mrs. Freeling?"

"I—I need time to think it over." How the words had formed in her mouth she did not know.

"Very well. Three days. I'll be here. If I haven't heard from you by midday on Tuesday, I will have to assume you do not wish to cooperate, and you will have to pay the price."

Eddie opened the door and stood there, waiting, staring. As if in a trance, Virginia staggered out to the elevators.

CHAPTER TWO

On the stroke of midnight Walter entered the apartment. A small light burned in the hall, but otherwise all was in darkness. He thought little about Virginia these days but, from habit, glanced toward the far end of the hall to the rooms she occupied. The doors were closed, and he walked silently on the thick rug to his bedroom. As he opened the door, he heard a sound, looked around, but saw nothing. Inside the bedroom he began to undress, then to lay out what he would need for the next day. The bedroom was so stuffy he opened the door.

He heard a noise again and stopped to listen. He moved softly to the passage to glance again toward Virginia's rooms. A few steps along the passage, he realized a light was on in her bathroom. The thin line beneath the door was almost concealed by carpeting. He moved closer and stopped before the bathroom door. He could hear it now: sobbing, spasmodic and hardly audible, and the sound of motion, subdued. He heard what seemed to be glass breaking—a few pieces tinkling. Then a sharp intake of breath, an unmistakable low moan of desperation as the sobbing ceased. A piece of glass tinkled as it fell, perhaps into the tub.

The door was locked, and he crashed against it, using his shoulder with all the force he could muster and yelling Virginia's name. The flimsy lock gave way and he burst in. Virginia sat on the edge of the tub, her features unrecognizable, blood running from a cut on her wrist. Blood ran in a thin red line, staining her clothes and the floor. But the powerful pumping action to be expected from a severed artery was missing; the cut was superficial. As usual, Virginia hadn't succeeded.

"You damn fool, Virginia . . ." He grabbed a towel and pressed it to her wrist.

"I couldn't do it, Walter. I tried, but the glass wouldn't cut." She spoke like a child, her eyes enormous and staring.

"Why, Virginia, why?" He stemmed the flow of blood, bathed the wound with antiseptic, and bound it. "Put your hand on your head. Just sit there and don't move," he ordered and hurried out to bring a shot of brandy. "Here, drink this!" He held the glass while she drank.

She coughed as the liquid burned her throat, and the violence of coughing seemed to shake her out of her trance. "I'm sorry, Walter. I didn't mean . . . to give any . . . trouble." Her words came in small gasps.

"I want you to sit down while I call a doctor."

"No! No doctors!" She sat up as if electrified.

"Now, come on, Virginia. That's a bad cut, and you need attention."

"No doctors, Walter. If you promise not to call a doctor, I'll tell you why I did it."

"Put your hand back on your head; it helps stop the flow of blood. . . . That's better. . . . Now come in here and sit down." He led her into the living room and seated her. "Good, there's not so much blood now. In a couple of minutes I'll change the bandage."

With the second bandage, the flow was diminishing. "I'll be all right now."

"You have to learn to accept change, Virginia. This is an infantile thing to do. You should be thinking about making a new life for yourself. And I should have known things would go wrong, both of us living in the apartment like this. . . ."

"I didn't do it because of us, Walter."

"Then why?"

She had come to the end of the road. Virginia sighed deeply and began to tell the story of Eddie Branden.

The agent on the case had been exposed to Professor Plutz's course. He was big and bulky, and the professor had given him special attention so that he could lessen the chance of being spotted for what he was at fifty yards. Nevertheless, Patrick Muldoon still wore his hair so that it seemed to have been shaped around the edge of a bowl. They had gathered in Walter's office at the embassy.

"Okay," Muldoon was saying, "the situation is this. When we grabbed the guy, we were too late to stop him from shipping out the negative of the film to Moscow. So we tried to work out a deal with them—return the negative and they could have their man back. They weren't very interested, I'm afraid."

"They weren't interested in getting their own agent back?" Walter asked, surprised.

"He's not a Russian agent. Edward Brandenberg is an East German who operates out of Austria on a free-lance basis, selling scraps of information to the Russians. Vienna is swarming with people like Brandenberg, all trying to scratch a living."

"So he has no value to them?"

"Not a lot. They could make more capital out of following his original idea of releasing the film," Muldoon said. "He intended to, you know, once he had wrung Mrs. Freeling dry. It would have put him in good standing with his Russian paymasters. Anything that will embarrass and belittle Americans is useful to them. The Kremlin gets a kick out of creating a stink in an important diplomatic center like London."

"So there's no deal?" Walter dejectedly inquired.

"It's not entirely hopeless yet. I've been talking to my opposite number at the Russian consulate—and I may have convinced him that they should have Brandenberg back."

"Is Brandenberg no good to us? Can't we get some information out of him?"

"He's not worth his keep. We could buy him for ten dollars more than the Russians are paying. These guys consider they've made it to the top when they're taken on as double agents."

Virginia, seated in a corner, had aged twenty years. Shrunken, her hair tangled, and her face devoid of makeup, she mumbled, "I'm so sorry. It's so awful to have caused all this trouble."

"One of those things, ma'am," Muldoon said in an effort at kindness. "You weren't to know Brandenberg's a spy. It's been going on a long time, you know. But, if they do release the film publicly, it's going to be tough on both of you. Not much we can do about that, I'm afraid."

"My career will be finished, for one thing," Walter stated baldly. "The department doesn't forget. It's the way it has to be. I represent the American government, and that's a significant responsibility. If I can't handle my personal affairs, I have no right to hold this position." Walter straightened his back.

"I'm so sorry," Virginia murmured again.

The telephone rang and Walter picked it up. He handed it to the agent. "It's for you."

Muldoon listened for a moment, said, "Uh-huh," a couple of times, then, "Too bad," and put the receiver down. His glum expression told Walter all he needed to know.

"They didn't hand over the film?" Walter's voice was from down in his shoes.

"No. I must agree with you that this will be very difficult in the department, Mr. Freeling. Get set for it."

"I don't have much choice, do I?"

For the first time Walter looked directly at Virginia, the utter hopelessness on his face matching hers. No more need for the bland diplomatic facade, the expressionless gaze that revealed nothing. For once, he could allow his face to reflect the black despair in his soul.

CHAPTER THREE

"You look terrible, Walter," Nina said as she escorted him into the living room of her Belgravia home. "Would you like a drink?"

"Thanks. If you would, please."

She brought it. "Now sit down and tell me what's happened."

Instead, he began pacing the elegant room. "I haven't burdened you with this before, Nina, but I've had severe problems with my wife in the past. . . ."

"I gathered that. You clearly weren't on the point of a divorce without reason."

"She has had several . . . liaisons. I don't know how to say more. . . ."

"You needn't. I have a vivid enough imagination. She sounds like a really dreadful person."

"She isn't, that's the strange part." He was silent a moment, then said, "I think she needs more love than I can give her. That may sound inane, but it's the only way I can think of to describe what I feel. Even now, I still feel Virginia is a victim of circumstances not really of her making."

"Has she found someone new?"

"Yes, understandably. What I didn't expect was that she would pick up a Russian spy."

"What? My God!"

"The oldest trick in the business and one she was well aware of. We've heard often enough how the Russians use sexual exploitations to get information."

"What information could your wife give them?"

"They wanted her to pump me."

"And she did?"

"She never had the opportunity. Virginia wouldn't have done it, in any case. She can't possibly cope with anything so devious."

She refilled his glass. "Is that all there is to it—the man turned out to be a spy?"

"No. He has compromising photographs. They're quite bad. And a God-awful film. The photographs already are being circulated. They're in the hands of the press."

"Is there no way you can persuade them not to use the story?"

Walter's sardonic look was its own reply.

". . . I suppose not. We can look forward to a lascivious account in the Sunday tabloid. How will this affect you, Walter?"

"Me? Oh, I'm finished here in England. I'll be shipped back home pronto, you can bet on that."

"That seems unfair."

"What's fair or unfair? If I hung around here, I'd be an embarrassment to the department, a liability. I wouldn't want that." A silence fell between them for several moments. "It leaves us quite a problem, doesn't it?" he added quietly.

"Yes, it does." She was looking at him intently, but her green eyes were unfathomable. He hesitated before plunging on.

"I haven't said this before, Nina, but I know I'm in love with you. I want you to come back with me to the States, and as soon as I can divorce Virginia, we'll be married. I realize that I can't offer you the life you're accustomed to here, but with enough love on both sides—" He stopped because Nina had begun to laugh. Quietly, in the back of her throat. "What's funny?" he asked sharply.

"You are, Walter! God, you really are a fool where women are concerned."

"Are you saying you don't love me?"

"I can't think of anything more remote from reality. What does love have to do with it?"

"Please answer the question, Nina."

"Very well, the answer is no."

The directness of her response shook him. This time he went to the whiskey bottle himself. When he turned, his face was rigid. "Thank you for being so candid. I'll finish this drink and go."

"Why be so abrupt with me? Have I suddenly turned into a goddamn ogre for telling you the truth?"

"The way we've been together, I thought at least . . ." He left the thought incomplete.

"I didn't realize you were such a romantic, Walter. You surely don't think life is like the movies, where all problems end when the loving couple walk off into the sunset hand in hand?"

"Now you're being banal."

"I could say the same about you." A hint of cynicism crossed her lovely mouth, then was gone.

She turned away. "It's not quite as simple as you imagine. There's something you don't know. In these days of high taxation, it's becoming increasingly difficult to maintain . . . the quality of life, shall we say. I've been getting into financial difficulties, and I may lose Bolsover Castle. I would simply die if that were to happen. The place represents six hundred years of family history, entrusted to me, and it's more important to me than life itself. I was about to negotiate a deal with the National Trust for them to take it over and preserve it before this damn stupid scheme for a submarine base came along. Now they say Cumberland Dale no longer qualifies as a beauty spot of historic interest. That means I lose their support, and I'm no longer able to maintain—" She stopped, realizing how she must sound to Walter.

"You should have told me, Nina. I could have suggested other options for you."

"There's nothing you can do. But the same can't be said of Ambassador Fitzgerald. If he puts my case for compensation to the American government, they can't ignore it. It's the only chance I've got left, and I'm fighting tooth and nail for it."

When she turned to look at him, he could see a new fervor in her eyes. She was a different woman from the warm, lovely creature he knew—she was a tigress, and he knew instantly she would swat him unmercifully if he were to hinder her cause.

Then, just as suddenly, the fire was gone, and she was asking, "What will happen when you go back to Washington, Walter?"

"I'll be relegated to some minor job and never be heard from again."

"I've a suggestion, if you're interested. If you should prefer to stay in England, I could arrange a position for you. Possibly with a company doing business in the States. You're quite capable, and I'm sure you would rise to the appropriate opportunity. But it would have to be with the understanding that we would not—would never—resume our own relationship."

He shook his head. "I'm too old to change direction now. I'm a State Department employee—always have been and always will be. Best thing I have to look forward to is retirement and a pension."

He gave way to one more inescapable humiliation. "If I did stay here, you're sure we could not go on as before?" He studied her expression.

"No, Walter dear, I'm afraid not." She smiled but otherwise was unmoved. "What happened between us is now a part of the past. History—that's all!"

"I understand." He put down his empty glass. "It's been lovely knowing you. I don't suppose we'll meet again. Good-bye, Nina. . . . And thanks."

"Good-bye, Walter."

He wondered briefly if he should kiss her. He decided not, turned, and walked briskly to the door without looking back.

For a change Hugh had stopped his incessant fiddling with equipment and sat looking at Jordan with an expression of dismay. "That's terrible," he said. "That's bloody *ter-r-rible.*" In emotional moments he tended to accentuate his rolling *r*s. "When are you going back?"

"Immediately. That is, within a few days."

"What's the bloody rush? The damage is done now."

"My parents are keeping a low profile. Keeping out of the way of reporters. It's bedlam at the apartment. I daren't go near there. We're staying at a house in Chelsea that the embassy found for us and trying to keep the address secret."

"It's tough on you."

"I've gotten used to the idea now. I have to admit it shook me badly when I first heard about it. That was on TV."

"Couldn't they have let you know first? It was damned unfair, letting you find out the hard way."

"They tried to call me at Oxford, apparently, but I was out for the day on a field trip. I'll be sorry to go. Not so much because I have to leave Oxford, but because I won't be coming here anymore."

"Can't you remain at Oxford until you graduate? You don't have to go back to the States just because your parents are going, surely?"

"No, but all the people at college know about what happened. They don't say anything directly to me, but their glances are enough. I'm beginning to feel uncomfortable, and in a way, I'm glad to be getting out."

"I understand. How about your two buddies? Have they been giving you a hard time?"

"Piers and Hakim? Oh, no, they're real bricks. Piers tells me I should see it as a great laugh, and Hakim pretends to be worried that he won't be able to crib from me anymore."

"They'd soon forget about it if you stayed. You have to develop a tougher hide, Jordan. Don't let the world kick you around."

"My father can't afford to keep me there, in any case. When he goes back, he loses seniority and the extra pay he was getting in London."

"Oh, if it's money that's worrying you, I can advance you enough to finish your studies. You can pay me back later when you have a job. That's no problem." When Jordan made no reply, he added, "Or how about the Arab boy? He throws money around like water, doesn't he? You've spent enough of his money on equipment to see you through to a professorship. He won't even miss it."

"It's not the same thing."

"Don't quote principles to me, young Freeling. Survival's the name of the game, and don't you forget it. It's not as if you won't be able to repay a loan one day, is it?"

"What I mean, Hugh, is I don't feel the same. I feel I've been wasting my time at Oxford. It's been something of a game, but now the game is over, and I have to think seriously about what I'm going to do with myself."

"You don't feel the same about the time you've spent with me, do you? You've become a computer expert I would back against almost anyone. That's no mean achievement."

Hugh noticed how the pale blue eyes, now three inches

above his own, had hardened into those of a man. "Now I want you to pay attention to this. Though I say it myself, I command a great deal of respect at IBM in New York for experimental work on computers I've done in the past. I'm going to write them about you and ask that they give you an opportunity in computers if you ever have reason to inquire. You could always have a backup career available if things aren't going your way otherwise."

"Do you think IBM really would take me on?"

"Someone I trained? My apprentice? They would fall over themselves!"

"I'll remember, and I'm grateful! Well, it's time I went home. We have a lot of packing to do. We're off in the morning."

"This is good-bye, then?"

"Yes, I won't be back. I appreciate all you've done for me, Hugh. I'll never forget it."

"I should hope not." Hugh's usual Scots tartness was tinged with fondness as, for the last time, he shook hands with the one he had guided between youth and manhood.

Jordan would go far. Of that, Hugh had no doubt.

CHAPTER FOUR

At Heathrow Airport a bright crisp morning followed early fog, and the volume of traffic circulating the terminal buildings was as great as ever. The taxi carrying the Freelings found a gap in the vehicles unloading at the intercontinental building and dived in.

Walter's diplomatic passport ensured that they circumvented the crowd and were taken to a special desk. Within minutes they were cleared through into the departure lounge, where it was cooler and less hectic.

As they approached their departure gate, a stream of passengers released from an incoming flight poured forth. The Freelings were making their way through the throng when a middle-aged, tough-looking but otherwise nondescript character, walking head down, slammed into Jordan and knocked his flight bag from his hand. The burly, unkempt individual in a rumpled suit quickly retrieved Jordan's bag and handed it to him. Beneath a bush of sandy hair peppered with gray, a rugged face wrinkled into an apologetic smile. The Freelings cleared the crowd and moved on to board their plane.

Sam Kilmartin, glad to be moving after sitting for hours, resumed his forceful gait toward the immigration desk. His manner of walking caused the bottoms of his pants legs, an inch too high above his shoes, to snap around his ankles. He reached for his passport and the documents that identified him as a longtime U.S. Treasury agent.

As he waited in line, he grinned ruefully at his clumsiness in running into the young American on the concourse. For most of the flight he had slept soundly, and he was only now coming out of the stupor. Dog-tired when he boarded at Dulles Airport, he had found it a welcome change to be able to lie back, with no telephone by his head to jar him awake.

The young man's face swam into Sam's vision again. He had discerned no surprise or shock on his face when the flight bag went sailing away, just dull acceptance. Sam had seen the look before, on the faces of people being arrested—a look of resignation. The lad's lack of reaction troubled Sam vaguely. It was his business to understand instinctive reactions. If reaction was not spontaneous, it usually was because someone was guarded, was hiding something . . . or felt distressed to such a degree that it dampened spontaneity.

That was it; something must be bothering the young fellow. Something pretty darn bad, he would guess.

It was an intelligent face, good-looking in its way, sensitive and untouched by the soiled fingers of worldliness. Sam remembered faces.

He felt a tap on his shoulder. The man who grabbed his hand was Ralph Heritage of Scotland Yard's counterfeit squad. "Welcome back, Sam! I've a real tough case for you."

Washington was disheartening, depressing, and like stepping back in time. Walter was back at the department in a thoroughly mundane capacity. Worse, the apartment he had found was cheaper, smaller, and noisier than the one they had given up to move to London.

"It's time we made some arrangements for you to complete your education, Son. We'll have to see what we can do about fitting you into a college."

"I've been thinking of it, Dad. Maybe it's time I took a job. I don't feel like going back to college. I'm considering a career in computers. I discussed it with Hugh before we left London."

"I've never been entirely happy with the influence he had on you. What future is there in being a computer mechanic? How can you compare that with a diplomatic career?"

"I could be a designer, or a programmer."

"Would you be satisfied working nine to five in some factory? Is that really what you want?"

Jordan was silent.

"I don't understand you, Son. Lots of people have hobbies, but they don't let them take over their professional lives."

"Undoubtedly, there are other ways to go."

"Why have you set your mind against the department?"

"I haven't! It's just that I think you got a raw deal. I don't want to spend my life worrying over whether my face fits, the way you've had to."

Walter looked at his son, appreciating Jordan's perception. "It isn't that difficult. The world of diplomacy has its inhibitions, but then so does every other activity. You get used to it, and the life can be rewarding, if you're successful. You get to travel a lot and meet people. There's a certain stature, too—"

"Aw, c'mon, Dad. What's stature worth in today's world? Money's the only thing that counts. With money a person doesn't need stature."

"I'm afraid I don't have money, Jordan. Not the kind of money you imply. Stature makes a good second best, even in your terms." He waited. "Look, you can't spend your time just hanging around the apartment. You have to make a move in some positive direction."

"I'd really like to take a course in computer science."

His father tried to object, but Jordan went on. "Not for a career. Just to get myself motivated and to take my mind off things. And to get a change of scenery."

"Where will you be taking the course?"

"I've been hearing about UCLA and what they're doing there."

"California?" Walter's surprise showed. "That's a little far, isn't it?"

"Far from what?"

A momentary, bitter spark in Jordan's blue eyes died instantly. But it burned a scar into Walter's heart and reminded him that Jordan was a loser, too, in the game of adult personalities.

"I think I could earn some money servicing computers, or something of the sort, in my spare time."

"Since we haven't heard from your mother, and it appears she isn't making a claim for alimony, I can spare enough for you to go west to study. On one condition."

"What's that?"

"I've told you, I don't want you working as a computer

mechanic. You're likely to ease yourself into that situation, so the part-time job is out, please."

"Dad, wake up! Working with computers is hardly the same as becoming a grease monkey."

CHAPTER FIVE

California! Hot, and so bright that Jordan was constantly wearing darkened aviator's goggles. He loved it, the room looking out over Westwood, the frenetic pace of Los Angeles. A call from an associate of Walter's had ensured that a place at UCLA awaited him. As a refugee from U.S. government policy in Europe, he was entitled, was the response.

The computer science course was easy, he found; principles and elementary stuff he'd long ago left behind. He quickly gained the reputation of something of a computer genius when it was assumed that he had swallowed the esoteric intricacies of microcode at a single gulp. One of his instructors, more astute than the rest, became suspicious of his phenomenal ability, so Jordan built a few errors into his programming.

L.A. was a great place, but he had one problem: Without a car he was seriously handicapped. If his plans didn't fit in with someone else's, he didn't travel. Public transport, other than up and down a few boulevards, was virtually nonexistent. The solution was a double-header, as Jordan saw it: buy a car or find a girl who had one.

He chose the latter.

He identified one girl who came regularly to the ice-cream parlor that could be seen from the window of his room. She drove a Mercedes sports convertible and was invariably alone. He knew she was a student because he'd seen her elsewhere on the campus. He guessed she attended a nearby tennis club, because she was always in a brief tennis outfit, with a lissome body that made him look again. She was almost as tall as he, with long golden hair tumbling over her shoulders and a California tan that gave her a sleek, oiled look.

He strolled the short distance to the ice-cream parlor, ordered a small vanilla cone, and sat at a table outside to eat it. Before long the Mercedes drove up. He watched her climb out and stride gracefully into the shop, long legs flashing. Now, as she was walking out, wrapping her tongue around an exotic looking double-dip cone, he tried to appear casual and offhand as he called out a tense "Hi!"

"Hello," she responded languidly.

"You're over at the arts campus, right?"

"Right. You too. I've seen you."

"You have?" He studied her generous mouth, cherry-colored against the pale ice cream.

"You live over there." She pointed at the window of his room. "I've noticed you watching me. You might consider being less obvious. More discreet, shall we say?"

He colored, and a dollop of ice cream ran down his chest. "Damn!"

"I'm Holly. Holly Benedict. What's your name?"

"Jordan Freeling."

She took another lick at the top of her cone. "Where you from, Jordan?"

"Washington."

"Studying?"

"I'm, ah—computer science."

"A number cruncher, huh? I've seen some of those. They go around with eyes on stalks."

"You noticed." He smiled for the first time.

"Oh, you can smile, too? Rather a nice smile, actually." She flicked her lashes at him twice, then went back to wearing down the cone.

"Where's your guy?" With a body like that, there was bound to be one somewhere in the picture.

"No guy. When you're going to be a tennis star and you spend all your time out of school whacking a ball, there's no time left for boyfriends."

"Tough. You're going to be a tennis star, Holly?"

"It's what my parents would like. My mother is nuts about the game, though she's never played. If her little girl could only make it into the state tournament, she'd be on cloud nine."

"Is her little girl going to make it?"

Holly shook her head. "I'm pretty good, but I'll never be championship caliber. Listen, Jordan, I have to go now. Got to whack a few balls around." She took a couple of steps and turned. "No wisecracks!"

"You said it, not me."

"Keep looking out the window. Who knows, maybe we'll meet again."

He felt slightly humiliated that she had so easily led him along. And yet she was quite a fascinating character, this Holly Benedict. Interesting, and more vital than most of the girls who hung out at Westwood, he thought. But he could see little prospect that Holly, with her independent way, would be solving his transportation problem, and decided he would have to look elsewhere.

No solution had offered itself two nights later when he stood behind his venetian blind to watch for Holly's arrival. This time he wouldn't go down, he resolved. He needed a driver, not a girl who was going to lead him around by the nose. Ten minutes later, he was about to give up looking, when she drove up, wearing a loose-fitting blue shirt and skintight jeans instead of her tennis gear. She sat down at what he thought of as his table and looked toward his window. He was sure she couldn't see him, but she continued to stare. It was virtually a challenge, one he couldn't resist.

"What took you so long?" she greeted him as he hurried toward her.

"I thought you weren't coming."

She didn't pursue it. "Notice anything different?"

"You're not playing tennis tonight?"

"I'm not playing tennis period. I told my mother contenders have to screw the organizers if they want to get into the state competition. That did it!"

"How long had you been playing, Holly?"

"Seriously nearly four years."

"Funny you should give it up suddenly. You have some other activity in mind?"

"What do you think?"

He couldn't believe his ears. Was this delectable female propositioning him? He swallowed. "What do you say we go for a ride, Holly?"

"Where do you have in mind?"

"The beach maybe. Santa Monica and north along the coast."

"Okay," she said agreeably.

She was a good driver, fast and positive, and the surefooted Mercedes suited her style. It was pleasant being driven along the Pacific Coast Highway with the balmy air caressing his face. At Malibu she turned off onto the beach, and they sat watching the sun sink on the horizon, turning the sea to orange.

When they kissed, the first hesitant, exploring contact, he responded strongly, immediately to her scent and the soft, supple movements of her flesh. They shared a wild moment of abandon as he crushed her to him, and their mouths blended together.

He was traveling in style, driven around town by Holly, who seemed to grow even more gorgeous and desirable as their romance blossomed. Now that she had thrown off the prohibitions of prospective tennis stardom, she was making up for the months of grinding practice she had endured, the enforced abstinence. It was tough aspiring to be another Tracy Austin.

They couldn't get enough of each other and went around fully aware that they drew admiring, sometimes envious, glances. Out of the public eye they spent hours locked in each other's arms, inhaling deeply of the incense of life they drew from one another and oblivious to the world. Jordan became familiar with every soft curve of her body, every graceful movement; when they weren't together, he could caress her in his thoughts. Holly became equally familiar with his physique.

They were creating their own small world, so that their names became synonymous among the students who knew them, and outside of class one was rarely seen without the other.

Because it was Holly who invariably came to pick him up and they had the privacy of his room for necking sessions, Jordan hadn't realized that he had never been to her home. One afternoon she told him her mother wished to meet him.

"She knows about me?" Jordan asked, unprepared for this development.

"Considering that I'm rarely home anymore, what do you think?"

"I hadn't thought about that."

"You're a real dummy, Jord, you know that? What's a mother to think when her daughter doesn't turn up night after night until the stroke of midnight? That she's turned into Cinderella? Sure she knows. I've told her all about you."

Holly's home was between Beverly Drive and Bel Air. In the warren of curving, shrubbed lanes that forms the exclusive residential section of Beverly Hills, they turned suddenly through iron gates set in a high fence surrounding what seemed to be a small park. An approach road swung across an extensive, immaculately kept lawn toward a mansion standing in regal, detached solitude. As the Mercedes accelerated toward the house, a pair of Filipino gardeners glanced up, recognized Holly with a nod, and got on with their work.

"You *live* here? You didn't tell me you were rich . . . your family. Not this rich!"

"You didn't ask."

"For Christ's sake, it's like a palace. What does your Dad do? Own a movie studio?"

"His company makes paper bags."

"You're kidding. I thought people who live up here were connected with the movies."

"That's what everyone thinks."

A few moments later he was standing in a large elaborate center hall, astonished to realize that Holly came from such luxury and wealth. Her mother descended on them. Martha Benedict was upright and full chested in a Balenciaga dress, diamond earrings, and a mountainous coiffure. She examined Jordan. "How do you do—I'm Holly's mother. I've been hearing a lot about you."

"Pleased to meet you, Mrs. Benedict."

"Do you realize that you are my daughter's first steady date?"

"I'm privileged, ma'am," Jordan said cautiously.

"He looks well enough behaved." She addressed Holly, but kept her eyes on Jordan. "That's something to be grateful for!"

"Aw, Mom, do you have to say things like that?" Holly asked, pained.

"He's not *that* sensitive, is he?" In response to her daughter's reproving look, she went on. "Oh, well, come along. Dad's waiting."

After meeting Martha Benedict, Jordan expected Holly's father to bite or at least roar. Paul Benedict was slightly shorter than his wife, thirty pounds overweight, and the heavy freckling on his face continued up over his forehead and through the few remaining hairs on his shiny scalp. He stood waiting with a mild expression. "Hi there, young feller," he said pleasantly. "Would you like a drink before dinner?"

"No, thank you, sir."

"Well, I'm no drinker myself, so let's get on with dinner. Call me Paul. I don't stand on ceremony."

In a sumptuous dining room, they were served by an elderly Mexican couple. Martha Benedict spoke to them so familiarly that Jordan guessed they must have been with the family for a long time.

"You do realize," Martha asked, over the salad, "that Holly is our only child?"

"Yes, I have gathered that."

"And you?"

"No brothers, no sisters for me either."

"I understand that your father is a diplomat?" Paul Benedict spoke up for the first time with an inquiring look.

Jordan shot Holly an annoyed look. He had instructed her specifically not to discuss his private affairs with anyone. He might have known she would make an exception of her family. "That's correct, Mr. Benedict. He's a career man with the Department of State."

"Say, that must be quite a life. I guess he travels a lot?"

"We've been on station in a number of countries."

"You always go with your father when he's working abroad?"

"Right from when I was born."

"Your mother, too, I take it?" Martha put in.

"That's right. It will be different now, though."

"Why is that?"

"They've separated."

"Oh, that's too bad," Martha said. She looked at her husband, eyebrows raised slightly.

"Besides, I don't think my father will be going abroad anymore. He expects to stick to Washington from now on."

"How about your education, Jordan? Makes it a little tough on you, doesn't it?" Paul inquired. "How old are you, by the way?"

"Not really. Most American embassies have a setup that takes care of families. When the children are older, they usually go on to university. And I'm nearly twenty-two."

"Did you study in the States before coming to UCLA?"

"No, I was at Oxford. Unfortunately, we were shipped back before I could graduate."

"Say, tell us about that," Paul said with interest.

"Don't forget to eat," Martha reminded Jordan. "You've hardly touched your food."

Jordan ate while telling them about Wynchgate and Oxford's Balliol College and relating stories of his friendship with Piers and Hakim. He left out Hugh Auchterlonie's important role.

"I understood from Holly that you're taking computer science. Isn't that a career course?"

"Yes, sir."

"It's graduate level, too, Dad," Holly put in.

"Hey, you must be a pretty smart lad," Paul said. "I like that. I think I'm a little paranoid about education. Where I come from—Hoboken, New Jersey—it was tough. Very few people could afford to educate their children. If you got past the ninth grade, you were considered an egghead. I only made eighth myself."

Jordan was amazed. "And yet now you have accomplished enough to own all this?" He gestured at their surroundings.

"There's another kind of school, son," Paul Benedict said. "The school of life. That's where I got my real education. These days I have people with degrees working for my company at three plants. I couldn't even tell you how many, not without checking. And a few thousand other folk, too."

"Gee, that's incredible, Mr. Benedict," Jordan said, with genuine admiration.

"Tell me, Jordan. Am I really missing the boat by delaying the whole business of converting my operation?" Paul Benedict was doubtful.

"Computers are already revolutionizing every aspect of our lives, in time, Mr. Benedict."

"I realize that. The reason I ask, I'm being badgered by my directors to approve a system of computerization for the company. So far I'm not too keen. It's costly, and I get the feeling I'm being sold a bill of goods. Our operation is not complex in a numerical sense. A lot of paperwork, it's true—invoicing, records, and all that. The paper drives us crazy. We get buried in it."

"You have no alternative, sir."

"You're that positive?"

"Operations like yours should be relatively paperless by now. Some people do find it hard to accept. They're used to the old ways. If you don't computerize, you'll get left behind."

Benedict's eyes narrowed, and he rolled his cigar in his mouth. Eventually he said, "I'm going to tell you the truth, son. You're a little young, but I can see you're an aware type, so maybe you'll understand." He paused, then spoke in a rush. "The friggin' things frighten the shit out of me. . . ."

"Mind your language, Paul," Martha bit off icily. "You're not out in the plant now." Holly grinned and studied her hands.

"Sorry," Benedict muttered. "Jordan, do you understand what I'm saying? A guy like me, from the old school, I'm completely out of my depth when it comes to computers."

"I'd be happy to advise you on a suitable system for your business," Jordan said. "One you can read and understand."

"No way, son! I'm defeated before I begin."

"You can count, can't you? Say, one to a hundred?. . ." Benedict nodded warily. "And as far as a thousand?"

"What help is that?"

"Forget the complexities. I'll program the system so that it answers your questions simply, by numbers. What you have to do is make up a list of questions to ask: amounts incoming, outgoing, daily totals, weekly totals, balances—anything you want. We'll give each question a number. And we can add on later, too, when you've got the hang of it. You'll have your personal code that will bring your personal program on line. Your name will do—PAUL.

Or you can have a secret code, if you want. All you'll do then is type in the number, and the machine will answer the question that fits the number."

"That doesn't sound difficult."

"You won't have to ask anyone a thing, unless you want to. You'll have a terminal in your office that will enable you to put your finger on the pulse of the business any time you want."

Benedict had forgotten his cigar. "That coding thing. Can I really have my own secret code? One the others won't know?"

"Sure."

"I'm getting ideas, son. With you behind me, I'm not going to look like the goof they're all expecting to see. Right?" Jordan nodded again. "Hey, maybe I'm jumping the gun here. Are you willing to help me with this thing? I'll see you don't lose over it."

"I don't want anything, Mr. Benedict. I'm pleased to do it."

"That's one swell boyfriend you have here, Holly." Beaming, he turned to his daughter. "Maybe now I'll get a little return on those goddamn tennis lessons I've been paying for."

CHAPTER SIX

Dear Hugh,

Thank you for your welcome letter. I'm glad to hear you are well, and I am okay, too. I am now well into the computer science course here at UCLA, but it's kid's stuff compared to what I was doing there with you. The only positive advance I'm making is in microcode, where I've been expanding my programming knowledge through some material recently released by NASA.

I've got myself a smashing girlfriend. Her name is Holly, and her old man is stinking rich. She has a figure like you've never seen and drives around in a Mercedes sports car. That kind of solves my transportation problems because if you don't have a car here in L.A., you're dead. I get along fine with Holly's old man, and I've designed a computer system for his business. He was leery at first, but now he can't get enough of it, and he's got me to show him how he can keep tabs on what everyone in the outfit is doing. He found out that one of his directors has been cheating on false supply invoices for twenty years and reckons I've saved him a million dollars, but I think he's exaggerating. He's offered me a job, but I don't want to spend my working life in the paper bag industry.

That's about all I have to write for the present, and I will let you know of any developments careerwise. I will have to make up my mind soon whether I want to take up my father's suggestion of trying for a position in the department. I can't seem to work up a great deal of enthusiasm, but with his backing, it would seem to offer the best career prospects.

I'm still missing England. If Professor Plutz is around, please give him my regards.

As ever,
Jordan

When Walter walked from the office that evening, he was in a daze. His career, already on the wane, had received yet another critical blow. His supervisor had explained that he would now be subordinate to a much younger man. At first he had managed to maintain an equilibrium. But now it was all overboard. His whole life's work was out the window, and he couldn't do one damn thing about it. Not that he even wanted to. To hell with them all!

As he left the department, he ignored his car and walked to the Lincoln Memorial. He wandered into Constitution Garden and spent a half hour absently studying the Reflecting Pool. He began walking again and lost track of time. When he tired of walking, he stopped to look around. Anything would be better than returning to that dismal, lonesome apartment, he thought. A bar's flashing neon sign beckoned.

He took a stool next to a big man with straw hair and a weather-beaten face who was steadily drinking beer but apparently finding no pleasure in it. Wearing a denim suit and cowboy boots, he looked even more grim than Walter felt. Walter ordered a scotch and water and downed it quickly. He felt a sudden desperate need to converse, and when he ordered another, he asked the stranger if he could buy him one.

"I appreciate that, sir. I'm drinking Bud." The barman brought over the beer. "Name's Chuck Bellows."

"Walter Freeling," Walter said. They shook hands.

"Sure meet some fine people here in the big city. Don't often get the chance to talk to an important-looking fellow like you back where I come from."

For the first time in weeks, Walter found himself smiling. It was mandatory that he present an impeccable appearance at the department: white shirt, club necktie, pencil-striped suit, polished black shoes.

"Where are you from, Chuck?"

"Oh, a small place near Elk City, far side of Oklahoma.

Out there in the sticks—the name wouldn't mean a thing to you."

"In Washington on business?"

"I guess you could say that. I'm off for home in the morning. If I start at dawn, I'll just about make it to my field by the time the sun goes down in the Panhandle. It's just about halfway across the continent. You can spit on Texas from where I live," he added by way of explanation.

"There's no way you could drive that distance in a day, Chuck," Walter said.

"I ain't driving. Got my own Piper Pawnee. That's a crop duster. Empty, she'll cruise 125 knots all day."

"Oh, you're a pilot."

"Sure am. That's why I'm here in Washington. Came all the way up here to hang one on those smart dudes over at the FAA. Of course, I couldn't find anyone who was willing to take responsibility, so I'm heading back disappointed."

Walter decided they both needed another drink. The whiskey was warming him and neutering the pain and anguish that washed over him whenever he made the mistake of thinking about his predicament. "I gather the aviation boys did something you don't like," he said after a while.

"That's right. They took away my license. Fact is it expires midnight tonight. I'll be flying back home illegal tomorrow."

"Is that wise?"

"Don't give a shit!"

"What did you do to lose your license, Chuck?"

"Nothing—some goddamn Okie doctor decided I couldn't pass my medical. Hell, just look at me. I'm strong as a bull!" Chuck flexed his arm muscles, then downed the rest of his beer. "Want another?"

"Sure, why not?" Walter drained his glass and slid it across to the barman. After he tasted the fresh whiskey, he commented, "You look good to me, Chuck."

"Yeah, I got another ten, twenty years flying in me yet. Can't convince that goddamn sawbones, though."

"What does he say is wrong with you?"

"Says it's the lungs. Don't remember the medical term for it. A sediment . . . something like the coal miners get from years down the pit, breathing that bad air. Comes of flying upwind into the chemical spray when I'm dusting. Kind of an occupational hazard." He gave a rueful grin. "Can't do the job right unless you're down there sitting on top of the crops."

"I've seen you fellows do that, racking a plane around and coming back low. It sure is skillful flying."

"Gets so you can fly through the eye of a needle." Pride showed through in Chuck's voice.

"Have another beer, Chuck?"

Chuck nodded.

"Barman, fill 'em up," Walter called out.

It was late and dark by the time they rolled out of the bar. On the sidewalk they shook hands and parted, walking in opposite directions. Walter had no idea where he was, only that he had not reached the oblivion he had sought. He'd had a snootful, he knew, realizing he was a little unsteady on his feet. But he had no real sensation of being drunk.

The flyer's problem bothered him. The man had nothing to live for. He, too, had nothing to live for. They were two of a kind.

Inwardly he blamed himself for what had happened. Virginia, knowing about Nina, had gone on living in the Knightsbridge apartment while he flaunted another woman. He knew why she had stayed—her love for Jordan.

Poor Jordan, he found himself thinking. His brilliant son, a boy with a mind faster than a calculating machine, his education now in ruins—and all because of a father who hadn't the judgment to perceive what was going on around him and to react decently.

Suddenly his eyes were full of tears, and with the rain, everything had become a wet blur. Funny, he hadn't realized it was raining, yet he was soaked, and water was running out of his hair in rivulets and down his face.

Through the mist he could see lights coming along the street. A kind of moving Christmas tree that splashed, rattled, and roared its way toward him. He couldn't see exactly what it was, except that it was a huge moving vehicle, huge enough to put an end to all his troubles.

For just an instant, he hesitated. But so deep was his misery now that he gave it no real second thought. As the howling monster drew near, he stepped off the curb and walked straight into its path.

CHAPTER SEVEN

It was a cold, damp day, and the mourners could be counted on the fingers of one hand as Walter Freeling, lonesome in life and now permanently lonesome, was conveyed to his final resting place. The unruly crowd that had gathered to await the cortege had spilled across the somnolent lawns of Whitecross Cemetery, trampling on carefully laid floral tributes decorating nearby graves. Several reporters and photographers, scrambling for vantage points, jockeyed for position.

When the hearse appeared at the cemetery gates, a murmuring arose as people moved forward to observe the occupants of the only passenger car. When its door opened, Jordan stepped out first, offering his arm to his mother. Virginia's veiled appearance was the signal for a popping of photographers' flashbulbs. Two reporters, bolder than the rest, moved up to question Virginia, until the disgusted funeral director, fuming, informed them in a penetrating whisper that he would flatten anyone who lacked the common decency to stand back until the completion of the ceremony. Her face white behind the veil, Virginia drew back. Resolutely, Jordan reached for her arm and led her away from the car.

It seemed endless, the pathetic little ceremony, the lowering of the coffin into the grave, and the struggle to get out of the cemetery. Now they were back in Walter's lifeless apartment, and the worst was over.

When Virginia removed her veil, Jordan looked at her anxiously. "You okay? You're not looking too good. There's some brandy here. I think we can both do with something. . . ." He poured out two large shots and handed one across to his mother. He swallowed his and coughed. Ordinarily liquor had no attraction for him, but now the fire it induced evoked a sensation of comfort. "Drink it, Mom. You need it."

"I feel so helpless, Jordan." Virginia sighed. "I only wish I could support you until you finish your course at UCLA, but I can't be certain."

"I only have a few months to go, and I'll manage. As I say, I'll find a job. Don't you go worrying yourself about it." He had in mind that Holly's father was obligated for work he had done. Although Paul was in his debt, Jordan hadn't intended collecting. But now things were very different; he would have to seek ways to have a real income. For a moment Jordan considered explaining how he probably could manage to complete the course at UCLA. But that would have meant explaining about Holly, and it didn't seem an appropriate time. He noticed a different expression on his mother's face. "What's on your mind, Mom?"

"The thing is," she said, "I have to go back to work in the morning. I'm fairly new at the job, and I can't take advantage. They know my whole story, and they've been very kind about it. It's that sort of family."

"Me, too. I think I'll go back to California in the morning. Except for you, there's nothing more for me to stay here for." He was silent a moment, then added, "You know, I just realized something."

"What's that, Jordan?"

He spoke quietly, betraying a determined strength of conviction. "I hate Washington! I hate everything it represents."

Virginia looked at him. "Me, too," she said. "I never realized quite how much until now."

CHAPTER EIGHT

Holly was waiting impatiently when he arrived in his room in Westwood. She threw herself into his arms, as if he had been away for months, and for ten minutes they kissed while embracing tightly.

"You look different somehow," he said at last. "It's weird. I've been away only a few days, yet somehow you seem . . . kind of grown-up."

She looked at him, her eyes deep and passionate. "I think being apart has made me realize just how much I love you. I mean it, Jordan. I couldn't stand it. I've been counting every minute."

"I don't have to be away to know I love you, Holly. You mean more to me than anything in the world."

She kissed him. "Did you think of me every moment?"

"Whenever I could. But it's been one hell of a rough ride. It almost got me down."

"Of course, with your father dying that way. Why couldn't you have told me what had happened? When I got your message that you were going to Washington, I didn't know what to think. You might have explained. I was so upset reading about it in the newspaper. Upset for you! You needed me, and I wasn't there."

"It was even worse than I expected. It was horrible." He shook his head at the memory. "It would have made no sense for you to be there, too. A funeral's no fun, and this one was worse than most."

"I didn't mean to make you miserable as soon as you got back!"

"It's okay," he answered dejectedly. "What happened is over. It won't go away, so there's no point in trying to hide it."

She brightened. "Let's talk about something else. Let's talk about us!"

"Yeah," he said, but still looked downcast.

"I have to find a way to cheer you up." She took his hand. "I think I know how to do it."

"There's not a thing in the world that would cheer me up right now." He tried a smile, but it came sadly.

"Oh, no?" Still holding his hand, she pulled him toward the bed. "Maybe it won't make you sing and dance, but what I have in mind will take your mind off things." She released his hand and reached for the buttons on her blouse. "Last one in bed gets to do all the work,"she said pertly.

Much later they sat drinking coffee when Jordan said suddenly, "Let's go over and see your father. I think that I should not seem to be avoiding him because of this."

The alarm that flitted across Holly's face surprised him. "I don't think this is a good time to see him, Jord," she said. "In fact, I think you should stay away from the house for a while."

"I don't get you." Jordan was completely bewildered.

"He's a little worked up over what he read in the papers. He's one of those people who believes everything he reads." She watched Jordan rise from his chair and walk to the window. "I told him it was probably pure sensationalism, but he wouldn't buy it—"

"Come on, Holly. Your father's no fool. He can't be swallowing all that crap."

"Listen to me, Jordan. I know him. He can be a real bastard when he wants, and right now he's furious about the publicity your family is getting—and that I'm associated with you. Give him some time to cool off."

"But Paul and I are friends. We understand each other. If I go over there and tell him what happened, that will be the end of the problem."

"He told me not to see you anymore."

"You're kidding."

"He's hateful when he gets this way. And as stubborn as a goddamn mule if he gets an idea in his head; nothing can budge it."

Jordan reached for his sweater. "We're going over there right now and speak with him."

"Please, Jordan, I know what I'm talking about," she pleaded. Her face was lined with anxiety.

"The hell with it," Jordan snapped back. "I've got nothing to be afraid of. I'm going right now. Are you coming or not?"

"No, I'm staying here." Holly rolled herself up into a protective ball.

"See you later!" He made for the door.

"Wait for me!" Holly had changed her mind and leaped up. "I'd better be around to clean up the blood."

As she drove, Holly tried repeatedly to talk Jordan out of the encounter with her father, but he sat stonily, making no reply.

Less than thirty minutes later Jordan stood facing Paul Benedict in the big house. "I don't remember inviting you here," Paul said with a frigid stare. "But as long as you're here—in the next two minutes—I'll give it to you straight. I've told my daughter not to see you anymore. I guess she has to see you to say good-bye—she's that kind of girl—but I warn you I'm going to see that she never has anything more to do with you!"

"Dad, this is monstrous—" Holly began, tears springing to her eyes.

"I'd like to speak to the young man alone, Holly. What I have to say isn't for your ears. Please leave us right now and close the door."

"I'm not leaving here, no matter what," Holly declared rebelliously. "Don't you have the balls to say to me—"

"Please, Holly, do as your father asks." Jordan's voice was controlled.

"No, I absolutely refuse to go." She glared at her father.

"I think your father is being perfectly reasonable, Holly."

"Well, if I leave you, will you call me when you've finished talking?" Her resolve was cracking.

"I'll call you myself, when he is ready to go. And that will be very shortly," her father said through his teeth, returning her angry glare.

When the door closed, Jordan said, "I'm ready."

"I didn't get where I am by kidding myself. The man who kids himself is never going to make it. Maybe you haven't seen enough of life to understand what I'm saying, but take it from me, it's a fact."

"I can understand that, Mr. Benedict," Jordan said.

"Okay, so now I come to Holly. My daughter is our only child. One of these days what I have is going to be all hers, and I expect to look out for her best interests. You're on the make for Holly. You know she's a good catch, and you think you've found a meal ticket for life. Usually it's the girl who's the gold digger, but in your case it's the other way."

The anger that boiled up in Jordan blinded him. "You're crazy. You have no right to say that!"

"All that nonsense about your proper upbringing. The diplomatic life and a terrific education in England. You were trying to dazzle me with your so-called background."

"That was Holly's idea, to tell you all those things—not mine. I don't go around boasting. I've got nothing to boast about."

"You can say that again."

"I don't know why she's trying to impress you. You got the wrong idea about me, Mr. Benedict—"

"You bet your life I did. Reading about your family in the newspaper straightened me out."

"I never said he was anyone important."

Paul plunged ahead: "I'm prepared to make it worth your while if you'll promise to stay away from Holly. As you've been riding around in her car, you presumably need one. Go down to one of the dealers in the valley and choose yourself a compact. I'll pick up the tab. It's worth it to be shut of you!"

The rest of his words were lost as Jordan turned and strode from the room. Once out of the front door, his tears blinding him, he ran down the driveway until he was well beyond the gates that protected the Benedicts from unwanted guests such as himself.

Hours later Holly came to him as he lay in darkness in his room. She switched on the light. "Please, Holly, turn it off," he said thickly.

It clicked off again, and she was kneeling beside the bed, rocking him in her arms. "Oh, my poor darling." She licked away his tears, and the fresh tears on his face were hers. "I could kill him! I'll never speak to him again as long as I live."

"You don't mean that, Holly."

"After what he did to you? He has no right to hurt you the way he did. Not that I know what he said to you, but it must have been something terrible, from what he said to me afterward."

"He just told me the truth as he sees it. Your father is an honest man, in his way, and I respect him for that."

"He's so cruel when he wants to be. But you're different. Maybe that's why I love you so much." She kissed him, but Jordan continued to stare blankly in front of him.

"He taught me something tonight. A lesson I'm never going to forget," he said slowly. In the artificial light that came through the window, she could see new determination in his eyes. "Funny, but I'm almost grateful to him for that." She was about to respond but sensed that he hadn't finished. "When I came back here, I was lost—totally lost," he continued. "Losing my father was like losing part of myself. I've never felt so vulnerable in my life. He always made the decisions, decided where I was going and what I was going to do. Now I have to make my own decisions. Get out there and fend for myself, or the world will trample over me."

"And where do I figure in your plans?" Holly whispered.

He heard real fear in her voice; her grip on him tightened and didn't relax until he said, "We love each other, and we have to fight for what we want. That's part of what I just learned from your father."

The tears cascaded down her cheeks. "Oh, I'm so glad. You don't know how happy it makes me to hear you say that."

"Don't cry so, Holly."

"I'm crying from happiness, darling. I have some news for you. Maybe it's not the best time to tell you, but I can't keep the secret any longer. If I don't tell, I'll bust. I'm pregnant!"

"Oh, my God!"

"I'm going to have the baby, Jordan! I want nothing more in this whole world than to have our baby. Even if you leave me, I am still going through with it."

"I'm not leaving you," Jordan said in a hoarse voice. "Never!"

Their kiss was fierce and seemingly endless. When

they eventually parted, Holly murmured, "Wouldn't you like to be on hand to hear my father when I tell him?"

Irrationally, excitedly, they both burst into laughter.

CHAPTER NINE

He read the letter from Hugh again. It ran:

Dear Jordan,

I was terribly sorry to hear of your father's death and especially sad that it happened under such distressing circumstances. Kindly convey my condolences to your mother. I take the view that she has been shabbily treated by both the press and the authorities, and you must not allow this incident to sour you in any way. You must always remember that you are the product of your upbringing and that your finer instincts are a reflection of your parents' true aspirations for you.

You probably need some cheering up at this time, so on a lighter note I have to tell you that I had a good laugh at the latest batch of computer scams you sent me. I don't know how to classify your abundant interest in computer crime—I can only say, God help any computer interests that you might want to rip off. With your expertise in microcode, they wouldn't stand a chance. Maybe you should call Fort Knox and ask if they use computers—you might as well start at the top!

Seriously, though, I recognize that with your father now gone, your opportunity of a career with the department may be much less. I have taken the liberty of getting in touch with an acquaintance of mine who is a highly placed executive with IBM. His name and New York number are on the separate enclosure. I explained your circumstances to him and your potential. He ought to be happy to take you in for training in their procedures. It could mean a good job with them and an assured future. And they pay very well. Of course, you don't have to take advantage of this thought if it does not fit your plans. Nevertheless, if you do decide on a career in computers, this could be one way to go.

Yours truly,
Hugh

P.S. Professor Plutz sends his regards.

Jordan's second reading was slow and deliberate; he paused most thoughtfully over the words, "With your expertise in microcode, they wouldn't stand a chance."

And then he walked up and down the room in mounting excitement, stopping occasionally to gaze out his window while his mind summed up the ideas that were racing wildly, clamoring for the logical place in a developing sequence. *If I were to do this, then I . . . No, I should . . .*

His brain was sorting out possibilities that Hugh's good-humored references had created for him. *First of all,* he reflected, *friend or no friend, I'd better lay off all my innocent chatter about computer crime if I write to Hugh again; no more of those clippings.*

As Hugh had accurately pointed out, he did have expertise in microcode. Not only that, but progressive insights that would serve well, if . . . His knowledge of the intricacies of computerization in broad scope would serve well in almost any situation that might arise. . . . Again, the *if* arose. And his ability to hold in the back of his head the most fantastic array of minutiae should be able to prevent his tripping himself up with contradictions, oversights, tricky loopholes. *If!*

Where to begin actively mapping out such a subversive campaign? Not at Fort Knox, surely, though Hugh's joking mention of that citadel did serve to put the much less formidable bastions of American industry and commerce into perspective. Some of them could be sitting ducks for the kind of enterprise that Jordan's thinking was now taking. IBM, for example, to pick up Hugh's further reference. But perhaps that revered concern should serve a wholly different purpose for him—contributing information that could be turned to his advantage elsewhere. And contact inside IBM could provide, as well, credibility, credentials for later operations.

Grave risks there'd be, but the reward could be well worth not only the risk but any reasonable cost. And what an opportunity to show that sonofabitch Paul Benedict what his despised son-in-law could do!

Holly appeared at his door, a McDonald's bag in her hand. "That's one more day you've skipped classes," she said accusingly. "You haven't been to school the whole week."

"I've made a decision. There's only one thing I know about—really know about—and that's computers. I could get a job in business quite easily, but it would lead nowhere. Nine to five, if I'm lucky, for the rest of my life. It would take the fun out of it, and I'd end up a sour, frustrated old guy. That's not good enough for me, Holly. I've seen how the other half lives, and I want mine. I'm going to place myself where I can capitalize on what I know."

"Why don't we just go away and get married and live happily ever after? That's what people do, isn't it?"

"Not from what I've seen," Jordan said. "Not unless you want to spend your time washing diapers and trying to eke out what I earn so that we can even eat."

"Others manage."

"I'm not others. We're not others. It wouldn't last. What we have would fall apart."

"Dad would never let that happen—"

"Let's understand something, Holly. I'm my own man. I don't want to go through life leaning on your father. If I'm going to fail, then I want it to be my own failure."

"Oh, you're such a pessimist, Jordan."

"No, I'm an optimist," he contradicted. "If I weren't, I wouldn't be planning—" He stopped abruptly.

"Planning what?"

"To make use of what talent I have to the best advantage."

"Why are you being so secretive?"

"It's safer for both of us if you don't know."

"Is it dangerous?"

"No. At least, not in the sense you mean."

"You mean illegal?"

"I don't want to discuss it."

"You say you'll make a lot of money?"

"Yes, a bundle."

"How much?"

"I don't know." He added perfunctorily, "Far more than we'll ever need, I guess."

"That sounds implausible. Does this have anything to do with the diplomat business?"

He shook his head, then added slowly, "It will take me some time. I'll be away the whole while. We won't even be able to be in touch."

"What!" she cried and jumped off her chair to face him. "Are you crazy, Jordan? I couldn't stand our being apart like that—not even knowing where you are or when I'd see you again." The reality of his proposal finally penetrated. She threw herself into his arms, to bury her face in his chest. "I'll just die, just plain die!"

"Aw, Holly, don't cry." He held her to him and whispered awkwardly. "There's nothing to cry about, dear. Think of the life we'll have together after that."

"Don't leave me, Jordan! Please don't leave me. I would just die!"

"Look at it this way: It's nothing but a business proposition. A little tougher than most, but the reward's bigger, too. When I come back, we'll be together for good, and you can have anything you want to make up for the separation. That's my promise."

She continued sobbing on his chest as if she hadn't heard him. "How about the baby? You haven't mentioned that."

"We go ahead. I want you to go ahead and have it."

Holly said miserably, "I know marriage doesn't count for much these days. But I was hoping we'd make it legal."

"Sure we will. We'll get married before I go."

"We will?" She blinked and the flow of tears eased.

"But not around here. We'll slip over the state line into Nevada. And some day we'll be married again."

"Well, Mom will be pleased, at least." Holly pulled back from him to wipe away her tears.

"That's, ah, that's something else," he said. "You don't tell anyone we're married, not even your parents. As far as you're concerned, I've disappeared. It's the only story you'll need if someone comes poking around."

Holly was staring again.

"That's the way it has to be, I'm afraid," he told her gently. "I'm marrying you now so that you'll know I mean everything I say. Just for us. You, me, and the baby. We'll do our celebrating later. I promise."

"Darling," Holly responded bravely, though not without a tremor in her voice, "if you must carry out this really dangerous—and foolhardy, I think—business, then I insist that you let me share in it in the only way I can. I've told you that I have fifty thousand in the bank from a legacy. It's yours to use—whatever part of it will help to keep you safe, well, comfortable, successful, alive!"

Reluctantly, Jordan agreed that he would plan on finding some effective and discreet way to transfer funds and that he would accept her help. Her money would, in fact, ease major hazards in the risky course he had chosen.

In Las Vegas, after a quickie wedding in a commercial chapel, they parted tearfully at the airport. Jordan had saved, until then, the news that he was not even planning to return to Los Angeles, but instead would be proceeding directly to his unstated destination. His parting promise was to repeat that after his return they would have a "real" wedding, with her parents—and their child—on hand.

Holly watched him resolutely stride toward the entrance to his plane before sobs of loneliness and uncertainty began to shake her uncontrollably.

CHAPTER TEN

He walked the streets of Manhattan, excited by the vitality of it all. Seediness jowl to jowl with the strength of underlying affluence. Limousines jockeying for position outside the Plaza Hotel, the opulence of the East Side. Central Park, around which it all appeared to revolve—a tranquil, green haven by day, a thieves' den at night. Times Square and Broadway, the neon capital.

Jordan found it stimulating. Yet above it all hung a threat that implied if he put a foot wrong, predators would leap at him from the shadows. If he failed, he would be devoured by them. But he was young and strong. He was the newest gladiator entering the arena. The price of failure was appalling, so he must not fail.

He took a room in a pleasant small hotel on the East Side, Lexington Avenue in the Sixties. He could have found something cheaper, but he wanted to avoid making himself conspicuous by the seediness of his accommodations. And, in any case, he liked the surroundings, the stability that recalled the conservative environment in which he'd been raised. Holly's funds already were coming in handy.

At IBM he found the executive with whom Hugh had been in contact. Malcolm Avery was tall, thin, balding and wore glasses with thick lenses that added to his air of erudition. "So you're the infamous Jordan Freeling?" he commented by way of introduction.

"I didn't know I was infamous, sir," Jordan said.

"According to Hugh Auchterlonie you will be, one of these days."

Jordan stiffened, wondering if his thoughts were transparent. He relaxed when he realized Avery was merely trying to put him at his ease.

"Hugh is always joking," Avery said jovially. "It's his Scottish sense of humor. We have a great regard here for Hugh. He's keen for me to take you under my wing."

"I've been specializing in microcode."

"Good. It will be a great help to you."

"What I would like is to take your course in programming, if that's possible," Jordan said firmly.

"But that's consumer-oriented, Jordan." Avery used a fatherly voice. "Hugh says you're something special, and I respect his opinions. Your talents would be wasted in programming." He corrected himself. "Not wasted, exactly. What I mean is that your capability could be better employed in design."

"I prefer programming." In response to Avery's look of disappointment, Jordan explained, "Design would take much longer to learn, and my location options would be limited."

"Well, I suppose I can see some sense in that, if you want to take a short-term view. If it's any help, we'll pay you while you're training in design. Subject to an employment contract," he added, as an afterthought.

"No, sir, I'm afraid it has to be programming."

"Very well, if you insist." Avery sighed, as if an opportunity was about to be sacrificed. He was quiet a moment, then, "I have an idea. The classes are small. Why don't you take both courses? Think you could handle it?"

"Oh, sure."

"That way you'll be able to make a balanced judgment at the end."

"Yes, I understand." Jordan was thoughtful. "Ah, if I take both, will I get paid?"

"I can arrange something. Again with an employment contract, of course. We would expect you not to run off and work elsewhere as soon as you were trained. Job-hopping is the bane of this industry."

"Naturally, sir." It was better than he'd dared hope. They were going to pay to teach him how to steal from them.

His principal instructor in both courses was a woman, he was surprised to discover. Pauline Hennessey was around thirty, nearly as tall as Jordan, with a superbly trim figure. She walked with quick, vital movement that was exceptionally attractive, he thought; Pauline clearly was aware of this quality.

Ash blond hair complemented a peachlike complexion. She fastened her gaze unwaveringly, almost challengingly, on anyone to whom she spoke. Jordan noticed that she could talk for minutes without blinking. It happened to be a characteristic Professor Plutz had cited as revealing sound nerves. Her tasteful, quietly expensive clothes imparted a businesslike aura. She could hardly disguise the fact that she had very shapely breasts, however, and at times Jordan had to make a conscious effort not to stare at her figure. He was undeniably a breast man, he decided.

Looking at her four pupils in turn, Pauline indicated a dozen thick ring-bound manuals stacked on a shelf above a filing cabinet. "Those are the program listings," she told them. "In order to successfully complete the course, you will have to get to know them like the backs of your hands." She smiled for the first time and added, "I can tell you now, it's questionable whether you'll be able to stand the pace. This is, by design, the toughest programming course in the business, and I have learned not to expect a one hundred percent success rate. Perhaps you can prove me wrong this time."

Having thrown a glove into the arena, Pauline dismissed her smile, reached for the first program manual, and started work.

Completion of the courses meant a hard grind for Jordan—not that he really needed to work as hard as he actually did. He could have breezed through Pauline's curriculum, despite the complexities she built into it. It was no problem to find time for the other course in computer design and operation. Having an entire range of equipment available made his subversive exploration of its potential easier. And now he was ready—the owner of an imposing official certificate testifying that he was a competent technician. He gazed at it with barely disguised pride the day Pauline handed it to him in a little ceremony. As she had predicted, only three pupils had survived; the fourth had been lost along the way.

"You can feel proud of yourself, Jordan. It's quite an achievement, though I say so myself."

"It's funny," Jordan said. "This is the first time I've ever actually completed a course. Gained a qualification of any sort. I suppose it's not a qualification, really. Just a record of completion."

"It's a qualification inside this company, one you can be proud of. There aren't many people with one of those."

"You're a snob, Pauline. I've always suspected it."

"No, I'm not," she said pleasantly enough. "Besides, what the paper certifies isn't very important. It's what you do now that matters. You should go far with us, Jordan."

"I'm looking forward to my first real job."

"Have you spoken to Avery yet? He'll want to see you, to discuss location and that sort of thing."

"Okay, I'll go along to his office."

"You could discuss salary with him. I'm sure you'll find him amenable."

"Is that a tip?"

"Kind of. You have a good report from me."

"Sounds like good advice."

"You're not staying in New York?"

"No, I think I'll go back to the West Coast."

"Good-bye, then, Jordan. We're two of a kind, you know, you and me."

He hesitated a moment.

"You give your life to the company, don't you, Pauline? Don't you miss being married—having a family?"

"How can I miss what I've never known? Get going, pal; Avery's waiting to see you." The moment of frankness had passed, and Pauline was back to her businesslike ways. She turned and walked off briskly without looking back.

Malcolm Avery came around his desk to shake Jordan's hand. "I always personally congratulate everyone who survives Pauline Hennessey's courses. She's a tough cookie."

"Oh, she's not too bad," Jordan responded.

"She turns out people who can maintain the company's reputation. That's important to us. Now, Jordan, I understand you'll be moving back to the West Coast."

It struck him, then, that he had discussed his intention with no one other than Pauline. She had been reporting, it appeared, to Avery on whatever he said. "I'd like to vacation first, before I report in Los Angeles."

"How long?"

"I had in mind sleeping through most of May. I'm feeling pretty shattered." He never had felt better and was primed for action.

"Sure, I understand. Let's see. . . ." Avery looked at his desk calendar. "It's the twenty-fifth of April now. Shall I pencil you in for the first of June? Okay, you'll report to John van Weiss in Los Angeles on the first. That's just fine; you'll be helping them out on their vacation scheduling. Always a difficult time."

"Okay. Anything else, Mr. Avery?"

"You'd better let me have your Los Angeles number, Jordan." He sat with pen poised.

"I don't have one yet. I'll be around New York for a few days. I'll call you before I leave for the Coast."

"I'll expect to hear from you."

"Good-bye, Mr. Avery, and thanks again."

"Jordan—don't you want to discuss your salary prospects before you go?" Avery's face held an inviting grin.

Jordan thought for only a moment. "No, sir."

"I would have thought . . . Well, don't worry; I'll let Van Weiss know you're worth a bit more than average pay."

"You can say that again," Jordan said, leaving Avery puzzling over this parting remark.

And now he was eager to try out his brand-new qualifications. It should ease his progress considerably, he had calculated, as he moved around from company to company.

He studied computer industry magazines and chose the advertisement of an important-looking agency. When he called, the voice on the other end of the line sounded receptive and invited him to meet a personnel officer. Seated before a desk the following morning, he faced an interviewer who smiled interminably.

"We have a great number of openings for programmers," the interviewer, Sy Hartnett, was saying. "Numbers count. We're talking about five billion dollars' worth of equipment. That provides jobs for a lot of computer programmers."

"Sure does," Jordan agreed. "Do you think there's an opening there for me?"

"No question." Hartnett waved a hand. "I can offer you a virtually limitless choice."

"I'd like to work in Manhattan. Preferably at one of the larger banks. I like the banking environment." Jordan said by way of explanation, "Less hectic than in industry."

"I know exactly what you mean. I once even considered a career as a librarian—peace and quiet and browsing among books. Let's see what we have here. . . ." He consulted a file. "How about a job in Wall Street? Would that attract you?"

"Sounds like a good possibility."

"One of the foremost banks. And one of our biggest clients, incidentally. I've never known them to turn down someone this agency has recommended. Now, may I please see your CV, Mr. Freeling?"

"My what?"

"Your curriculum vitae. I'd like to make a couple of copies, one for our records, and one for your potential employer."

Jordan made a show of looking through his pockets, giving himself time to think. "I don't seem to have it."

"Well, perhaps you'll mail it to me." Hartnett took up his pen again. "Meantime, you could give me a few details. Where did you graduate?"

"I, ah, I've just completed what's probably the best programming course there is." He took out his certificate and passed it across the desk.

Hartnett studied the certificate. "A house course? I'm surprised they let you go. It's not often a good man gets away from them."

"I feel I need some experience in the field, Mr. Hartnett. The company is too much of a protected environment."

"I understand. The spirit of adventure and all that. You didn't say where you graduated. Is your degree in computer science or data processing?"

Jordan considered the question. "I haven't graduated, Mr. Hartnett. I haven't completed an accredited course, other than that one." He indicated the certificate.

The smile on Hartnett's face faded. "I don't understand. How could you have passed through this course if you weren't properly primed?"

"I was recommended. I've had a considerable amount of experience on some heavy equipment."

"I see. Can I make some notes on that?" His pen hesitated above a note pad.

"It was kind of classified. I can't tell you about it, Mr. Hartnett. Won't the certificate be sufficient?"

"I'm afraid not." Hartnett's pen dropped to his desk. "It's more than I dare do, to recommend someone who has no formal qualifications. Our clients are important companies and institutions. You may be the finest programmer in the country, but unless I can put forward a presentable résumé, you won't even be considered. That's the way it is, I regret to say, Mr. Freeling. It works both ways, you see, protecting the good name of this agency as well as the interests of our clients. I'm sure you understand."

"Yes, of course."

"I'm glad you see my point. Good morning, Mr. Freeling."

Jordan emerged onto Fifth Avenue and began walking, deep in thought. Hartnett was so suspicious of him that he had intended to check the certificate's authenticity, Jordan was sure, and might even do so yet, out of curiosity. It would make little difference now that he was launched upon his path. What bothered him was that he had run into a brick wall. He was now left with a big problem: How to go job-hopping without the means to gain access to new employers.

Oblivious to the crowds on the sidewalk, he continued until he found himself in Grand Army Plaza. He dodged the traffic to cross Central Park South and strolled along until he found an empty wooden bench.

After intense concentration, the solution came to him. He sat chuckling, knowing that he had found the key to ensure the success of his plan. All he needed was to be bold. It was fitting, for the whole damned scheme was bold. He rose from the park bench and began walking briskly.

Holly squared her shoulders, emotionally preparing herself for the confrontation with her parents. They were spending a relaxed evening with television and desultory efforts at conversation.

Paul and Martha had made no comment about Jordan's absence, since his banishment could be presumed complete. But they had noted Holly's withdrawn attitude, her expressed intention of dropping out of UCLA as soon as the term ended, and her general air of abstractedness.

Get it over fast! Holly told herself as she abruptly snapped off the television, commanding her parents' surprised attention. And rapidly indeed she blurted out, dry-eyed and with steady voice, the facts of her pregnancy, of Jordan's supposed abandonment of her, of her expectation to bear the child. She had finished before either of them could utter an astonished, outraged word, then added, "I'd like to stay on here, if I could."

Martha's sobs of dismay for "my baby" as she embraced Holly were more than matched by Paul's bellows of rage and revenge. The news of his forthcoming status as a grandfather seemed to have passed over his head, and whatever concern he might feel for his daughter was totally subordinated by his desire to hunt down Jordan Freeling and kill him.

Three days later he had calmed down enough to take part in a rational conversation, recognizing that his first priority must be Holly's welfare and her need for emotional support rather than a wild chase after the scoundrel.

In keeping with her pact with Jordan, Holly kept the fact of her marriage secret—thus making the Benedicts' wound more poisonous—and so Paul's team of private eyes never had Las Vegas as a proper starting point in trying to track down Jordan's route of departure. The trail, already cold, proved to be an impossible one. Jordan had left behind no clues as he cleared out of his rooming house and the university. His records at UCLA were useless.

After a shakily nervous beginning brought on by the new tensions, Holly—growing lovelier weekly as she fleshed out in the early stages of motherhood—settled in again at home. She was intent on maintaining healthy habits for the sake of her unborn child and on keeping faith with Jordan's need for secrecy. Nothing else mattered.

Only gradually could she bring herself to accept her mother's loving attentiveness, and together they formed a team to seek Paul's confidence and forgiveness. Not long before the baby was due, he was won over totally when Holly volunteered the promise that if she had a son he would be named Paul and that a girl could be named Deborah for his mother. And when little Deborah was born, he assumed the role of the most loving of fathers and grandfathers.

Unconsciously she shut Jordan from her mind, and it was her farher for whom Holly asked after she left the delivery room. Their reunion was complete.

CHAPTER ELEVEN

The Swissair Boeing 747 bore on into the night above the Atlantic. Dinner had been served, a movie shown, and the lights turned down so that passengers could rest. Alone on a seat at the rear of the economy section, Jordan let down the seat back, drew a blanket up to his chin, and stretched his long legs out as far as he could. He closed his eyes, but sleep refused to come. He was too full of excitement, too aware that he was on the first leg of a great adventure. In his thoughts he again ran over the details of his plan, seeking a glitch. None was to be found, nothing he could anticipate at this stage. Doubtless, bugs would appear, and he would have to deal with them as they came along. But he was an expert at debugging, and if the master program was sound, the rest was a matter of diligent application, was it not?

Jordan moved under the airline blanket and opened his eyes to stare at the dimly lit cabin roof. The coming phase of the operation was the easy part: opening a number of bank accounts in different identities in various parts of the world. Tracing the money as it bounced among the various accounts would be extremely difficult for any investigator and would require the cooperation of banking authorities in each country. It would also take some time, far more than he needed to collect the money in a master account and disappear. The master account would be in Switzerland, of course, where banks disapproved strongly of inquiries into their clients' accounts, no matter what the allegations or who was inquiring. Both he and the money would be out of reach.

He had been looking forward to this part. At last he would see some real action after the intense study and rigid personal discipline. This was phase two and would provide a respite before he was plunged into the key function: arranging for his eventual receipt of lots of money—other people's money.

At Zurich's Kloten Airport, an immigration officer gave Jordan's passport a cursory glance and passed him through. The passport was issued in the name of Richard Elegan, born eight months before Jordan. The photograph was correctly one of Jordan—except that his hair was now black instead of his usual tawny blond and he wore an ample dark mustache. A heavy black frame for thick but plain lenses gave him a serious, professional look. The subtle changes should be enough to confound any random inquiry. His knowledge of passport procedures had made it easy to obtain one fraudulently. An obituary announced the death, from blood poisoning, of one Richard Elegan, a young New York resident; Jordan had simply assumed the dead man's identity. A duplicate birth certificate was his for a small fee. It was the primary document for the issuance of a first passport, containing a photograph of Jordan in his current disguise. The only hitch might have arisen if a passport already had been issued to Elegan. Jordan had precluded this possibility by first telephoning, as Elegan, to report the loss or theft of his passport. When he was told that no record of a passport in that name could be found, he knew he could safely go ahead with his fraudulent application.

Now, as Elegan, he took a taxi ride to the Bahnhofstrasse, and on Paradeplatz found the most successful banking retreats in the world, the homes of the Zurich "gnomes." Jordan chose the Union Bank of Switzerland. It was surprisingly easy opening an account in the name of Richard Elegan. His cashier's check was accepted as a matter of course. Asked whether he wished the account to be referred to by name or number, he opted for a number. The bank officer, who spoke perfect English, showed no surprise and made the necessary notations. Jordan informed him that the account would be inactive for some months, after which some unusually large sums could be expected. The officer accepted the information with courtesy, and Jordan assumed that after his departure a further notation would be made of his remarks, to be kept with the account.

In a surprisingly short time he was out on the sidewalk, clutching a slip bearing only the bank's particulars and an eight-digit number.

Germany was next, he had decided. At a travel agency, he booked a flight to Munich. By midafternoon he was walking through the immigration section of the airport. Again the Elegan passport saw him through without query. He took a taxi and sat back in the rear seat as the black Mercedes charged into town, hurtling over a bridge crossing the river Isar.

On a broad shopping avenue called Sonnenstrasse he was welcomed with typical German efficiency at a large branch of the Deutsche Bank. An English-speaking assistant manager opened a checking account for Mr. William Bender, of Minneapolis. Bank statements were to be held in Munich until called for. Jordan explained that the $1,742 check was merely a token amount to establish the account and that the account should not be considered "dead" if no other movement occurred for some time. Ultimately, he said, the sums arriving would be of a magnitude of seven figures, and some important transactions would be passing through the Munich account.

The assistant manager, duly impressed, asked if he might inquire of Mr. Bender's business. Jordan implied, with a hint of confidentiality, that the most famous product of the region being beer, the banker might care to speculate on some very big futures business in the brewing industry. The man decorously escorted Jordan to the door.

He left the Deutsche Bank knowing full well that a record would be made of his remarks and that, accordingly, forthcoming transactions of a substantial nature might be expected on the account.

He had originally contemplated Milan as the next stop on his tour but now realized that the Italians, in their volatile economic policies, were likely to obstruct him in the free flow of money in and out of their currency. According to what he had been reading in the financial pages, if the money entered the country in dollars, it remained exportable. The licensing procedure had not been explained in detail, and he had no patience with the idea of chasing licenses to facilitate the free movement of his own money. *His* own money? Jordan smiled to himself and decided to skip what might turn out to be an unnecessary problem.

He had the choice of several financial centers around the world, so why ask for trouble?

He took a plane over the border to Strasbourg, the French center of European Economic Community participation. It was a busy, beautiful town hardly an hour by air from Munich, and he was installed in a hotel by midday. Less stark than the one in Munich and more luxurious, it teemed with what appeared to be senior civil servants from a variety of Common Market nations. He could easily achieve anonymity among such a diverse gathering. In another guise he completed his business with the Credit Lyonnais by six in the evening. He had no further reason to remain in Strasbourg.

Air France surpassed itself on the flight to Brussels. Seeking, perhaps, to impress the EEC functionaries who appeared to fill the passenger list, the airline served a gourmet dinner that was the best meal Jordan had eaten in days. He even enjoyed the champagne. He was in bed by midnight. Varying the subtlety of his disguise once again, he opened an account at a prime Belgian bank the next day. Heelless shoes and an excess of padding at waist and shoulders gave him a squat appearance. As Plutz had explained, he would be remembered as several inches shorter than his true height.

Now it was Friday, and he would have to let the weekend pass before he could continue his round of European banks. He returned to his hotel room and sat down to think. He was memorizing all the details he would need: the variety of names he was employing, bank account numbers, and bank codes needed for money transfers. It was also necessary for him to store in his mind precise details of the differences in his appearance at each of the establishments he had visited, in case it ever became necessary to pay a personal call. He had virtually total recall, but it was always possible that he might miss some minor but vital point. This represented a genuine hazard, and whenever he permitted himself to think of the consequences, he shuddered at the chilling realization.

CHAPTER TWELVE

In bright early-morning sun, Jordan stood at his London hotel window, watching traffic in Park Lane, and beyond, the green, wooded lushness of Hyde Park. To the left, behind the smart royal military barracks, was the location of their old Knightsbridge apartment, and his gaze strayed there for an instant before returning to the traffic way below.

He found it highly familiar, and nostalgia flooded over him. It was a painful familiarity, yet in its own way a comforting one. For him England had a sense of reality that he had missed. His real life had been here, a life carefree and serene. A life of Wynchgate and Oxford, the companionship of Piers and Hakim. And Hugh Auchterlonie, with his knowledge ungrudgingly given. Jordan wondered what Hugh would think if he knew his protégé was, at this moment, less than a mile from Grosvenor Square.

London offered excellent facilities for his purpose, and his understanding of procedures here would be a big help. He took particular care with his disguise. Conservatism was to be the keynote this time; it was pointless to chance evoking raised eyebrows. He made himself larger and bulkier all around, with pads that gave him heftier shoulders, thick arms and legs, and a slight paunch. Contact lenses changed the color of his eyes to brown, and subtle cheek and jaw fillings gave him a fuller face that matched his new, heavier body. He made himself two inches taller with lifts in his extralong shoes and put on a suit of heavy tweed. He was ready to face the world of British banking.

He was coming out of Barclays Bank, the details of his new account and a receipt for the $1,742 deposit in his pocket, when it struck him—why not use London twice? So long as he kept the two accounts separated by not transmitting funds from one to the other, he could see no reason for failing to open a second account. He returned to the Hilton to work again on his disguise. As he was putting the finishing touches to his appearance, he realized that if he used a non-British bank in London, it would confuse the issue and further delay the inevitable investigation. Chuckling, he left the hotel, found a cab, and ordered it to the Cannon Street branch of the Banco de Bilbao. The manager would doubtless be pleased to know that he was considering a substantial future investment in Spanish property development.

Jordan had booked three nights at the London Hilton because he didn't want to feel rushed; he wanted to pause in the midst of weaving a web of complexity, a red-herring trail that would drive his pursuers to distraction. On the morning of the third day, he recognized how badly he wanted to see Hugh. Safety required that no one should know of his visit to London. On the other hand, he now reasoned, if an investigation had reached the point where Hugh was questioned, the game would be up in any case. That he had entered the country as Richard Elegan would mean nothing.

So what? he thought. They're going to find out anyway, and he could see little prospect of the investigation's getting to Hugh before he was out of reach. He reached for the telephone, picked it up, then replaced it; no point in needlessly establishing a record of his stay at the Hilton. He would use a coin phone in the hotel lobby. Eagerly he dressed for his visit to Grosvenor Square as Jordan Freeling.

"I don't believe it. It's actually you!" Hugh said exuberantly.

"Who did you think was on the phone—a ghost?"

They pummeled each other. "My God, I do believe you've grown another couple of inches." Hugh stepped back to study Jordan, now towering six inches above him. "If you've found pills for growing, you might at least let me have the prescription."

"No pills, Hugh." Jordan's face was split in a grin. "I guess I'm a late developer."

"Late or not, you're a full-grown man now, and no mistake. The callow youth I knew is no more. Now that you're here, I can't work. Too excited! Let's go along to the cafeteria and have a good old jaw." Hugh set off promptly, in his usual manner, with Jordan trailing behind.

Over coffee Jordan said, "I'm sorry I didn't let you know I was coming, Hugh. It was something of a surprise trip."

Hugh didn't ask for an explanation. "Well, I'm delighted you remembered to come along and see me. I was beginning to think you'd forgotten me. And I'm sorry about your broken hand."

"Broken hand?"

"You haven't written in months."

Jordan grinned. "I've been kind of busy. You'd have heard from me sooner or later."

"Keep in touch, laddie. I told you when you left, it's too easy to lose contact."

"I'll remember, Hugh."

"You'll be starting work in California soon, then?"

"What's that?"

"It must be a month since you finished the course. Avery wrote to tell me you completed it and were taking a vacation before moving to the West Coast."

"Oh, that's right," Jordan said quickly. He added, "I may be extending the vacation."

"It must be marvelous to have such a carefree, irresponsible life."

"I'll be reporting in L.A. sooner or later." He didn't like telling Hugh a direct lie, but he couldn't explain that in this case "sooner or later" would mean never.

"They got you signed up, I take it?"

"Yes, I signed," Jordan agreed.

"They don't let their best people go if they can help it. You'll have a good career with them."

"I know." Jordan was looking into the middle distance.

"Something troubling you, laddie?"

"Nothing special." Jordan looked back toward him and smiled disarmingly.

"You're looking very serious, as if you have a big problem on your mind."

"I thought I was smiling."

"Ah, you forget. I know the difference." Hugh didn't pursue the point. "Well, tell me about yourself. I don't suppose I have to say again how sad I was to hear of your father's death. How are you bearing up now?"

"I've about got over it," Jordan said quietly.

"And your mother?"

"With luck, she'll manage to put her life back together."

"It must be tough for her. I never really knew her, of course, but please give her my kind regards once again. And the girl—Holly, isn't it? Is she still taking care of your love life?"

"Holly?" Funny, Jordan thought, except for noting a probable date for the birth of their child, he hadn't allowed himself much conscious thought of Holly.

"You were saying?" Hugh interrupted.

"Sorry, I was miles away. Holly and me, we're still friends, I guess. Haven't seen her for some time, of course." He must not let Hugh know he and Holly were married. He changed the subject quickly. "I think I've found a way of putting in a program patch that can't be detected," Jordan quietly said.

At the mention of computers, interest came into Hugh's eyes. "Well, of course it won't be detected, you idiot. If it's a patch, it won't appear in the program listing."

"No, I mean when the program is run. No indication will appear on the printout. There's no record under test."

"What purpose will that serve?"

"I don't know. I'm trying to think of one," he said offhandedly. He was taking a chance, explaining the technique to Hugh, since Hugh was aware of his interest in computer crime. On the other hand, even if Hugh came to suspect that Jordan had been exploring methods of computer scam, he would do nothing. It was no crime merely to contemplate crime. On the other hand, if a potential fault existed in the technique, Hugh probably would spot it immediately. It seemed worth the risk to run the program past his mentor.

"Okay, let's hear it," Hugh said.

"I'll explain it in terms of a hardwired machine. . . ." Jordan began, then stopped. If he wanted the real benefit of Hugh's profound understanding of the subject, he would be a fool to try to obscure the extraordinary potential of what he had devised.

"No, forget that," he said. "Let's take the normal method of translating assembly language into microcode.

The progression is, for example, assembly language into microprograms, microprograms into microinstructions, each microinstruction of seventy-five bits, right? We divide up the seventy-five bits into the proportions we require so that we now have a corresponding arrangement of high and low voltages that will open and close the circuit gates in the necessary order. Now, when we run a set of encoded numbers through the arithmetic and logic unit in the normal way—"

"Just a minute. I gather you're going to talk about trapdoors," Hugh interrupted him. "It sounds as if you intend going into some detail. If that's the case, I'll need some more coffee."

"Yes, sir!" Hugh was already a jump ahead of him. He got up to fetch two more cups. Coffee was the computer expert's mainstay, and no extended conversation could proceed without it.

When he returned, properly supplied, Hugh listened to his novel method of potentially wreaking hell among contemporary computer security operations.

It was when Hugh began to relax and smile that Jordan knew, beyond a shadow of doubt, that his technique could be made to work.

CHAPTER THIRTEEN

The din was unbelievable. Jordan marveled that the citizens of Hong Kong could spend their entire day in the midst of it and remain sane. The colorful street market in Wan-chai was alive with energy and sheer noise. Store after store sold radio equipment, hi-fis, tape recorders, and televisions, and every variety between. It seemed that each store vied with the next in playing music intended to attract potential customers; they competed with the output of a number of cassette stalls. And it all was regularly drowned out by an excruciating racket from the jackhammers of a construction crew. The vigorous cries of traders had to be loud enough to defeat the background cacophony; this in turn forced up the level of conversation among the throngs in the street, so that a constant, involuntary hum was added to the willful pollution of the air. All in Chinese.

Merchandise spilled from the curbside stalls. Household goods, hand-tools, clothes Eastern and Western, and articles that, for Jordan, had no known application. Food was offered in great variety—hot, cold, and raw. There were individual hawkers not tied to stalls and even a street musician.

Hong Kong! Vital, industrious, and teeming in a way he had never seen.

The Hong Kong and Shanghai Bank was cordially cooperative. The officers pointed out ways in which his money could earn interest totally tax-free and beyond the concern of revenue authorities anywhere. Interest on the money was currently Jordan's least problem, but it was good to know of a potential source of income.

Two days later, satiated with vitality, noise, and color,

Jordan left Hong Kong and moved to Venezuela by way of Manila, Hawaii, and Panama. It was a journey nearly half-way around the world, across the Pacific at its widest, and he was so exhausted, and his inner clock so confused by jet lag, that he fell into bed at the Caracas hotel and slept through the night and the following day, too.

When he awoke, he couldn't, for the moment, recall where he was. Then awareness came flooding: He was in the Venezuelan capital.

It was certainly a luxurious room, Jordan thought as he walked across the carpet to the French windows. From the balcony he looked down on the city, spread out far along the valley—a shimmering vista pierced by the vaulting towers of skyscrapers and apartments. He could make out the various centers of activity in the valley by the movement of traffic, heavy in certain sections. When he looked straight down to the foot of the building, he could see people playing on a miniature golf course. The sound of their laughter floated up to him.

Back in the room he phoned down for the time and found that locally it was two P.M.

Well behind schedule, he went to work quickly with his disguise kit and left in time for the after-lunch reopening of the banks. He took a cab to the twin-towered Centro Simon Bolívar, an ultramodern commercial complex. On a dazzling new plaza he met with a representative from Banco Central and arranged for a deposit of $1,742 in the name of Howard Levitt, of Seattle. His business was promptly completed once he had been assured, as before, that an external account meant the money could enter and leave the country without hindrance.

Late that evening he boarded a Pan Am flight back to New York.

CHAPTER FOURTEEN

Jordan was glad he had chosen Greenwich Village as his new home. It was cosmopolitan and full of people with unusual characteristics—which was good, because nobody took much notice of his nondescript profile. He avoided striking up even passing acquaintanceships.

In the identity and appearance of Richard Elegan, he rented a mail drop and phone-answering service from an accommodation bureau high in an office building on Madison Avenue. The address, with its 10022 zip, looked good on the stationery he'd had printed: The Digidata Computer Consultancy—Specialist Programmers. It was a simple way around the problem of obtaining direct employment. As an employee of the Digidata Consultancy, supplied on a contract basis, he would not be subject to the same intense career scrutiny he could otherwise expect. It had the advantage, for an employer, that it eliminated the risk of being saddled with someone who might turn out to be unsatisfactory. If his services were inadequate, or in any way unsuitable, they could always throw him back at the consultancy.

The careworn saffron blond operating the desk service from a shabby little office tried not to show her suspicion of his motives. It was Jordan's guess she was suspicious of most of her clients but needed their business. He decided that it might be prudent, to avoid inquiry from an unexpected source, to put her mind at rest. "You see, it's just a way of increasing my earnings, Mrs. Williams," he said. Her name was on a plaque among the grimy ashtrays on the desk.

"I've never had a computer person before." She took his

money for her advance fee. "Most of my regulars do mail order or envelope stuffing—that kind of thing."

"You'll hardly know I'm on your books. I don't expect many phone calls, and mail won't be more than one or two letters a month."

"How will you make a profit on the overhead?" she began, then checked herself. "Sorry, that's not my business, of course. I'm not really concerned, just so long as it's a legit operation. Too many people think they can get away with mail-order fraud, using a bureau," she added.

"Let me explain," Jordan said. "What I do . . . well, it's something like the way a temporary typist works, only on computers. You see, I'm restless, and I don't like to stay with one company for too long. I get bored with the same surroundings, the same faces."

"Yeah, I'm that way myself." She patted her brittle hair into place.

"My way, I get to see the latest technology, too, by dealing with firms with the newest equipment. That's important in my business."

"I remember hearing about that. How quickly a new computer can become yesterday's cold potatoes."

"That's a fact, Mrs. Williams. I have to keep hot, if I'm going to be competitive. There's also the question of money. I get a higher rate than standard for a temporary position. And then there's the matter of a consultancy fee for supplying my services." He grinned conspiratorially. "The hiring company doesn't need to know I am the consultancy, get it? The way it works out, the extra fee darn near pays my taxes. It's like working tax-free. How many people you know can say that?"

"Say, that's a good idea. Why don't more people in your business do the same thing?"

"A matter of enterprise, Mrs. Williams. If everyone was enterprising, there wouldn't be much left over for you and me, right?"

"I'm glad you told me about it, Mr. Elegan. I'll be able to explain to Inspector Donnelly when he comes nosing around."

"Inspector Donnelly?" Jordan became instantly alert.

"Post office. Always looking out for mail-order scams. If I think someone is suspicious, he checks them out for me.

It works both ways when you keep on the right side of the law, know what I mean?"

"I trust you won't be revealing my private business," Jordan said warily. "Computer users are often sensitive to information about their affairs. You could lay me open to charges."

"Don't you concern yourself, now, Mr. Elegan. He'll only be told you're a new client and that I'm satisfied you are legit."

"I hope so."

"There's nothing wrong in having an angle. Everyone who gets on in the world has an angle."

He left the office feeling slightly concerned but soon got over it. He had nothing to fear, fundamentally, and would not have for some time to come. The worst that could be said of him as yet was that his mode of gaining employment was unethical and that he was using an alias. No ulterior motive could be shown, and an explanation even was possible, in that despite his capability, he was improperly qualified. It didn't mean he couldn't deliver, as any potential employer would quickly learn.

Satisfied he could safely proceed, he walked to the nearest bank and opened an account in the name of Digidata. The "consultancy" would be receiving fees for his services, and he might as well let the establishments that were going to take him on pay for his sustenance while he arranged, from their funds, for more substantial long-term comfort.

Jordan reasoned that, as it was money he was after, a good place to start would be a bank. With the Digidata Computer Consultancy providing a curriculum vitae that validated his qualifications and experience, he was quickly installed at a central branch of Chase Manhattan.

When he learned what he would be working on, he could hardly believe his luck. He was presented with a program ideally suited to his scheme. His immediate superior, a blasé senior programmer named Chris Castelis, asked, "How's your microcode?"

"Pretty good." Jordan felt the pace of his pulse increase.

"Bores the shit out of me!" Chris said moodily. "The trouble here is there's so much of it. On this bitch of a job it runs out of your ears."

"What's the job?"

"A long-term payments program. It's a cooperative effort, financed through the International Monetary Fund on behalf of the United Nations. Some kind of international handout to aid underdeveloped countries. The trouble is, from what I hear, nobody trusts the administrations in these countries to handle the money. You've heard the rumors, how the money ends up in the pockets of some bigwig local politician, or goes to buy guns to strengthen some military junta. Sounded a bit farfetched to me until I came up against this job. Now I can believe it. The payments are not made to governments directly, but always to international contractors engaged on big projects in those countries. Like the new dam in Tanzania—a German contractor is handling that, with a number of subcontractors. Or the electrification of South American railways. That's being handled by a French consortium."

"So what's the problem? Sounds straightforward enough to me."

"Oh, yeah?" Chris took off his glasses and cleaned them. It was his nervous habit, as Jordan was to discover. "Let's look at some of the variables: Stage payments for work completed are made on the basis of progress reports from the contractors, confirmed by teams of international inspectors. These stage payments are drawn on a reserve account maintained jointly by the donating nations here in New York. Now no donating country wants to pay in more than it has to, naturally, or one day earlier than the money is needed. If they pay early, they lose interest—we're talking about large sums here. The system works like this: When a payment is called for, an automatic withdrawal occurs in a predetermined percentage of the total, in a debit on each country's national bank. Are you with me so far?"

"I'm listening. Go on." Jordan was concentrating on the possible implications in Chris's information.

"There's a second set of payments, to cover overhead, financing of equipment, static charges, even things like our costs. Again these payments are not enacted until the last moment. It sounds simpler than the first lot, but it isn't, because it's subject to inflationary factors that we feed into the computer every month after they're agreed to by all the banks. Now comes the crazy part. The inflationary factors are written in terms of each nation's currency, giving and receiving, and you can imagine how that runs, varying from three or four percent per annum for Switzerland to over one hundred percent for countries like Argentina and Israel."

"It's all done in English, I assume?"

Chris looked at him. "We're only concerned with numbers," he went on. "Now we come to additions and cancellations. The whole thing is always on the move, like a goddamn jelly. Around ten percent of the schemes never reach fruition. Usually we learn about a cancellation after we've rewritten the program. With additions, it can be worse. There's a new scheme coming up for an Egyptian development. We were told initially payments would be made over a seven-year period. As soon as we had patched it into the program, the period was changed to ten years, and we had to start all over again. Are you beginning to get the picture?"

"I think so," Jordan said guardedly.

"Okay, so now we come to the fact that politicians say one thing but mean another. One or another of the donating countries always is seeking to reduce its commitment because of changes in its internal economy. When that happens, and it is agreed to by the rest, all the numbers are out the window and we start again."

"Running variables will cover all the factors you've mentioned so far," Jordan observed.

"Some features I haven't mentioned so far. A donating country may be unable to meet its commitment, on a temporary basis. An internal budget may go haywire. For example, when oil prices jump about. That can really hit a country that has to import all its oil, like Germany or Japan. What happens then? We move that country's contribution over into a ghost account. In reality it's a debit account maintained by the International Monetary Fund. All the inflationary factors are applied to that account, too. We began by writing it in as part of the master program, but it got to be too complex, so we took it out and rewrote it as a separate entity." He looked sharply at Jordan. "I think I'll start you off on the ghost account."

"Whatever you say, Chris," Jordan responded.

Chris changed his mind immediately. "No, what I'd like you to do first is get the hang of how the bank makes its charges. That's important. Let's face it, at the end of the day we're only in the deal for the money."

"You can say that again." Jordan patiently mouthed another platitude.

"How's your memory?" Chris asked.

"Above average."

"Good. We apply over one hundred and twenty formulas to this operation to determine our costs. If you can memorize them, you'll save yourself a lot of time."

"I'll try."

"Okay, we'll get started. Come with me." Jordan followed through the quiet, air-conditioned, humidity-controlled computer room. Chris stopped to open a door that revealed a small room lined with shelves of thick, carefully bound, numbered volumes. Jordan knew immediately that they were operating systems. "The blue ones are old programs and failures," Chris said. "The red ones are active. We'll start here." He reached up for the first of a series of red volumes, and the sigh he emitted did not escape Jordan.

Chris was making heavy weather of the complexity of the United Nations program. Jordan could eat it up and spit it out, he knew before they had even begun, and the knowledge gave him a warm, satisfying glow.

It was an orgy, a feast of computer technology. In a blizzard of microcode, Jordan had rewritten the fundamental operating system within a few weeks. "It's clear what has happened," he told Chris Castelis. "With the revisions and refinements that came along, nobody stopped to question whether the basic operating system could carry the load. It needed a radical approach."

"Hell, I didn't originate it," Chris said defensively. "When I took over the job, the program already was creaking. I've had my work cut out trying to keep up with the amendments."

Jordan didn't comment that it was part of a senior programmer's task to question the integrity of systems fundamentals. The last thing he wanted was to start up some form of rivalry with his immediate superior. "Sure, I understand. That's why I was brought in. Sometimes a fresh approach can make all the difference."

"Right," Chris agreed, relieved that Jordan didn't intend making him appear inefficient.

"And I want you to know I appreciate how you've let me

get on with rewriting the operating system," Jordan added. "I couldn't have done it if you'd hit me with all the revision drudge coming in." His objective was to assume as much responsibility for the program as he could. This way, he would remain the authority on the new setup and be left to his own devices.

"When will you be ready to convert over to the new system?" Chris queried.

"I'd like to make a few more dry runs first. A few days—maybe a week."

"Okay. Let me know when you're ready. What we'll do is run the two systems side by side until we're satisfied the bugs are out of the new one."

"It shouldn't be necessary—"

"Just a precaution, Mike." His new name was Michael Collins.

Jordan hadn't argued. With Chris satisfied that the new program could cope efficiently with all their requirements, he would drop the old one like a hot brick, Jordan was certain. Outside of his own purposes, he had designed an operating system that was far superior to the old method. He was pleased that his engagement wouldn't prove a total loss to the bank and that he'd been able to bring about a technical improvement in the programming department. In a perverse way, it justified his entire motivation, he considered.

And now the new system had been in operation for a couple of weeks, everything was running smoothly, and he could think of no reason for further delay. It was time for him to enact his mission, to insert into the U.N. program an unidentifiable trapdoor that would trigger off, at some future date, an illicit payment into one of his overseas accounts. It was all done by numbers—a number represented the amount to be transferred. The transfer took place from a number representing the relevant section of the U.N. account, identified at source by a number that was the appropriate bank sending code. The credit was received by yet another number that distinguished the destination bank from others and routed to an account that could be none other than the number representing it. Every number was a face, subtly different from all the other faces, just as no human face has its perfectly identical match. It was all so simple and fundamentally foolproof, provided the correct buttons had been pressed. Except that, like a maggot in a barrel of apples, it all went wrong if an unexpected element was introduced. And Jordan had perfected that unexpected element.

He chose his German account in Munich for the first receipt. Several German contractors were involved in the Tanzanian project, which was just now getting into its stride, with completion anticipated in three to four years. He instructed the computer to pay exactly $500,000 into his Munich account on a given date in the future. It was not a large amount relative to the sums to be paid from the U.N. account at the height of the Tanzanian project. It wasn't even necessary for it to lie alongside other German payments, strictly, as it wouldn't show up until the periodic audit slated for sixty days after the transfer. Even if the payment was discovered immediately, the amount was insufficient in the scale of the operation to invoke a special audit, a formidable task that took weeks to organize.

He closed the trapdoor by keying in a few special commands, then ran the appropriate section of the program through the computer as a final check. The big line printer at one side spewed out a mass of concertina-folded paper at high speed, then stopped suddenly. He ripped off the printout and began studying the rows upon rows of printed numbers. Nothing: No indication whatsoever of the subversive commands that would be activated by the program on the day of payment. Nor could there ever be, for anyone unfamiliar with his method. And because his method was unique, to his knowledge, it meant he was unquestionably the only one who would ever know fully what had happened. Examination of the tapes after the event would reveal nothing, moreover, since his program change included a command to erase all traces of his trapdoor device after the completion of its function. It would be a total riddle to an investigator, no matter how expert.

Jordan removed the tape and returned it to its place in the security rack, in line with the other master tapes that were kept ready for use, in chronological order. Early in the procedure he'd had to ask permission from Chris Castelis every time he needed a master tape from the security rack. But after a while, when he was deliberately disturbing Chris several times a day, though many of the tapes were in his care for reprogramming, Chris asked for authorization for Jordan to have unrestricted access to the masters.

It had been easy. Placing a trapdoor in the Tanzanian master program had taken less than ten minutes, in broad daylight, in the middle of the working day, in full view of the entire computer department. Yet that relatively simple operation was the culmination of many months of preparation and hard study. He wondered why he didn't feel more excitement, a sense of elation, a thrill, instead of nothing. As he moved away from the security rack, he became aware of a single drop of perspiration on his forehead. He flicked it away and went in search of Chris.

Jordan had finished what he had come to the bank to do, and any more time there would be wasted. He needed to move on to other places, to other computers.

The senior programmer was in a bad mood that morning. When Chris Castelis was in one of his moods, everyone in the department avoided him. It was a good time to pick a quarrel with him. And what better cause could he want, Jordan thought, than friction with a superior? What better reason to walk out in a huff?

CHAPTER FIFTEEN

Jordan had considered, early in his calculations, the possibility of scoring one big hit, of wrenching free a massive sum from the computer processes of some financial institution and making a run for it. The prospect of drawing attention to himself would increase immeasurably, however, if he were to try that daring plan, and he rejected the tempting idea.

His carefully devised scheme had all the earmarks of success, if only he could contain his impatience. Even more important, it would make possible a realistic goal of quietly collected wealth as opposed to the certain, dramatic pursuit of a big-time fugitive. The elements of diffusion and confusion were important to his scheme, and he resolved to stick to his plan.

Arriving in Detroit from New York, he decided he didn't like the city, especially the hotel, the weather, the people—or the job with General Motors. But GM was running a computer program that suited his purpose ideally, and he was glad when a job offer was confirmed.

The Digidata cv had produced an odd result. A personnel officer at General Motors, eager to find permanent employees for the financial section, had tried to woo him away from the "consultancy."

"You're just the kind of person we're looking for, Mr. Maynard," the personnel officer told Jordan. "Young, well qualified, good background experience."

"I'm looking forward to working here," Jordan said agreeably.

"I don't think you get my meaning. I'm talking about permanent employment with General Motors."

"I haven't given that any consideration. I was only

planning on working out the contract you negotiated with Digidata."

"If it's the money you're thinking of, you should know that we're flexible. I'm prepared to talk to the financial comptroller about you, if you want."

"That's very good of you, Mr. Hill. I'll certainly give it some thought."

"Of course, that's subject to your performance. I'm assuming you're going to fit in here and make yourself a valued member of the computer team."

"Naturally."

"It's my guess there will be no reason for doubt on that score. I pride myself on being a good judge of character." Hill smiled with pride at his own qualities. "Are you married, Mr. Maynard? It says nothing here, so I'm presuming not."

"That's correct. I mean, I'm not married."

"Well, you'll be getting married one day, I presume. You could do worse than cast your eye around the members of our staff's social club—salaried staff, of course. We have some fine families here, and we're a somewhat close-knit community. I can guarantee you a hearty welcome."

"Sounds terrific." So Hill wanted to be a matchmaker, too. Jordan wondered how the personnel officer would react if he had any inkling of the new employee's true purpose.

"The company has a special scheme for those who make a real effort to identify with General Motors. I'm talking about housing, an advantageous mortgage rate. That's important, when a man marries and starts a family."

"Sure is," Jordan commented. "It's no great life, living in a hotel room."

"Exactly. When you're settled in, why don't you come and see me again? Maybe I can fix it for you to stay with one of our families."

"Sounds fine," Jordan said, with another smile.

"Now don't forget. You think about those things I said to you."

Before coming to Detroit, Jordan had no concept of how immense the General Motors operation was. With revenues equal to the budgets of some nations, it was a Goliath of modern industry straddling the entire spectrum of the American economy. Its extensive financial operations handled many facets of accountancy under the corporate umbrella.

All these varied activities held no interest for Jordan. He was concerned only with the kernel, the very heart of finance around which the gigantic operation revolved. It took the form of a special unit within the department that handled major loan accounts. A woman named Marilyn Garcia had told Jordan about the special accounts unit, where she worked as a secretary. Jordan had gone to some trouble to make her acquaintance. Marilyn was twenty, dark, and intelligent, of Spanish-American parents. Her mother had felt she would have her best chance with an "American" given name and named her first child after an actress.

"It's a special investment department for big loans," Marilyn told him. "The stock market's not the only place we raise money."

"Nothing would surprise me."

"We're handling a heck of a lot of Arab money, Jeff. They try to keep it under wraps, but lots of people know about it. It seems the Arabs have so much liquidity they're desperate to recirculate their cash in every major Western industry."

"Property, too, so I've heard. They're buying into city centers wherever they can," Jordan put in.

"We handle all kinds of institutional loans," Marilyn went on. "The big stuff that doesn't get into the newspapers. Pension funds are our biggest investors outside of the Arabs. The pensions people have to be able to predict their income way ahead, you know."

"Oh? How far ahead?"

"Five, ten years. I don't know how our people can guarantee a dividend so far ahead, but they do. They must know what they're doing."

"Sure they do. That's why they're the biggest in the business."

"We have lots of individual investors who place big money with us. Sometimes they're handling it for others—investment counselors operating trusts, and that kind of thing. We're writing deals all the time. Last week we came to an arrangement with an African country to pay them their interest in trucks." She looked doubtful. "Maybe I shouldn't be telling you which country that is."

"I don't want to know any secrets," Jordan said, "but I'm interested in your long-term computer programs. That's my specialty."

"It is? Maybe you should speak to George Wittner."

"Who's he?"

"Head computer planner. He's always moaning about the quality of our programs. He says he can't find the caliber of people he needs to operate the department efficiently."

"I guess he doesn't know I'm around." Jordan smiled.

"You know, Jeff, I just love your dimple, when you smile," Marilyn said.

"Ah, this Wittner. Do you think you could mention me to him sometime?"

"Oh, sure. I see him most days."

"Thanks, Marilyn. I'd appreciate that."

"Will I be seeing you at the club tonight?" Her soft brown eyes had grown a little in expectation.

"Yeah. What do you say we go out to dinner first, just you and me? That place down the road, Chick Chox, it looks good. I've been thinking of dropping by there one day."

"I'd like that."

"Meet me outside the club at seven. And can you drive your car? That would make things even nicer!"

Later, when he met George Wittner, he decided that the head computer planner was making hard work of his job. It must be a syndrome among computer experts, he concluded. They lived from day to day with complexity; it was their *modus operandi*, yet it was this very aspect that drove them to distraction. He sensed that perhaps it was his extraordinary memory that made things so much easier for him. After all, a computer was merely an elaborate memory device, and in a sense, he could identify with it. That was crazy, wasn't it—identifying with a computer? Yet at moments he genuinely felt he was responding to a challenge, that he stood toe to toe with a metal box full of wires, wheels, plastic, nuts, bolts, and silicon.

"So you think you can do better, do you?" Wittner growled suspiciously.

"I'm quite certain of it, sir," Jordan said. "It's not a matter of better or worse, it's a question of development. You know how quickly things change in our business. There's always something new. A person like yourself, in an executive position, has his work cut out handling administration and at the same time keeping up with what's going on in development."

"Well, that's true enough, Maynard, I have to admit," Wittner said cautiously. "I'm having to miss out on quite a few interesting seminars I'd like to attend. And how people can find time to read all the publications pouring onto the market these days, I just don't know."

"Exactly, Mr. Wittner. It's the reason our business makes nonsense of traditional attitudes to skills. But, of course, there's one way you can use your position as an executive to good effect."

"Oh, how's that?"

"By utilizing someone like me. By putting me to work on the tacky problems. What you do is let me beat my brains out while you get on with the man's work."

Wittner wasn't as susceptible as Jordan had imagined. "You think you're pretty good, do you, Maynard?"

"It's a question of my exposure, sir," Jordan said patiently. "As I'm with a consultancy, I move around a lot, and that way I get a broader view of what's going on out there. I get to know of any hot developments and can check them out in the field."

"That makes sense. But at your age you can't have been around to that extent."

"I started very young, sir." It was a lame explanation, but Wittner didn't question it. The affinity between youth and computers was an undeniable phenomenon.

"I come back to my first question: Do you think you can improve on our existing systems? Without major reequipment, that is? My projections are already over budget."

"In general I have to say no, sir. I can suggest some improvements, but they wouldn't be worth the upheaval. The department looks in pretty good shape to me."

Wittner looked pleased for the first time.

Jordan went on. "In one regard I know I can bring about some significant advances in the operating systems. I kind of specialize in long-term programs, and I try to keep up with developments. I haven't yet seen the company's applications in that sector, but unless you're up to date with what's happening—and I mean as of yesterday—I can show you what you're missing."

"The heavy iron, huh?" Wittner looked at Jordan with new respect.

"Yes, sir. Most people fight shy of it. The sheer volume of microcode puts them off. I eat it up—it kind of turns me on. Just a quirk of character, I guess. It's not something I'd admit to everyone." He looked suitably embarrassed.

"I'm glad you're being so frank with me, Maynard, and there's nothing to be ashamed of in being good at your job." Wittner was silent while he thought the situation through. "I suspect you have a useful capability there, and I'm going to put you to the test. I want you to move into this section on Monday and start a survey of our long-term programs."

"It'll be my pleasure, sir. And thanks for the opportunity."

Gaining Wittner's confidence had opened up the path he sought. It was easy while studying the set programs to gain access to an appropriate section of the command tapes. He found an instruction for payment to an Arab consortium of $700,000, to be executed two days after his Chase Manhattan bonanza was due through. It was ideal for his purpose. He inserted his trapdoor into the program with the instruction to change the receiving code from that of the Bank of Tehran to that of his Hong Kong bank and to credit his account there. No alteration in the program would appear until nanoseconds—billionths of a second—before the command was due to be enacted. And just as quickly, after the payment had been authorized, all traces of the trapdoor would be wiped from the program. It had taken him precisely twelve minutes to engineer his enrichment by $700,000.

At the end of the first week, Jordan reported to George Wittner that he found the systems in use admirable and could recommend only minor improvements. Wittner, full of grand expectations as a result of Jordan's buildup, promptly kicked him back to the general department.

On Monday of the second week, Jordan reported to the personnel officer. "I'm packing up and going back to New York right away, Mr. Hill," he said. "I can't stay here a moment longer."

"What's wrong, Maynard?" Hill looked alarmed. "I understand you're doing well here. I've been getting only good reports about you."

"The job's fine." He caused himself to look miserable. "It's woman trouble."

". . . That Garcia girl? I've seen you together at the social club," Hill said quizzically.

"I'm madly in love with her."

"What's wrong with that?" Hill smiled optimistically.

"If I stay around here, I'm going to end up marrying her. I can see it coming."

"That's nothing to be afraid of, young man. Most of us take the plunge sooner or later. My advice is not to keep sowing wild oats until the store runs out." His smile broadened.

"You don't understand. It's my parents. They're prejudiced, you see—the most prejudiced people possible. My old man is a big shot in the Klan, so you can imagine. If I took Marilyn home as my wife, they'd throw us both out. I couldn't live with that."

"My God, that is a problem." The personnel officer's face screwed up in sympathy. "The only advice I can think to give you is that you have to live your own life. Sometimes that means making a break with what you're used to. On the other hand, I wouldn't want to feel responsible for advising you to fall out with your parents. . . ."

"I've made up my mind, Mr. Hill. I'm making a clean break, before I get too involved."

"I can certainly sympathize with you. It's an unfortunate dilemma."

"Good-bye, Mr. Hill. And thanks for your advice."

"Any time you want to come back, just call me, Maynard. There's always room here for a straight arrow."

Jordan had so many variations of disguise that even his awesome memory was being stretched to new limits. Although he could remember, in its entirety, when he stopped to think, everything that had happened to him, he found a new factor creeping in, a disturbing element that might have resulted from his endless deceptions. It was a fading of his perspective—a diminishing view of his grand objective. Where he had expected to be rejected, he had instead been accepted; where he had expected a difficult working environment, he had found pleasant, amenable circumstances. This changed his outlook.

Time had passed since his traumatic experiences and

the death of his father, and he was finding himself again. He realized he could make a satisfactory life, or at least a livable one, without resorting to the extremes to which he was committed. But it was too late. If he hesitated now, he would be risking everything.

Frequently he found himself thinking about Holly, almost against his will. He had made a rule of consciously dismissing her from his mind, of leaving behind all memory and all conjecture. But often in the still of the night, she refused to be banished from his dreams. The warm softness of her, the ache of her loving, pervaded his being so that he basked in the joy of her aura. Her absence left a void in his life that no woman could ever fill. He was incomplete without her, and the hunger that consumed him had become part of the force driving him. And their child—the thought of her—him?—was more than he could sustain.

Holly was missing him, too, he knew. He longed to rush away, to fly across the continent that divided them simply to hold his wife and baby in his arms for even a single stolen moment. He dared not, for their sakes as well as his. Such a foolhardy move, he knew, would destroy all his equilibrium, and everything would be lost.

Jordan shook his head violently from side to side, forcing himself to eject any thought of Holly and the baby. The action served to throw a solitary tear from his cheek.

Attracted to Texaco, he was mindful of Caracas and the Venezuelan connection for the simple reason that Texaco purchased a great deal of oil from the South American state. Caracas was where he intended to dispatch a large slice of Texaco loot, if, of course, he could get near enough to the master tapes to arrange for a convenient transfer.

Obtaining employment with the oil company had been easy. They had jumped at the opportunity of acquiring, even on a consultancy basis, a programmer well enough qualified and experienced to be a systems analyst. Mention of EDP audit experience was enough to get him into the appropriate financial section. For the first time he had exaggerated his ability, but as the company apparently was in need of a troubleshooter and he was so fast at debugging, he hoped to bluff his way through. The worst they could do was fire him, he argued to himself. And save themselves a fortune.

Jordan did not get the sack, and they quickly found a way to use his talents. But again he found himself outside the section where the real action was taking place. Several times a day he passed the glass division that isolated the central accounting unit. In there, he had been told, the big money operations and the long-term payments were handled. He could see what was going on, but he was unauthorized to go beyond the glass division, much less to operate any equipment on the other side. Unless he could find some way of getting at the program listings and the appropriate tapes, he would never have the opportunity of reducing Texaco's disposable assets.

Because of a strict hierarchy of staffing levels, he couldn't even get past the boss of his section, despite strong hints that his specialty was long-term programming techniques. He was given to understand that the central unit was an efficient, satisfactory operation, and they weren't interested in ambitious interlopers.

Jordan was on the verge of writing off Texaco when he saw a possible opening—if he cared to go far out on a limb. He hadn't needed to go to extremes previously, but here he would have to try harder.

That evening he remained behind in the office. He locked himself in a toilet just before quitting time and didn't emerge until the building seemed entirely quiet. When he finally sauntered out, he was the sole occupant of the big open-plan office, still fully lighted. At his desk he slipped his jacket over the chair back, rolled up his shirtsleeves to give himself a worklike appearance, and sat down, staring at the central accounting unit.

The hydraulic swish of a door controller and female chatter broke into his thoughts. The cleaning crew was on hand. He reached out for a stack of computer printout on his desk, drew it to him, and began ticking off entries. Because it was not unknown for someone to stay late, the cleaners took little notice of him. In an hour the hum of vacuum cleaners had ceased, he'd been asked to turn off the lights when he left, and he was alone again.

From his seat he studied the central unit. Outside the powerful twin computers he could see little in the unit—once the big gray metal cabinet was locked, that was. The cabinet interested him. It contained racks that held rows of thick operating manuals and master tapes. At the end of the working day, all tapes and manuals were carefully placed in the cabinet, its doors were closed, and the combination lock spun. Not a high degree of security—more a matter of order, of avoiding loss, accidental damage, or perhaps even petty vandalism. The information on the tapes was not confidential, but concerned a volume of important financial transactions.

He was losing time. To achieve his aim, he had to get at the material inside the cabinet. The trouble was it would have to be done so that he left no telltale signs behind. When he finally rose and walked to the central unit, he had no idea how he could attain his objective.

He tapped the cabinet; its heavy metal responded dully. He looked for hinge pins that he might remove, but the hinges were concealed within the structure. He studied the combination lock, then spun it. It responded smoothly, with a pleasantly solid mechanical action. He was no safecracker, he decided, which canceled out the combination lock as a means of entry. He returned to his desk and put his head in his hands. How to get into the damn cabinet? He allowed his imagination to roam.

The next he knew, a uniformed security guard was standing by the desk. "Are you okay?"

"What?" Jordan shook himself awake. "Oh, sure, I'm fine. Gee, I guess I must have fallen asleep!"

"Well, now, that's understandable, working here long hours, with all that brain work you people have to do."

"Yeah, you can say that again." Mechanically, Jordan shuffled a few papers on his desk.

"Will you be staying long, Mr. Ainsley?" The guard had glanced at Jordan's ID, pinned to his jacket lapel.

"No. I'm bushed, to tell the truth. I think I'll pack up right now."

"You don't have to go on my account. The reason I ask, it's zero hour in fifteen minutes. Nine o'clock is when I turn on the automatic security alarms. The elevators go off, and the building is wired through to the police. You'll need to call me if you want to leave after that time."

"It won't be necessary," Jordan said. "I'll be on my way in five minutes."

"Okay, Mr. Ainsley. I'll be downstairs at the entrance ready to let you out."

"Thanks."

Zero hour! For Christ's sake, Jordan thought, like "going over the top," and "bombs away." The security guard evidently had an overripe sense of drama. With the man gone, the office was still again. He stood upright and slowly slipped on his jacket. Zero—what was so significant about zero? His head was still thick. And then he remembered that the combination lock on the cabinet had stood at zero before he'd spun it. It was still a clear picture in his mind, the vision of the pointer on the round, numbered face when he had reached for it.

Now why in hell was that? He knew of no reason for resetting the pointer to zero after securing the lock. Perhaps the person handling the lock was a fastidious type who would be pleased to see the number. Logistically, zero was the most significant in a random set of numbers, and the place was running alive with mathematicians. But then, come to think of it, habitually resetting the pointer to zero served a purpose after all—it eliminated the possibility of leaving the final setting number on the dial after locking up. Ha, so there was a purpose!

Pleased that he'd solved this little problem, on the way he reflected that zero was a starting point, a base from which to work, better than a random start on the dial. All he needed now were the numbers in the lock's combination.

A chuckle froze in his throat, and deep in thought, he hardly responded as the guard bade him good night and let him out of the building.

Every day for a week Jordan watched discreetly, from a distance, as the cabinet was opened at nine o'clock and closed at five. One man always handled the chore, one of the seniors from the central unit. And, as Jordan observed through a series of sidelong glances, he habitually reset the combination lock to zero. Fortunately the glass enclosure permitted him to watch everything that went on within it.

Before the end of the week, he had acquired the most sensitive cassette recorder he could find. With an inbuilt microphone, it was thin enough to go easily into the space behind the cabinet. He acquired double-faced adhesive tape and plastered the face of the machine. Now he was ready.

He waited impatiently for the weekend to pass. On Monday morning he entered the building at eight, hoping to find no early starters in the department. He had the office to himself. He walked quickly across into the central unit and slipped the recorder behind the cabinet. When the adhesive had stuck, he switched on the recorder. The time was six minutes past eight; the recording tape would run for one hour and pick up every sound in the body of the hollow cabinet when the combination lock was operated.

He found it hard to concentrate on his work during the day. At last alone in the office that evening, he recovered the tape recorder and took it to his desk. When he played the tape he almost whooped with delight. The sounds of the combination lock's functions had traveled through the metal body of the cabinet and imprinted themselves clearly, as a hollow grating sound, on the sensitive recording tape. Five distinct and separate movements, representing the changes in direction of the dial; the fifth was the resetting to zero. The periodicity of the lock's action was perfectly apparent. Now the only thing Jordan didn't know was the direction, right or left, that started off the sequence. It meant that each sequence he tried would have to be duplicated but in the opposite direction.

In less than fifteen minutes he had the cabinet open and was gazing at the operating systems manuals and master tapes.

He was too excited to work on them that night. By the next day he had calmed down, and that evening, when the office had cleared, Jordan began a leisurely investigation of the Texaco payments programs. The amounts remitted were staggering; sums ranging into seven and eight figures were commonplace; even nine-figure totals sometimes entered the Venezuelan transactions.

He didn't want to be greedy, but he found that the most

convenient date for his purpose coincided with a planned transfer of $2.3 million. Swallowing hard, he began work on the appropriate tape to ensure that the funds would be redirected to his Caracas account.

CHAPTER SIXTEEN

Jordan liked Sunnyvale almost as much as he had disliked Detroit. An air about the Santa Clara Valley was almost intoxicating. The people thought like him, behaved like him, and many even looked like him.

He had returned to California not because it meant he was close to Holly, or even because of its climate, which he again found stimulating. He was there because he happened to see a newspaper in a store that sold microcomputer equipment. The *San Jose Mercury* was bursting with computer-allied advertisements.

He had never before thought of visiting Silicon Valley, although he was well aware of its role in his professional gestation. He knew how it all began out here in 1948 when Shockley, Brattain, and Bardeen had produced an extraordinary little device known as a transistor, then afterward received the Nobel Prize in recognition of their contribution to technology. What had at first appeared the ultimate electronic miracle soon became subject to American enterprise, and the race to produce a "five-cent transistor" was on.

All this was not part of Jordan's conscious thought as he leafed through the pages of the *Mercury*. Instead, he sought a semiconductor application that fitted his grand design, and he found it in an offer from Lockheed.

It would be easy to jockey himself into a position from which to manipulate payments. From choice he found himself working on a long-term capital payments—repayments program for the purchase of foreign equipment, compensation remitted abroad for licenses, fees, and patents. Among contracted purchases were Rolls-Royce aircraft engines from England.

Jordan programmed the computer to pay the price of an engine at the appropriate time into one of his London accounts. Afterward, upon thinking about it, he went back and repeated the procedure, so that he would also receive the cost of a Rolls-Royce engine in his second London account. He was astounded to find that the inflationary formula would provide nearly two million dollars for each account. The sheer weight of numbers took his breath away. It was a full day before he could think rationally again.

Now that his mission in the Santa Clara Valley was complete, he realized that he was not unaffected, as he had thought, by his proximity to Holly. His iron self-control was wilting, and the urge to see her, even from a distance—to know that all was well with his wife and child—was becoming almost unbearable. At night he lay awake in the rooming house in Sunnyvale, listening to the traffic on the nearby Bayshore Freeway. Outside of town, he knew, it merged with the old El Camino Real to become the route south. A single day's hard drive, and he could have Holly in his arms again. As simple as that. But if he did, if he surrendered to his emotions, he could be sowing a seed that might ultimately destroy them both. It was vital to retain control of himself. Yet again, perhaps he could hit on another alternative, a partial satisfaction. He sat up in bed and formed a plan.

She was a large, heavy girl with a puckish face that reflected a sense of fun as well as a self-confidence that sometimes came out as arrogance. Sylvia Lawrence was a data entry operator in his department at Lockheed, and he cultivated her because she didn't mind giving him occasional lifts in her T-bird and again he was finding it hell without wheels.

"Sylvia," Jordan asked one afternoon, "how come you're so rich? You own a house, a car, and an airplane, and some people here making twice what you must earn can't even pay their mortgages."

"It's simple, Steve." Sylvia stopped whacking her keyboard to fire up a cigarette. She blew a cloud of blue smoke in his direction. "I married a man with one hell of a lot of money." Relaxing, she leaned back in her chair and cocked a surprisingly small foot on a desk.

"I didn't know you were married."

"I'm not, anymore. I divorced him. I took the house and two hundred thousand dollars to salve my broken heart. Now that it's feeling better, I'm thinking of doing it again. How are you fixed?" She regarded him with mock relish.

"Me?" He laughed. "At the end of the month I don't have a cent to my name. Look, I want to ask you a favor. I was remembering what you said, that you fly down to Los Angeles some weekends to see your family?"

"Sure, it's true. Why should I lie?"

"I don't know," Jordan said. "I never knew a girl who's a pilot. Seems funny."

"I always wanted to fly. When I got the settlement, I went straight out, took some lessons, and then bought myself a plane." She blew him another cloud of smoke. "What should a girl my shape do—become a model?"

"Don't knock yourself, Sylvia," Jordan murmured. "Plenty of others around will always do it for you."

"I'm a realist, kiddo." For a moment she frowned, then was back to her ebullient self. "So what if I fly down to L.A.? You want to bum a ride?"

"Yeah, I guess I do."

"I wasn't counting on making the trip this weekend. But just so I can show off for you, I'll change my plans. We can fly down Saturday, come back Sunday."

"Gee, thanks, Sylvia."

"It'll cost you half the gas," she added as an afterthought.

Early Saturday morning Sylvia picked him up in Sunnyvale and they drove out to the Palo Alto airport. She parked near a high-winged red-and-white plane, and Jordan helped her unload her flying gear.

They strapped in. Sylvia went through her preflight checks, called the tower, and soon the Cessna was waddling along the periphery track. Jordan sat through it all, intrigued by Sylvia's proficiency. They were on the runway, and she was firewalling the throttle. Then they were airborne.

They were an hour into the flight, and the insidious tiredness was catching up with him. The sun reflecting off the engine canopy was hitting him straight in the eyes, and he regretted not bringing sunglasses. Below them the California coast crept slowly along, and the engine developed a hypnotic beat. Sylvia had been silent for some time, and he found his eyelids drooping. He was dozing when he realized that something was different.

The engine had stopped! His eyes snapped open, and he jerked upright.

"I thought that would wake you." Sylvia was grinning as she reset the throttle and brought back the power. "It usually works."

"Please don't play games with me, Sylvia," Jordan said disapprovingly.

"Don't go back to sleep," she said. "It's time for you to join the club."

"The club?"

"The Mile High Club."

"What's that?"

"You don't know?"

He shook his head.

". . . You'll see."

She pressed a white button on the panel and slid her seat fully back and unbuckled her seat belt.

"What are you doing?" Jordan wanted to know.

"Getting in the back."

"Who's going to fly the goddamn plane?"

"It can fly itself for a while. It's on autopilot."

He watched her climb over and flop down in the rear. The plane lurched with her weight, and he saw the wheel move slightly as the plane's trim was automatically adjusted. His throat felt dry. "You mean this thing is flying itself?"

"That's right. It's quite safe. Come on over." Sylvia had pulled her blouse over her head. Her large breasts hung pendulous in an outsize bra. She reached behind her to unclasp it.

"Hey, you're kidding, Sylvia! Aren't you?"

"Never been more serious! Have to get it where I can. Come on, it's time to pay your fare. A ride for a ride. That's reasonable, isn't it?"

"What if I don't?"

"I'll frighten the shit out of you, dear boy. I've just finished an aerobatics course, and I just love throwing this thing all over the sky." She was pushing ample jeans over her thighs.

"I'm coming!" As he clambered over the seat, he inadvertently kicked the control column. The plane lurched before righting itself. It was enough to throw him into Sylvia's arms. She reached for him hungrily. He never did have a chance to remove his slacks.

Sylvia was picked up by her parents at Santa Monica Airport. They dropped him off on Wilshire Boulevard. Sylvia's parting instruction was for him to be back at the plane by midday tomorrow.

He fought a battle within himself. To rent a car he needed a driver's license, and the only one he had was in his own name. Perhaps it was foolhardy to leave a record of his presence in Los Angeles, but he had reached a point of rebellion about caution, and after all, the risk seemed minimal. He took the license from his pocket and walked toward a Hertz sign. There he rented a Mustang and drove it to Beverly Hills. Seeing Holly's house was like a stab to the heart. It was as if nothing had happened, as though things were exactly as he left them. But things *had* happened, and he was now irrevocably committed to a course that had one of two predestined endings. He brought himself under control and found a place, in the narrow lanes outside the Beverly Hills Golf Club, where he could watch Holly's house unobserved. While he waited, he took from his pocket the few extra items of disguise that should make him indistinguishable, even to Holly. He slipped into ragged jeans and pasted on scraggly whiskers and a hairpiece that had some characteristics of a crow's nest.

What the hell was he doing here? It was growing late, he was stiff and uncomfortable, and he could see no sign of activity in the Benedict household. The chances of a brief look at Holly were receding.

Then a door of the big Benedict garage was tilting smoothly up. Someone had entered a car from within the house. A dark Continental came down the drive, swung out through the gate, and turned toward him. As it passed, he caught a glimpse, slumped low in his seat, of Holly's mother at the wheel. Beside her, Holly, her face partly obscured, gave her attention to a baby on her lap.

He was headed the wrong way. Frantically he started the engine, wrenched the Mustang around in the narrow, arboreous lane, and shot off in pursuit.

Martha Benedict was a careful driver, and he caught up

with the Continental as it turned out of Beverly Drive onto Santa Monica Boulevard. He hung back and followed at a discreet distance. When it passed the Avenue of the Stars and turned into the big underground car park beneath Century City, he followed carefully, keeping way back. He parked three lanes away in the lot and watched Martha, Holly, and the baby emerge from the car. His heart flipped when he realized he had a daughter. Their destination was Bullock's department store. He kept them distantly in sight.

He was feeling content, though still curious. All seemed well with Holly and the child.

He feigned interest in a rack of suits, hoping they would take no notice of a hippie type in torn jeans, long hair, and a scruffy beard. They passed behind him, their familiar voices chatting, while he stood rigid. Without looking around, he judged that they had reached the end of the row. He stepped back in the opposite direction. But now, from the corner of his eye, he could see that Martha had stopped in the middle of the aisle and was staring back at him curiously.

He walked quickly away. As soon as he was out of the nearest exit, he ran. He gunned the Mustang out onto Santa Monica Boulevard and away from Century City. He drove around for an hour before he stopped to find a cheap motel in Venice where he could spend the night and await the flight back to Palo Alto.

CHAPTER SEVENTEEN

Jordan reviewed, as he did virtually every day, the intricate details of his efforts. The amounts that would suddenly accrue to his credit in foreign banks at the appropriate date in the future now totaled in excess of $9.6 million. The total had been swollen within the past several weeks by his quick forays—each worth slightly over a million dollars—into a large manufacturing company in Atlanta and an insurance giant back in New York City.

After a series of rapid transfers between the various accounts, the money would eventually repose, source unknown, in total safety in Zurich.

Not that he intended for the money to remain there permanently. But the solid wall that Switzerland presented to a fiscal investigation would give him breathing space. He did not naively assume that U.S. authorities could never persuade the Swiss to disgorge him and his ill-gotten gains—eventually. They *might*, if they ever caught up with him.

The $9.6 million bothered him. It was near enough to a round total of ten million to be an irritant.

It remained only to decide whether he was satisfied or if he wanted to shoot for double figures. The factors enabling him to engineer this extraordinary feat still applied. Enough time was left, and if he truly believed in his own ability, he should see the task through to its proper conclusion. He had another reason—ten was the cardinal number, an important fulcrum for a mathematician.

He decided to steal the final half million.

Casting about for a likely final mark, he recalled from his stint at Chase Manhattan that the most problematical computer input had been that originating at the U.S.

Treasury. It was not so much a question of a baser standard of work as one of motivation, he thought. It seemed that the necessity to achieve pristine correctness somehow became less imperative when multitudinous columns of figures on a computer printout represented little more than statistics. The trouble was nobody handled actual money at the Treasury. Sometimes the impact of reality lost its influence. Drowned, perhaps, in the clanking of an overburdened bureaucratic machine.

Studying job advertisements, Jordan had become aware of how the government competed for computer skills in the labor market. So he decided to put a plan into action.

He found Washington made him feel strangely nostalgic, considering that he had never liked the place, and he was careful to avoid familiar parts. A subtle disguise and yet another identity, one that aged him ten years, discounted the possibility of his being recognized by someone from his past. He confined himself mostly to his hotel room and the Treasury Building.

A personnel man named Billings was studying Jordan's CV. "Your qualifications and experience appear quite satisfactory, Mr. Barret," Billings was saying.

They should be, Jordan thought, since they had been freshly minted that morning.

"I'll pencil you in for your tests at the end of the month."

"I beg your pardon, sir?" Jordan said politely.

"Is that inconvenient?"

"Which tests are we discussing, Mr. Billings?"

"Why, the necessary tests before you can take up a position here as a programmer."

"Perhaps I have it wrong, sir. I understood you needed someone immediately."

"Well, we do. But it's the rule that nobody can take up employment here at the Treasury unless that person can meet our standards."

"Ordinarily that's understandable, Mr. Billings. But aren't you overlooking something? I'm already employed —by Digidata."

"Oh, I see what you mean. Let me explain. We make a practice of not varying the tests rule, even for people employed on a temporary—or agency—basis. We are a department of government, after all, and we have standards to maintain. It's a rare occasion for us to take on outside help, so it's never been a problem."

"I get you." Jordan started to rise. "I think we're both wasting our time."

"Just a moment. I can fix the tests for some other time, if it would suit you better."

"From what you say, you need me immediately. I'm available to start work now, and I don't see any reason to hang around for any tests. My time is valuable—if you study the CV closely, you'll find you're getting a systems analyst for the price of a programmer. I don't think you quite appreciate that, Mr. Billings, or that I'm familiar with the latest computer developments. You see, the Digidata Consultancy rarely has someone like me available. I just happen to be between two major contracts, and I'm filling in time. I don't suppose I should say this, but from what I know of the work of your computer section, it would benefit from my experience. I specialize in highly complex long-term programs, and maybe I could be useful in instructing some of your people. Economy of operation, for one thing—chances are I can reduce the major programs ten to twenty percent by using combination functions. That would be a big saving for you."

"Yes, indeed." Billings looked interested.

"Pity we can't work together. Thanks for seeing me."

"Perhaps we can come to an understanding," Billings said quickly. Jordan waited. ". . . I can't vary the tests routine, but I could start you immediately, and you can take the tests later, in the course of your work. Just treat them as a formality."

"Sounds okay."

"We'll bring them in line with the procedure for checking on your credentials. Probably have the whole thing cleared up in three or four weeks."

"Why do you have to check up on my credentials? Surely the fact that I come from Digidata should be good enough for you. They take full responsibility, you know."

"Yes, I appreciate that, Mr. Barret, but government departments have their own way of doing things. I assure you we won't embarrass you, or compromise your career in any way, if that's what is worrying you."

"I'm not worried, Mr. Billings. You just go ahead and do what you have to." Jordan smiled openly.

He would have to move fast, damn fast. Just as he was beginning to regret his choice of targets, his luck held. In only three days he gained access to an appropriate payments program.

At 3:10 P.M., on his fourth day at the Treasury, he inserted into a forward welfare-funding program an instruction to pay, for the benefit of a New York account he had established in another bogus name, $650,000. He was obliged to keep the payment within the United States since a different section handled external accounts and he had no time to attempt an infiltration. By 3:19 he had closed the trapdoor on his entry, working openly at a console and under the noses of other employees. Now they could run the program back, forth, or upside down, and perhaps they would, but nothing would be revealed of his entry. At 3:35 he was on his way out of the building without a backward glance.

He was not happy about having programmed a payment into a New York account. He would have to arrange with the bank that the money, when it arrived, be dispatched immediately to one of his foreign accounts. Or more than one. And he had a nagging feeling about any investigation of his credentials by Billings. Suddenly he decided what he had to do.

From a pay phone he called the Treasury.

"Uh, where are you, Barret?" Billings asked.

"I'm outside the building. I've left."

"Are you saying that you're not in the computer section at this time?"

"No, I told you, Mr. Billings, I've walked out on the job."

"Is this a union matter?"

"Nothing to do with a union. It's personal."

"Somewhat unprofessional of you, don't you think?"

"I'm sorry. You see my mind is in a turmoil."

"Your mind? Could you please explain that remark?"

"It's that girl!" It had worked once, Jordan reasoned—why not twice?

"Which girl is that, Barret?"

"I don't want to mention any names. One of the girls in the section. When she walks past, it's like I can see right through her clothes, and I get this sudden urge."

"I'm not really interested in the fact that you find a certain girl attractive, Barret. I have better things to do—"

"You don't understand. I have the sudden urge to rape her."

"You *what?*" He could picture Billings sitting up, startled.

"I've done it before, you see. But I've got control of myself now. These days when it happens, when I get the urge, I get out of sight of the girl and stay where I'll never see her again."

After a silence: "Ah, now, how far has this gone, Barret? I mean, just between you and me, as friends. Have you ever been apprehended for something of this nature? You really should tell me, you know." His voice dripped with caution.

"I'm afraid so, Mr. Billings. Fact is I've done time for attempted rape—twice. That's why I'm calling you."

"To tell me you have the urge?"

"No, sir. Just to let you know that you won't find my credentials checking out. It would have been all up with me, in any case, once you had the replies. Maybe it's just as well I got the urge again. You see, I've been fooling everyone, including Digidata. The information that I gave them—the stuff you read on my CV—it just isn't true. Oh, I can do the work okay, as you'll find out if you ask in the section. But I can't give my real details because then it would emerge that I have a prison record, and nobody would employ me—"

"Hold it, Barret! Am I to understand that you've been deceiving the computer consultancy that employs you?"

"Yeah. They don't know about me."

"Didn't they check you out? It's remiss of them, if they didn't check you out."

"It's the way it happened—I kind of fell into working for them. One time I did an emergency job for them, on a self-employed basis. Then a couple more, and since then they've come to trust me. I don't let people down on the job, you understand. It's the other thing. Sex!"

"I see." There was silence from Billings, then, "Does your section head know you're not coming back?"

"No, sir. I was hoping you would tell him for me. Kind of explain and give my apologies. I dare not come near the building again."

"Very well, Barret. You do realize that I'll have to write a stiff letter to Digidata about this?"

"Do you have to, sir?" Jordan managed to get a plea into his voice.

"I'm afraid so, Barret. For the protection of others."

"Well, if you must, you must, I guess."

"And Barret, do yourself a favor and see a doctor, will you?"

"Yes, sir."

"Do that right away!" Billings added sternly.

So his mission was complete. Now he could turn to the execution of his personal plans—especially the "rescue" of Holly and their baby—while a series of well-coordinated dates for the maturing of the pieces of his fortune were checked off on the calendar. Meanwhile the recollection of him, in all his names and disguises, would dim and pass from the thoughts of Billings and all the others. Nobody would be putting the fragmentary clues together in a hurry, he felt sure. And, by the time they could, if they ever did, he and Holly would be living in luxury with their child. For the present all he needed to do was drop out of sight.

Florida seemed a good layover hideout for the time being. He'd lose himself in Fort Lauderdale, among the thousands of young itinerants heading for its beaches at this time of year. And then hurry to Los Angeles for Holly as quickly as the secrets of his trapdoors permitted.

PART THREE

CHAPTER ONE

Late on a muggy September night, Paul and Martha Benedict returned to their mansion from a charity ball at the Century Plaza. As they turned into the drive, they could see a light in their granddaughter's bedroom. Concerned that all was not well with Debbie, Martha urged her husband to drive more quickly the last few rods.

Inside the house they discovered that their daughter and granddaughter were nowhere to be found. They experienced moments of panic before they saw a note, left in a prominent position on the mantel. It ran:

Dear Mom and Dad,

We have to go away for a while. A certain someone finally came for us, as I said he would one day. I wish you could have seen his face when he first held Debbie in his arms. It helped to make up for all the lousy nights, all the anxiety. You know how tough the waiting has been. Now it is all over, and my heart is filled with happiness.

We can't say where we will be. You probably will not hear from us for some time, but you are not to worry, and you should know that wherever we are, we will be safe. When the time is right, we will be in touch.

Thanks from you-know-who for caring for us all this time, and a thousand hugs and kisses from Debbie and me.

We want you to know that we will always be thinking of you, wherever we are.

Please destroy this note immediately.

Your loving daughter,
Holly

P.S: Dad, I am to tell you that I will be kept in the manner to which I am accustomed.

CHAPTER TWO

Between them, the two men who sat facing each other across a scarred desk had seen forty-six years of government service.

Sam Kilmartin, senior Treasury agent, was the most experienced and capable field man on the force, despite an inclination to carry on a one-man crusade at times. He was tolerated because he was an unfailing, dedicated public servant and an idealist under a deceptively gruff exterior. The exploits on his record were legendary, a constant example to new entrants to the service. If citations were ever to be given, then his list would be a yard long, and everyone knew it.

A bland philosophy lay behind Sam's attitude, and it explained why, to him, currency was not money, but the lifeblood of the nation. It came from a profound understanding of a simple fact: that a country with a despoiled, debased currency was a country burdened and weakened. And no evil, self-seeking bastard, big or small, was going to kick the trestles from beneath that noble concept of individual freedom, that monument to human dignity that was the United States of America. Not while Sam Kilmartin was around.

Chuck MacCaskey was Sam's contemporary and his boss. "I don't get it," Sam exclaimed, looking at a slim folder on Chuck MacCaskey's desk. "Chuck, this is a job for the FBI. How come it's landed up here?"

"I don't understand either, Sam, to be honest. I've queried it upstairs, and the only answer I get is 'Follow orders and get on with the job.' "

"That's it, huh?"

"Yeah. There's no mistake."

"And there is no currency connection whatsoever?"

"None that I can see. For the present, all we know is that something like six hundred fifty thousand dollars has disappeared, sucked out of the Treasury computer accounts, and nobody seems to know how it was taken."

"It's theft or embezzlement. That has to be the province of the FBI," Sam said stubbornly.

"Look, Sam," Chuck said with patience. "Don't let's keep going over this point. What we have here is an in-house crime. The department chiefs don't want to look like fools by bringing in the FBI to tell us what's going on in our own backyard."

Sam was unimpressed. "At the risk of boring you, how about the computer angle?"

"If you want, I'll have someone sent from the computer section to advise you."

"What has been done so far?"

"Nothing external. They thought at first it might have been a technical error, or machine malfunction, or even a simple accounting mistake. It takes time to check up on these things, with computer entries running into the billions."

"And when did the actual money transfer take place?"

"Over two months ago. The deficiency was discovered in the second monthly audit of computer accounts. As I understand it, the discovery was pure chance. There's no machinery for reviewing payments, only discrepancies and errors."

"You're kidding, Chuck."

"No, I'm not. Reviewing the billions of dollars handled would double the work load, and that negates the very purpose of computerization. There are built-in checks, of course, and if this was deliberate theft, then whoever did it knows one hell of a lot about the computer system used, because it didn't show up as an imbalance in the totals. Fact is, if it weren't for an eagle eye in the accounting department who happened to recognize the receiving bank code, we might never have known about it."

"So whoever stole the money has had time to cover his tracks?"

"Sam, we know so little about how it was done we're not even certain, at this point, that the money was stolen," Chuck said resignedly.

"Hell, that's not difficult," Sam said. "You only have to establish whether the money is still at the host bank in New York. If it's been incorrectly transferred, it can be returned."

"Oh, yeah? It's not that easy," Chuck said laconically.

"I'm not with you."

"Believe it or not, we don't know if the money's still in New York or if it's been moved on. The New York bank is being cagey. What it amounts to, the bank is not prepared to make a single move out of line, for the government or anyone else. That translates for us as our needing a court order to examine a client's account. How do you like them apples?"

Sam stared. "So get a court order. What's the problem?"

In New York a sullen bank manager named Stevens read every word of the court order Sam slapped on his desk.

"You might have saved me the trouble of getting this," Sam complained. "When the government wants to see details of an account, it's going to see that account, come hell or high water."

"I'm not prepared to discuss the matter with a public employee who has no knowledge of the subject," Stevens said haughtily. "Shall we get on with the matter in hand?" He picked up a telephone and barked a curt instruction into it. "I want the Gregory Whitefish account records."

They sat in uncomfortable silence until a secretary arrived with details of the account. Stevens glanced through the papers first, then condescendingly handed them over. While Sam examined the contents of the folder, Stevens carefully filed away the court order in his desk, placed his hands flat on top, and sat waiting.

"Could you please explain something here to me, Mr. Stevens?"

The manager responded immediately. "The court order requires only that I open the books of account for examination in regard to this client, not that I make an assessment of the client's financial conduct—"

Sam cut him short. "Look," he exploded, "let's get something straight. What I'm investigating is the possibility of a major theft from public funds. Maybe you don't care about that? So let's understand each other, and I'm only going to say this one time: If I don't get some cooperation from you, I'll be back here with a team of Treasury accountants who will tear your bank apart, account by account. If we find one irregularity, no matter how small, I'll recommend prosecution. Also, I guarantee that my people will be so careless with your records you'll have to close your doors to the public for a week before you're able to operate. I guess that's illegal, too, but just try and prove it."

Sam was out of order, and he knew it.

"Very well, Mr. Kilmartin. I'll do what I can to cooperate." Stevens had gone pale and was subdued by Sam's unexpected outburst. "However, I want it on record that I do so under protest."

Sam had quickly brought himself under control. Speaking now in a purposely mild tone, he pointed to the documents. "Am I correct in assuming that this account was hardly used before the funds were received in September?"

"Yes. It was opened with a deposit of one thousand, seven hundred and forty-two dollars in June of the previous year, as you can see, and only two minor transactions took place between then and the time the large sum was received. Sufficient to avoid the account's being considered dormant."

"Was the one thousand, seven hundred and forty-two dollars in the form of a check?"

"No, it was cash."

"This Gregory Whitefish—did you have any prior knowledge of him?"

"No. Whitefish came unrecommended."

"And this is the Social Security number he gave?"

"Yes, it is."

Sam made a note of the number. He was certain it would turn out to be bogus. "You say he left a memorandum; can you explain in simple terms what it says?"

"Yes. These are the instructions how the capital sum was to be handled when it arrived. It was to be forwarded immediately to a bank in Venezuela. These are the details—"

"But this memo is dated when the account was opened, June of last year. Are you saying you had instructions on what to do with the six hundred fifty thousand dollars fifteen months before the money arrived?"

"That is correct," Stevens said, calm now. "The amount

wasn't specified, except that it would be in six or seven figures."

"*Seven* figures?"

"As I was saying," Stevens continued, "this is the information on where the money was to be sent. International bank code and account number."

Sam began making notes. After a moment he put down his pen. "I'd be grateful for a photocopy of all this, Mr. Stevens."

"The order says examination of Mr. Whitefish's account. . . ."

"I can take these papers away for examination if you prefer."

"Very well, I'll arrange it."

"And I'd like to speak to the member of your staff who opened Mr. Whitefish's account."

"It's a Miss Helen Morton." Stevens was becoming more relaxed. He picked up the phone without being threatened.

Helen Morton was a plain, efficient-looking woman. "I don't remember much about his appearance, sir," she said, her brow creasing. "It was a long time ago, and I don't recall seeing the customer since."

"Try hard to remember, Miss Morton," Sam urged.

"Well, I probably wouldn't remember him at all after all this time if it weren't for the funny name and the unusual forwarding instructions for a big amount. Over half a million, he said. I open quite a few new accounts every week, but most of them are small, domestic accounts, you understand."

"So you do remember what he looked like?" Sam asked hopefully.

"He was quite young, I guess," Helen Morton said. "I remember that he was kind of . . . hairy. Yes, he had a bushy mustache, kind of a ginger color, and his skin was very pale."

"Good. Was he a big man or small?"

"Fairly tall—I don't think he was about six feet—my fiancé is six feet, and I tend to remember men that size."

"You're doing just fine, Miss Morton. Anything else?"

"Oh, yes, he had a slight limp."

"A limp?" Sam felt the excitement rise in him. A limp would mark him out in a crowd. "Right or left foot?"

"I don't remember, I'm afraid."

"Anything else?"

"I don't think so." She was shaking her head.

"One more question. Is it normal practice to accept a post office box number for a bank account?"

"It happens. We have no rule against it."

"Thanks, Miss Morton, you've been a big help."

When Stevens's secretary arrived with the photocopies, he could do no more there, and Sam left the bank.

He went directly to the post office, where the box number yielded a name and address across the city, in Queens. No such place appeared in the postal scheme of the city, and a call to the police confirmed that the street didn't exist. Sam called his own office and asked them to run Whitefish's name through the national computers. In minutes they were back with the information: The Social Security number belonged to a man named Bellamy in South Dakota, and no record could be found of a Whitefish—driver's license or anything else. Sam didn't have to look farther. Whitefish could be nothing but a red herring.

He arrived at La Guardia Airport late, grateful to find that the plane to Washington was half-empty. As it leaped, lightly loaded, into the night sky, he watched the lights spreading out below that were the panorama of New York, then all became dark on the ground. He dropped the seat back and eased himself down to think. Flying concentrated his mind wonderfully, he found. No telephones, no callers, no distractions. Just a predetermined period of peace in a comfortable aluminum tube barreling powerfully along.

This was no random event, he had already decided, but a highly sophisticated crime by an expert or experts. Planned well in advance, for Christ's sake.

The implication of the Venezuelan destination of the money was ominous. He could hardly bear to think of the thousands of miles he would travel if it turned out to be necessary to follow the trail.

The young man who knocked and entered his office appeared little more than a boy, Sam thought. Small and thin, with sandy hair and an unlined face and hands that were delicate, like a girl's. "Mr. Kilmartin?"

"Yes. Who are you?"

"I'm Robert Halpern, from the computer section."

"*You're* their expert?" Sam caught himself. "I expected someone older. Take a seat. I'm Sam." He extended his hand. "How old are you, Robert?"

"Twenty-five. They tell me I don't look my age." A wry flicker crossed the young face.

Sam cleared his throat. "I need some help here, Robert. I'm trying to establish how the money came to be transmitted to New York. You're familiar with what happened, I take it?"

"Yes, I've looked into it from the computer angle. An instruction was entered into the computer accounts from this end. Once the instruction is effected, a money transfer goes through the banking system to the destination bank without further question, among thousands that go out daily. Unless the receiving bank raises a query, why should the payment be reexamined? Automatic balances throw up anything that doesn't check out. And then there's the audit, but that's just another computer function in reality, and it's based on the information fed in initially."

"The person who did this knew one hell of a lot about computers—is that what you're telling me?"

The young man's eyes glinted for a second, and he didn't answer directly. "I have established that the order to pay originated here. It could only have come from an instruction in the master program."

"What can you tell me about this instruction?"

"Nothing."

"I mean, did he use a special technique—was there something about the way it was done?"

"Mr. Kilmartin, I can find no instruction in the master program. I've been through it several times, and it's exactly as it was set up originally, precisely according to the operating system."

"Could the order to pay have come from an outside source—from somewhere in the banking system, for example?"

"No, the procedure is too involved, and it would have shown up. It originated here, no question of that."

"I'd like you to go over the whole thing again and then let me have an analysis in writing."

Halpern lifted his thin shoulders, indicating the hopelessness of the assignment. "I'll try again, if you want, but it's a waste of time."

"And try to keep the report simple, Robert. I mean, no computerese, just plain English, if you can manage it."

Looking sadder than ever, Halpern wheeled around and departed.

Sam had drawn another blank, and the case was now looking even more mystifying. If he could glean no helpful technical information, then at least he could find people to investigate. He called the computer section personnel officer. "Billings, this is Kilmartin. I've been talking to young Halpern. Are you sure he's the best expert we have?"

Billings sighed. "It's a phenomenon you have to understand," he said. "The world of computers is run by kids. Halpern is so well qualified and so good at his job that any commercial employer in Washington would be happy to get him. It's my constant worry that these people will be grabbed by industry."

"He sure as hell doesn't know how the money was ghosted out of here."

"If Halpern doesn't understand it, you have a real problem on your hands."

"Is it possible he was involved personally, do you think?"

"Most unlikely, going on his record."

"I'll need background material on anyone in the computer section who might have had a hand in this. I'll leave it to you to determine who has access to the equipment and sufficient knowledge."

"Don't try to throw it on my shoulders, pal! Dozens of capable people work here. I don't want to have to choose likely suspects. That's your job."

"Just do your best. And let me have copies of those records as soon as you can."

CHAPTER THREE

He was off on the "Gregory Whitefish" trail.

What a ridiculous name, Sam told himself. Evidently the criminal had little fear of drawing attention to himself. And wasn't it a typical trait of a young, inexperienced person to use a humorous pseudonym? He couldn't imagine the hardened currency hustlers who were his usual adversaries adopting a name like that. In his mind he was trying to build up a picture of someone who would fit the description given by Helen Morton, the bank clerk: tallish, a bushy mustache, nearer twenty than thirty, and very pale. Pale! Robert Halpern was so pale that it seemed he rarely saw daylight. And so young . . . a hairy face looked older than a cleanly shaved one. As for the limp, he would disregard that for now. If the man was trying to disguise his appearance, a limp would be simple to effect.

As the Pan Am jet bore on toward Caracas he mulled over the various possibilities. A good height—say five ten or eleven. It wasn't much to go on.

He had a few frail strands but no way to knit them together into a rope of substance. He gave up worrying about it and settled down to sleep the remaining four hours to Caracas.

He had taken the precaution of bringing along a letter of introduction from Banco Central's New York office. On the glittering new plaza of the Centro Simon Bolívar, he was warmly surprised by an assistant manager's welcome. "My name is Eduardo Riva. Please accept the apologies of our manager, Señor Escobar. He was expecting you but received an unexpected invitation from an important client."

Sam handed over the letter of introduction. "All I need is a small amount of information."

Riva read the letter. "How may I help you, Señor Kilmartin?"

Sam borrowed a scratch pad on Riva's desk and wrote a number.

"Do you recognize that number, Señor Riva?"

"Yes. It would be one of our accounts."

"I would like some details from that account, if you please."

"That presents a problem." The assistant manager picked up the letter and read it once again. "It asks here that we extend you our cooperation. Unfortunately, I would be breaking the law if I were to reveal the contents of the account."

"I represent an agency of the law, Señor Riva. The person operating that account may very well be involved in illegal activity."

"You are speaking of American law, Señor Kilmartin, not Venezuelan law. I would much prefer it if you could wait until Señor Escobar is available, so that he may make the decision."

"When is he expected back?"

Riva suddenly brightened. "Ah, I remember that account. Excuse me for just a moment." He jumped up, hurriedly left the office, and returned brandishing a statement folder. "As Levitt is an American national and you are an official of the United States Treasury, I do not think I am committing an impropriety. The law is specific only in regard to the accounts of Venezuelan nationals."

"Levitt?" Sam repeated.

"Howard Levitt, of Seattle, Washington, is the name of the account holder."

"May I ask how it is you immediately recalled that particular account, Señor Riva? After all, it is one among many here in your bank."

"A coincidence. I had a note in my diary to review this account ever since it was opened with a deposit of one thousand, seven hundred and forty-two dollars. The anniversary is coming up this week. Instructions were left by—"

"Hold it! Did you say one thousand, seven hundred and forty-two dollars?" Sam queried. It was exactly the amount used to open the New York account.

"That is correct, Señor Kilmartin. We were informed by Señor Levitt that the account would remain inactive until approximately September of this year. We were then to expect some substantial sums, which were to be dealt with in a somewhat complex manner, using several foreign banks. That was the reason for the note in my diary, you see. I wanted to check that Levitt's instructions had been complied with."

"One of the large sums was the six hundred fifty thousand dollars from New York, I presume?"

"That is correct." Riva consulted the statement folder. "Not the largest, by any means."

"Oh? And what is the largest?"

"When the account became reactivated, the first payment through was two point three million, from Texaco. It doesn't say so here, but I happen to be familiar with the Texaco bank codings."

"Two point three million bucks, you say?"

"Yes. We dispatched the entire amount to Hong Kong immediately, as instructed."

Sam was silent a moment. "Tell me something, Señor Riva. How much money, in total, has gone through this account?"

Riva ran his finger down the top document. "Something over ten million dollars, in all. Do you want an exact figure?"

"No, that'll do for the moment." His mind was racing but getting nowhere. It was now painfully obvious that the Treasury scam was part of a much wider scheme. Riva had placed the bank documents before him on the desk. Before he bent his head to examine them, Sam had one more question. He knew the answer before Riva spoke. "How much money remains in this account now?"

"Why, none, Señor Kilmartin. The account is closed."

Sam stared at the account details in silence for a couple of moments. "What do you remember of this Mr. Levitt? Was he a young man—midtwenties, say?"

"Oh, no, señor. I recall him as older than that. And considerably overweight. His belly bulged out around his belt like that of a beer drinker."

"Was Levitt kind of pale faced?"

"No. Red cheeks and even a hint of a red nose."

"A mustache?"

"No, I would have remembered that. His hair eludes me, though. It was nothing special."

"How tall?"

"About one point eight meters, as far as I recall."

Nearly six feet; the height checked. Sam stored Riva's recollections away in his mind. It seemed possible that young Whitefish was not alone and that he was up against a conspiracy to defraud. Its size was indicated by the volume of money passing through the Levitt account. Was ten million the grand total? The implications of what he might find elsewhere were riveting. "Would you do me a favor, Señor Riva?" Sam asked.

"If I can, of course."

"Please list for me the origin of each payment you have received into the Levitt account. Name and location of the sending bank and originating account details. As much information as you can give me."

"My pleasure, Señor Kilmartin." Riva began making notes.

CHAPTER FOUR

In Brussels, Sam met with outright refusal to disclose the contents of the client's account. The Belgians declined to mar their reputation as a crossroads for continental finance by randomly opening their books to some government snooper, no matter which government he represented. They would not even tell him if the account was dormant or still active. Information, he was told sharply, could only be divulged as a consequence of the appropriate legal procedures. *Hell!* Sam thought, as he walked from the regal building on the Rue Belliard.

He could remain in Brussels while he goaded the American consular staff into action, but he decided against it. If he could exhaust the Whitefish trail quickly enough, the money might still be within reach, wherever it was. He canceled his booking for a second night and was on a plane out of Belgium by early afternoon.

In Strasbourg he got little more help. The French were pleasant but nearly as obstructive as the Belgians. At the Credit Lyonnais he was told only that the account currently held no balance, but because they had received no instructions to close it, they considered it still open.

Sam realized he had to come to terms with the question of bank secrecy. As the French manager explained, a bank executive considered confidentiality a most important aspect of his function; his clients trusted him in the same way they would trust the family doctor or solicitor.

At noon Sam was on a plane to his next destination. He was not prepared to waste time in Germany, as well, if he could help it, so he had called ahead for assistance. At the Munich airport he was met by a consular official named Hillier, who examined Sam's credentials carefully.

On busy Sonnenstrasse, they were conducted into the office of the Deutsche Bank manager. After an exchange in German with Hillier, he sent for a subordinate. "I have asked that we conduct the conversation in English," Hillier said from the side of his mouth. "It doesn't do to make things easy for them."

The manager introduced Herr Albers, his assistant.

Hillier introduced Sam. "This is Herr Kilmartin. He is an official of the United States Treasury in Washington. I am a vice-consul of the U.S. Government." Hillier took out his ID and asked for Sam's. He waved them briefly.

"How may we be of assistance, gentlemen?" Albers asked with formality.

"I regret to have to tell you there has been an allegation of serious irregularity here within the Deutsche Bank," Hillier said coolly. "Herr Kilmartin has just arrived here in Munich and we have decided to come directly to your bank to establish the facts before we proceed further with our inquiries."

The two Germans had a hurried conference. Looking concerned, Albers turned back. "Would you please explain the nature of this irregularity?"

"A theft of official funds from the United States Treasury is involved. It is suspected that the facilities of this bank are being used to transmit the stolen money."

"We cannot answer for the moral conduct of our clients," Albers responded.

"You can if the client is in collusion with a bank employee."

"Can you give me the name of this employee?" Albers demanded sharply.

"Not until we have had an opportunity to examine the evidence."

Albers translated for his boss, who began looking angry. "What is the nature of this evidence, Herr Hillier?" Albers asked.

"It is an account held here. This one . . ." Hillier handed over a slip on which Sam had written the account number.

"Just a moment." Albers walked quickly from the room. He returned with some documents and went straight to his boss. Together they discussed the account before Albers turned. "I am most concerned, Herr Hillier," he said.

"This is an account which I personally opened for Herr William Bender, of Minneapolis, Minnesota, U.S.A."

"Some months ago?" Sam inquired.

"That is so. I hope I am not being accused of some crime. I can assure you, gentlemen, that you are quite mistaken."

"Well, as we now know, the account number refers to an American connection," Hillier said cryptically.

"I do not understand. These figures are subject to constant audit. We are quite confident they are correct."

"Probably they are, from your angle, but it is our information they refer to stolen money," Sam said.

"And how is an employee of the bank involved?"

"If you will allow us to see the accounts, perhaps we can tell you."

The manager impatiently called for Albers to translate. Sam could see that Albers was becoming anxious. The manager was looking reluctant when Hillier added, "Will you kindly inform your superior that we shall be applying for a court order on Monday to examine these documents? It will save time if we can see them now, and you can still have the official order on Monday, if you require it for your records."

Albers rattled off something in German to his boss, clearly concerned that the implied stain on his character be erased as quickly as possible. Suddenly the manager acquiesced, shrugging his shoulders. Albers turned to hand over the documents with a sharp, angry motion.

In one glance at the bank statements, Sam had what he wanted to know. The list of transactions was similar to that on the Venezuelan account. The total that had entered and flown the Deutsche Bank in a flurry of payments again exceeded ten million, and Sam's finger stopped at a payment of $1.4 million. Beside it was a code that matched none of the others. "Switzerland?" His eyes swiveled to Albers, whose gaze followed Sam's finger. "Yes, it is."

"Can you give me any information—name, account number, or location of the destination bank?"

"I'm afraid not, Herr Kilmartin." A knowing smile slipped across Alber's face, then was gone.

"Okay." Sam straightened. "That's all I need to know. I'd be obliged for a copy of these, and then we'll be on our way."

"Ah, in the matter of a bank employee whose conduct is

under suspicion—I am waiting to hear your conclusions," Albers objected with obvious concern.

Sam let Hillier do the talking. "Oh, we're happy to tell you there's no question of a problem in that regard, Herr Albers," Hillier said generously. "These documents clear up that aspect of the investigation nicely."

Outside, in the car, Sam said, "Thanks, pal. You and me, I guess we make a good double act."

"My pleasure. What happens now?"

"You take me to the airport. And if your driver could get this sauerkraut trolley rolling real fast, I'd be grateful. There's a plane to London at five o'clock."

Hillier ordered his driver to the airport. "Do you T-men always rush around this way?" he asked lightly.

"For ten percent of the yield, you'd rush around too, my friend, I assure you."

He sat back in his seat. All the way out to the airport, he avoided the querulous glances of Vice-Consul Hillier.

Sam had called ahead and left a message at Ralph Heritage's Scotland Yard office that he was inbound to London. But at Heathrow nobody awaited him.

"Your message is still on his desk, Mr. Kilmartin," a secretary at the Yard told him. "The commander's in Wales on a case. We don't know exactly where, and we don't expect him back before tomorrow."

"Damn!" Sam said softly.

"If it's vitally urgent I could have the Welsh police alerted. Perhaps we can locate him, sir," she offered.

"No, thank you, that won't be necessary." Ralph wouldn't thank him for activating a police region's search facilities. "I don't know where I'll be staying. When I'm fixed up, I'll call in again."

He asked a taxi driver to find him a hotel in town, something not too elaborate. "London's pretty full right now, guv'nor," the cloth-capped driver told him. "There are exhibitions on at Olympia and Earls Court. It won't be easy."

"What do you suggest?"

"Bed and breakfast for a night or two near one of the mainline railway stations. Then you can check out the better hotels in your own time."

"That will do. I'll be here only a couple of nights. Let's go."

In Sussex Gardens by Paddington Station, most of the converted Victorian houses displayed FULL signs. At the end of a terrace one had a solitary free room, and Sam thankfully dragged his suitcase up three flights of stairs. The room was narrow and dingy, but he hardly noticed. It was late evening now, and the traveling was beginning to catch up with him. He took out a bottle of scotch he had bought at the Munich airport and lay down.

He awoke to daylight. And the stench of whiskey; the bottle had drained its contents into his clothes and the bed. He showered in the little tiled stall behind a curtain in a corner of the room, shaved, and put on fresh clothes. Then he called the Yard.

"Where the hell are you?" Heritage's voice came over the line.

"The Viola Hotel." Sam began to read off the address from a card on a rickety table, when Ralph interrupted.

"Wait there, I'm on my way." In less than thirty minutes, Sam let his old friend in. They shook hands vigorously. "What in heck are you doing in this joint, Sam?"

"Came into town without a booking. I had to sleep somewhere." Ralph was wrinkling his nose. "Sorry about the smell. I fell asleep over a half pint."

Ralph was grinning. "Look, I wasn't going to tell you, but I guess you can do with a laugh. This is a place the street girls use—they bring the men here."

"Delightful!" Sam didn't find it funny. "It's not important. I'm only in London a day or two. Might as well sleep here."

"No way. Pack your bag and let's go."

"I can't impose on you every time I come through London, Ralph." Sam was determined. "I didn't call you for that."

"Don't waste your breath."

In the car Sam explained his mission. "I need your help to get these people to open their books. I don't have time to indulge their sensibilities."

"Okay. What we'll do, we'll be at Barclays Bank first thing Monday morning. What's more, we'll ask Barclays to get the Banco de Bilbao to bring over the account—the two banks are near each other. We'll let them do the running around."

"Monday morning? I was hoping we might be able to organize something for today or tomorrow."

Ralph sighed. "You know, Sam, sometimes you do things the hard way. These are institutions shut down tight for the weekend. God knows where the bank officers are. Probably away in their country hideouts. Maybe we could find them and, if we're lucky, get them to open up. Then we might hit the problem you've had all along, with one or the other. I can absolutely guarantee you'll see both London accounts at start of business Monday morning."

"How can you be so sure?"

"Because I won't be wasting the weekend. I'll arrange for a couple of magistrate's warrants to be issued informally, just in case we need them."

Sam was silent, grateful for the help from his friend yet reluctant to lose that much time. Ralph understood, but he had his own way of doing things. "Sam, if you ask me, you're just too late. The money's gone, and you can kiss it good-bye. The best you can hope for is that you'll eventually discover where and who is responsible. That's going to take time and patience. I shouldn't have to tell a man of your experience that you should pace yourself. Take it easy, Sam!"

He didn't respond immediately. He had no way to sensibly convey the feeling of urgency about the investigation. When he stopped to think about it, he could identify no reason for any such immediacy. The ball of yarn would unravel in time. Or maybe it wouldn't.

"Yeah, I guess you're right, Ralph," Sam said at length. "You're one hell of a laid-back guy, you know that?"

"That's another of your Yankee expressions I haven't heard before. Is it good or bad?"

Sam grinned, the first time in days. "I leave it to your imagination."

Thus, Sam unexpectedly spent a pleasantly relaxed weekend with Ralph and his wife, Sally, in a mock-Tudor house, in a leafy London suburb.

By ten-thirty Monday morning Sam, at Barclays Bank, was holding both the Barclays account and the one from the London branch of the Banco de Bilbao, which had arrived by messenger. Hungrily he consumed the cold figures on the sheets before him. They told the same story as the other accounts, and now he was positive he knew the entire complex pattern of money transfers, even though he hadn't seen the Hong Kong account. The whole operation was a tactic to ensure delay while capital was filtered out of the various accounts, to finally disappear into the Swiss banking system.

The Barclays foreign expert was Matthews, a gray-haired, dignified man wearing a stiff white collar over a shirt with broad stripes. "Mr. Matthews, is there no way at all to break down these Swiss codes?"

"I'm afraid not."

"There has to be somebody, somewhere, who can give me a lead." Sam was adamant.

"You are making a mistake if you think these codes will ever be of help. They are constantly being changed. And you'll get some idea of what you're up against when you realize that in Switzerland disclosure of confidential banking information is punishable by jail sentences. People have tried for years to get information from these codes, and no one has succeeded."

CHAPTER FIVE

Sam flew back to the States Tuesday morning, spent Wednesday and Thursday preparing his report, handed it in on Friday, and was told that he would be required to attend an executive meeting the following morning at nine. A Saturday meeting of Treasury brass was almost unheard of, except in times of dire financial crisis, and no one had told Sam of an impending crisis.

At 8:55 he was in the corridor leading to the upper executive boardroom when MacCaskey stepped out of the elevator. "What in hell's going on, Chuck?"

"Beats me!" Together they began walking toward the high doors at the end of the corridor. "I haven't been told a thing, except that I've heard the deputy comptroller is tweaking a few tails up here in the rarefied air. You know about as much as I do."

At the boardroom a uniformed security man awaited them. "Good morning, gentlemen. I must ask you to wait out here. You'll be called in due course."

Sam and Chuck sat on a couple of hard chairs in a row lined up against a wall, in increasing discomfort, until past ten, when one of the boardroom doors opened. The security man called out for Mr. MacCaskey, and Chuck disappeared through the tall doors.

Twenty minutes passed before Chuck reappeared. He signaled for Sam to go in and, saying nothing, strode off along the corridor, his face a serious mask.

The boardroom was very impressive. Its principal feature was a long, highly polished conference table. Around it were twenty or more high-backed chairs, empty except for four at one end. At the top of the table, Sam recognized Deputy Comptroller Mark Wesley.

"Do sit down, Mr. Kilmartin." Wesley gave him a brief nod of recognition. "I don't propose to introduce these gentlemen to you at this stage. Who they are is not significant to your part in this, but you'll be pleased to know that I've described you to them as the best man in the business."

As Sam sat, an instant of fleeting recognition of the man opposite flashed through his mind, then was gone. He was immediately annoyed with himself—he never forgot faces—it must have been long ago. Then his attention was captured by Wesley.

"We've read your report on the Whitefish matter," Wesley told him. "A copy of the Hong Kong bank account has been acquired, and it ties in with the rest, just as you speculated it would."

He had been unaware that the Hong Kong statements had arrived. "Look, Mr. Wesley," he said, "the theft of Treasury funds is an important matter, but I get the feeling there must be more to this than I'm aware of. As the investigating officer, I should be told what's going on."

Wesley glanced at the others. They were impassive, and his attention returned to Sam. "The fact is, we don't know a great deal more than you do, except that the potential in this case may be rather more significant than is apparent. I'd rather not have to explain right now, but you can take it that what I'm talking about has no bearing on your investigation. It won't affect it either way."

Sam sat in puzzled silence. Wesley could only be talking about the additional money Sam's investigation had unearthed. "I assume you're talking about the rest of the money, sir. I make it ten point two million, altogether. I haven't been instructed in that regard, but it must have been stolen, too."

"Yes, that's so. And now I'm authorizing you to widen your investigation to take in the other thefts. You'll find that a similar computer technique was used throughout and—"

"Excuse me, sir," Sam interrupted. "Wouldn't it help if we could determine exactly how it was done? The computer stunt, I mean. I know nothing about computers, but there must be someone with the savvy to analyze the technique."

"Who said we're unaware of how it was done?" Wesley's voice was brittle.

"I consulted with Mr. Robert Halpern, of computer section, sir. It was my understanding that they couldn't explain, down there, how the illicit instruction was infiltrated into the program."

"We're working on that one. We'll come up with a solution sooner or later, naturally."

"Knowing how it was done might just give us a lead to the wiseass."

Wesley scowled. "Yes, well, that is *our* problem. Yours is to follow through on anything you can dig up at the computer locations. The information we already have is on its way to MacCaskey, and you can work out any operational plan you like. We want this character, and we want him fast. The instigator, that is. Of course, all information you generate remains classified. I can't stress the importance of that too much."

"Yes, sir." Sam was too experienced to query such specific orders. "I have one further observation."

"Go ahead!"

"It seems to me an investigation of this nature is more in the province of the FBI than the Treasury. I was wondering why I've been given the job."

He had been able to get it in, MacCaskey or no MacCaskey. When the man opposite him blinked, he had a flash of recognition. Now he remembered the face: Norman Logan, the FBI chief with no official title. The policymaker and the man reputed to be more powerful than the director himself. Logan, the man rarely seen in public, the shadowy figure behind the FBI throne. What in God's name was Logan doing here?

"It has already been explained to you that we will keep this within the department," Wesley was saying. "Substantial Treasury funds were appropriated illegally. Isn't that reason enough to use our own resources?"

"Yes, sir, but we could spread a wider net using the FBI —"

"Have you any other questions?" Wesley cut him off abruptly.

"No, sir."

"Good morning, Mr. Kilmartin!"

Standing up, Sam carefully returned his chair to its place under the table's overhang. As he did so, he scrutinized the thin pink file that Logan had before him on the table. On its front was a number, and Sam read it upside down: 808. "Good morning, gentlemen," he said politely. He made for the door.

Later, sitting in his office, Sam reached a decision. The time had come for him to live up to his reputation and his own belief in himself. It was time to look out for his own end—no agent of his standing should tolerate working in the dark this way. He dialed the FBI number. "Extension ten-ten," a woman answered. He recognized the voice.

"Janet," he said, "it's Sam Kilmartin."

A pause, as if the call was anticipated and feared. "Well, hi, Sam. How have you been?"

"Janet, I need five minutes of your time."

"You can speak. I'm alone in the office."

"No, meet me away from the building. What time do you finish?"

"Five o'clock."

"Five-fifteen. The Kit Kat coffee shop. You know where that is?"

"Yes, I know."

"Tonight."

She came into the coffee shop looking gaunt, a woman of forty-five with hair beginning to gray, an upright bearing, and an intelligent face. When she saw him, her eyes skipped across the faces of other customers, seeking familiar features. Seeing none, she seated herself in the booth facing him. "There's been nothing, Sam. I swear to God, Billy hasn't put a foot wrong since that one time. He's nearly completed a course in motor mechanics, and he's been promised a job at the new Ford agency on—" Sam held up his hand and she ceased her rapid, nervous chatter.

"Good," he said gently. "I'm glad to hear Bill's getting along okay. Would you like coffee, Janet?"

"No, thanks. What do you want, Sam?"

"I need a favor. Are you still Norman Logan's secretary?"

"He's not always in the building. When he is, I do some work for him," she conceded cautiously.

"I'm on a case with him," Sam said, "but he's holding out on me. There's a pink file, number 808. I want to know what's in it."

"Oh, no, Sam. I couldn't!" Janet put her hand to her mouth.

"Look, it's not as if I'm a subversive or a spy. I'm a T-man, remember? It's a race between them and us."

"I've never done anything like that."

"What's a pink file? Is it highly classified?"

"Yes."

"Can you get at it?"

She hesitated, and her eyes said that she could. "No, I can't."

"You'll have to find a way."

"Are you threatening me, Sam?"

"No, Janet. I'm not. But you do owe me a favor, and I need to collect," Sam insisted in a low voice.

He could see it all again in her eyes: The time he made a bust and the youngster used as a runner in a stupidly amateurish counterfeiting operation turned out to be her son, Bill. Sam had known Bill's father as a G-man, one whose dedication had cost him his life. Sam had hauled Bill home and given him the rousting of his life in front of his fear-stricken mother. That was three years ago now, but Janet still lived in dread of any repetition.

"It's unfair, Sam." Tears began to form in her eyes.

"If you are caught, I'll come right out and admit I put you up to it. I'll take the blame, and I'll talk you out of trouble. Don't worry."

"What do you want?"

"I want a copy of what's in file number 808."

"I'll try."

Janet came through. It was in his hands at last, a photocopy of Norman Logan's report. Sam sat down to read the ten pages with an excitement rare to him.

The first four sheets consisted of a report from the computer section signed by Robert Halpern. At the end Halpern expressed bafflement over two complex mathematical equations gone awry. The fifth sheet, detailing the loss of six hundred fifty thousand dollars of Treasury funds, was little more than an internal accounting consolidation.

Then the documents began to get interesting—details of computer losses sustained by commercial institutions, from Chase Manhattan through Texaco to a variety of other top-drawer establishments, bringing the total to

$10.2 million. What Sam found intriguing was the series of dates. Before the Treasury loss, each earlier theft had been reported to the FBI. As Sam read on, he found that within two days of the Treasury loss the FBI had assumed that, because all the illicit transfers had taken place within four days, they constituted one big rip-off.

Sam's gaze lifted. So the secretive bastards had known all along about the other thefts—well before he had been ordered to investigate. Why hadn't he been informed? And now another nagging question took form: Why had no hint of all this ever reached the public? The caper was three months old, but not a word had been published.

Incomprehension clouding his eyes, Sam bent his head to the final two sheets in the file, and these made everything clear. Containing Norman Logan's views on what had taken place, they revealed his influence in FBI affairs:

Confidential to Principals. FBI/TREASURY

Preliminary observations in the matter of subversive penetration of computer installations herein described for the purpose of effecting a solution to theft or embezzlement by a person or persons unknown.

This office considers it of urgent concern that the method(s) used to effect unauthorized money transfers by electronic means is/are at present unknown. It is particularly significant that the computer departments of all institutions affected are unable to offer a technical explanation of how the crimes were executed. It follows that the technique employed must be determined without delay, in order that a remedy may be applied against further intrusion. To this end it is suggested that advice be sought immediately from appropriate sources of computer expertise, such as manufacturers. In the event a solution is not rapidly forthcoming, appropriate bodies such as SRI can be of assistance, and options of this nature should be established forthwith.

The hazards implicit in failure to correct the situation within a short time are self-evident, apart from the ramifications of computer vulnerability arising from these incidents. This office therefore suggests that the following be considered:

1. *Defense:* We cannot ignore the possibility that subversive commands may be introduced into computer

programs controlling defense equipment. Equally, agencies concerned with intelligence matters may be covertly penetrated.

2. *Federal Administration:* The multiplicity of computer operations employed in civil functions provides countless openings for regulatory abuse, extending, in the extreme, to debasement of the democratic process.

3. *Commercial/Industrial Considerations:* As distinct from serious fiscal loss, commercial organizations employing computer facilities may suffer additional harm from public knowledge of their vulnerability. For example, stockholders' suits alleging inadequate management techniques have been known to arise from aberrations of this nature, with consequent disruption to business, resulting unemployment, etc. *We have received urgent requests that strenuous efforts be made to conceal this matter from public view in the short term.*

These examples are not intended to represent a comprehensive survey of potential risk to the well-being of the nation. Many additional factors will occur. Unless a solution to the computer problem is forthcoming in the immediate future, recommendation should be made to the White House that it may wish to study the subject through the medium of an appropriate committee of inquiry.

In particular, this office is concerned with the part the FBI may be called upon to play, and it cannot be stressed too strongly that extreme caution is advised. In the event that the technical dilemma remains unresolved, investigation by teams of FBI agents seeking the perpetrator(s) will undoubtedly lead to premature revelation of the facts. The media ordinarily are quick to sense a major FBI inquiry. On balance, the value of apprehending the criminal(s) is outweighed by the anticipated loss of public confidence, if the vulnerability of computer functions becomes common knowledge.

This office therefore suggests that until the foregoing technical problem is solved, a most circumspect approach be adopted. The fact that the Treasury has suffered financial loss is adequate justification for deploying its investigative staff. Treasury agents are, of course, equal in status to ours, and enjoy the additional benefit that they ordinarily sustain less exposure. It is therefore recommended that, initially, a solitary Treasury field agent of the highest caliber and professional repute undertake investigative procedures. Furthermore, it is inadvisable that the full facts be made known to him, but rather that he be instructed only in regard to appropriation of Treasury funds.

For the guidance of FBI/Treasury staff, a full analysis of this matter will be undertaken when more information becomes available.

This office has, on several occasions, urged that a special section within the bureau be devoted exclusively to study of computer crime. The proliferation of this type of equipment demands that such an objective now be pursued with vigor.

Norman Logan's signature, without reference to his function, completed the document. Sam noted again the date by Logan's signature: two days before Sam received the assignment. A number of developments had occurred since, but one thing was certain: The computer riddle remained unsolved. He eased back in his chair, marveling at the degree of expertise that was confounding the computer people. Someone out there was so clever that he represented an awesome threat to the American nation.

CHAPTER SIX

A dozen miles south of Zurich, the small town of Stäfa nestled in the valley region of Toggenburg. It looked out across the still, slate-gray waters of the Zürichsee toward snow-capped massifs three miles distant.

Outside the town, concealed from traffic and built on rock that jutted over the lake, was a chalet.

In the enormous living room, curving glass formed an entire wall. Its panels reached up and out into space at a considerable angle. A little girl had managed to surmount the ledge and now was spread-eagled on the glass itself. She was fearlessly inching her way up and out so she could look down into the lake below. A great central fireplace glowed with its pile of burning logs. Not far from it, almost submerged in a davenport that snaked along one wall, Jordan was totally absorbed in a book. Holly, walking into the room, gave a sudden, frightened call and ran to grab Debbie and bring her down from the sloping glass.

Jordan looked up from his book. "Don't worry," he said calmly. "The glass is armored, you know. It would support a truck."

Holding Debbie in her arms, Holly gazed down into the water. Her slimly exquisite girlish figure had filled out in the right places, and she conveyed a glow of vitality and happiness. "It frightens me sometimes, being suspended out over the lake like this."

"Don't you like the house that much?" Concerned, he hurried toward her. "If you don't, we can easily find another. How about a chalet in the mountains? I have some brochures—"

"No, darling, I do love the house. Honest!" She put Debbie over her shoulder, caressing the fast-growing youngster fondly. "I love everything here. The country, the people, being with you like this. I just can't believe it's true. Sometimes I wake in the night and reach out to touch you, just to make sure you're really there."

Jordan embraced them both before Holly put Debbie on the rug, and the child, gurgling happily, toddled off to seek a small toy in the rug's thick pile. Holly linked her arm through his, and they stood together looking out over the panorama.

"Is it really all over now, Jordan? Can you promise me we won't ever be apart again?"

"You have my word. From now on only good things are going to happen to us."

"But you said last night you're planning to give them enough information so they can locate you if they wish to. I don't like the idea of that, darling." Holly's face reflected her anxiety.

"You don't have to worry, baby. I have considered it very carefully and decided that this is the way to go. We can't be on the run forever, afraid of our shadows, dreading the next knock at the door, unable to really be ourselves. Oh, we've got comfort, yes; but peace, no."

Jordan circled his arms over the blond hair that covered Holly's shoulders and gave her a loud kiss. "I thought at first the only chance I had was to hit and run. At the time it seemed to me that was as far as it went. It's possible for us to live in great style in certain countries that have no extradition treaty with the U.S. The American authorities couldn't get at us there."

"Are we safe here, Jordan?"

"Well, no. They could get me here, sooner or later, if they wanted."

"Then what in Christ's name are we doing here?" Holly's look had turned to one of alarm. "Why aren't we in one of those other countries?"

"Relax! Nothing's going to happen in a hurry."

"I still don't like it, Jordan." Holly's look was tremulous.

"Relax, baby. I still have an ace in the hole. A way of keeping them off our backs."

"Do you mean it—are you serious?"

"Sure I mean it. Later, when the heat is off, we may

even be able to return to the States. With the money, of course."

"Oh, Jordan, that would be so fantastic. To be home again." For an instant Holly revealed her regrets, but she recovered quickly. "I'll go anywhere with you, darling, you know I will. Being together is the only thing that matters. But if there's really some hope that we can go home one day—"

"Don't count on it, Holly," Jordan cut in seriously. "Maybe that's hoping for too much. But if nobody comes up with an idea to counter my latest, I think I can come out on top, wherever we are."

"What idea is that, Jordan?"

"I can't explain it yet. I'm still working it through the final phase."

"You're talking about computers, of course?"

"In a way. This is a new twist." He gave a quick, mischievous grin.

"Ah! That's what you've been doing in the den."

"I've been writing microcode, a great deal of it. But I've almost finished now."

From below, in the multilevel house, they heard the sound of the doorbell. Jordan felt a tremor go through Holly.

"Who is that?" She rushed to Debbie.

"Relax, will you?" Jordan stood and stretched. "It's only the new car. I told them to deliver it at eleven."

"You didn't say you were buying a car."

"Every family has to have a Rolls, don't they?"

"We have a Rolls-Royce?"

"That burgundy color you like, as near as I could match it. You'd better go to the door. I arranged for you to have an hour's instruction. They say you need to know a couple of things to drive it well."

"Me!"

"Yes, and you'll have to learn kind of quick. You need to be at Kloten airport at two-thirty."

"Airport—what for?"

"To pick up your mom and dad. I sent them two open tickets to Zurich on Swissair."

Holly stared at him, confounded.

"I thought you'd want them here for our wedding."

"Our wedding?"

"Our *real* wedding. Remember my promise to you—a white gown, flowers, the whole bit?"

"Oh, Jordan!" She threw herself at him, her eyes streaming. They kissed emotionally, to the doorbell's now insistent ring.

CHAPTER SEVEN

Sam was wallowing in computers and feeling lost.

At each site affected by theft, he had asked for three lists: first a record of current employees with access to the computers and the appropriate level of programming skill; then a list of similar past employees, extending back for a year; and third a list composed of any from the first two who may have been suspected of being disgruntled, dissatisfied, or bearing some kind of grudge. He added a further requirement: that anyone known to have an inordinate level of skill be flagged.

All the names had been processed for signs of criminality, but little was revealed. Motoring violations comprised the bulk of the recorded offenses, which were well below the national average, Sam observed. One case of wife beating was among them and one of malicious damage to a baby grand. The spectrum of larceny was covered by a couple of prosecutions for shoplifting. Clearly the preoccupations of numerical wizardry left little time for lawbreaking.

Impatiently he threw the lists aside. He didn't need them. Just as, in all probability, he had no need to go outside his own office looking for clues.

He closed his eyes to reflect. His investigative senses were bared, his antennae out in the wind seeking a notion, a suggestion, a nuance. Would it have been possible to influence, or bribe, seven prickly, highly skilled programmers, all at different locations? Of course not. It was out of the question, and this meant, since he had combed all the employee lists of all the personnel officers, that the man was using a false name in each instance.

The personnel people had scorned his theory and demonstrated the care with which they reviewed each application for employment. It made the water even murkier that photographs ordinarily accompanied the records of these key employees, and all had been satisfactorily identified at their various locations. No common face, no common identity appeared. Identity—name and face. Disguise had popped into Sam's head the previous day as a wild possibility. The man would have to be good if he were using disguise, which implied professional help or instruction.

Sam called the major theaters. In New York they knew about makeup, not disguise. And, they told him it was little different in Hollywood. It seemed nobody in the country knew a damn thing about *real* disguise, and no schools, no experts were around. Sam had tried the CIA as a last resort, and the best they could suggest was a professor based in London. An expert was said to be in Bulgaria, too, and the Russians had a couple, but they would hardly serve his need. The London professor would be his best bet—when he could get to it.

London! For God's sake, Sam thought, when he needed someone urgently here in Washington. He considered calling Heritage in London, but for the meantime made a note to be sure to get to this Professor Plutz. A different identity each time. The implications of that theory were astounding and must prevail until a better, more plausible one came along.

Sam had not spoken to Robert Halpern since early in the case, and though he had become leery of computer people in general, he conceded just a chance, now that he was more familiar with the details, that he might have missed something.

The young expert came up from the computer section in answer to Sam's call. He looked sullen, his eyes redder than ever in resentment. "I'm very busy, Mr. Kilmartin," he said. "I suppose you do realize that interruptions of this nature break my concentration?"

"I'm sorry to disturb you, Robert," Sam said easily, "but I'm getting no feedback on this case. I just want you to try to remember if anything unusual has happened in the section."

"When?"

"Just—ah, anytime. The point is, Robert," he said patiently, "you're one of the few people who has almost certainly been face-to-face with this guy. I'm ruling out that he's a member of the present staff, you understand. I'd like you to concentrate your thoughts on all the people, individually, who have worked here with you this last year or so."

"Five or six have now moved on."

"Six in all, Robert. With forty-eight in your section, it appears to be less than the national average for the industry. I gather that some prefer the stability of working for the government."

"The money's not so hot."

"I get the feeling money isn't always the deciding factor." He was trying to be pleasant, to warm up Halpern.

"Job satisfaction?" Halpern asked unexpectedly.

"Something like that, I guess," Sam said amiably.

"That's a crock. I have to pay the same bills everyone else does. And I work a damn sight harder than most. Why should I take less than the industry level?"

"Well, you certainly have a point there."

"Look, Mr. Kilmartin, why don't you go bother someone else—maybe the person who was doing my job when I was working over at the Federal Reserve Building. . . ."

"You were out of the department? Nobody told me."

"It was a while ago, when they were reequipping at the Fed, and the idea was to make their new installation compatible with ours. I was there six weeks helping sort out the mess."

"There's nothing on your employment record."

"Why should there be? It was a temporary assignment, on Treasury business."

"The period when Halpern was working over at the Federal Reserve—why didn't you tell me about that?" Sam asked Billings.

The personnel officer sat back and regarded Sam coldly. "You didn't ask, after all."

"It might have seemed to you it was important, that your best man was absent from the section for some time."

"May I remind you, Kilmartin, that you told me you wished to limit your inquiry to one year prior to the date of the credit transfer?"

"That was intended as a general guide."

"I wasn't to know that. You're the detective, not I."

Sam grunted. "Who took Halpern's place, in his absence?"

"No one in particular, it so happens."

"Then who did his work?"

"Much of what Halpern does is forward planning. It was simply laid over until he returned. It's true the section got into something of a pickle, when he was at the Fed. That was when we had a couple of key programmers leave in the same week. I wasn't able to replace those people immediately and had to call in some outside help. I managed to borrow a systems analyst and a data entry operator from Records. I tried the agencies, too, but there were no temps available, and the advertisements weren't getting any response. . . ." He stopped, his eyes rounding.

"What is it?" Sam said.

"I just remembered something, speaking of agencies. I took on someone for a short period. He was the strangest character and didn't last more than a few days."

"A programmer?"

"Yes."

"A good one?"

"I can't honestly say. The initial feedback I had was quite satisfactory; that I remember. On his CV he was good enough to be a systems analyst, but that didn't mean a thing. You see, his references were all bogus."

Sam sat up. "What was that you said?"

"Just a moment. I'll get the record." Billings rose and searched through a cabinet. "Yes, here it is. Reginald Barret. He came from the Digidata Consultancy, of New York."

"If he came from a consultancy, how could it be that his references were bogus?"

"He'd been fooling them, too, apparently."

"How do you know that?"

"He called me up to tell me so. After he quit."

"I don't get it. Why would he do that?"

"It was a weird business altogether," Billings continued. "Barret was probably fully qualified and certainly seemed to know his work. I'd have heard soon enough if he didn't. But he was using a bogus name because he'd been in jail. At least, so he said."

"Did he happen to tell you why he had been in jail?"

"For rape. Or attempted rape, I guess it was."

"I don't understand why he was in such a hurry to tell you about his past."

"That was his reason for quitting. He told me on the phone that he was developing dangerous tendencies over a girl in the office. He felt that, for safety's sake, he'd better put some distance between the girl and himself."

"Criminals don't think that way," Sam objected baldly.

"Perhaps he was rehabilitated. His conduct appears to indicate that fact," Billings said reflectively. "He didn't get fired from here, you understand. Just walked out."

"You said his credentials turned out to be fake. You would have fired him, sooner or later, when you found out."

"Oh, there's no question. He'd have had to go."

"How come you didn't check up on him before you took him on?"

Billings looked uncomfortable. "It was a matter of expediency. We were desperately short of help in the computer section. I even arranged for him to take his entry tests at the end of the month so that we could put him to work immediately. It's not as bad as it sounds. You have to understand it would have shown up within minutes if he weren't a competent programmer. I was relying on his CV from an accredited consultancy for his background."

"Had you dealt with this Digidata outfit previously?"

"Well, no, I hadn't. We use employment agencies at odd times, but a consultancy is somewhat specialized, and we have our own specialists, like Halpern."

"What did they have to say about this Barret incident?"

"To be frank, I haven't been in touch with them. The whole incident was over in three or four days. I had considered writing them a stinking letter, but as Barret had confessed to me and had presumably revealed the facts to Digidata afterward, I took it no further—"

"You were taken for a ride, my friend."

"Do you think Barret might have set up the Treasury computer?" His tone had risen.

"I don't know, but for the first time in this goddamn case I have a positive lead." He unobtrusively crossed his fingers. "I guess, as Barret was coming and going in the section, he was issued an ID?"

"Why, yes." Billings dipped into his file. "In fact, here's his photograph."

Sam reached for it with a grunt of gratification, certain he was gazing at the man who could take on the technological resources of an entire industry and emerge the victor. The full-cheeked, somber face that gazed back blankly gave no indication of such vaulting aptitude. Could this possibly be the shadowy Gregory Whitefish, too?

Hell, the face just didn't look right. An illogical disappointment stabbed Sam; illogical because he knew full well that the man's image on a photograph meant little. Yet it did, indeed, resemble a face that could dribble lasciviously through its bushy mustache over a voluptuous female form. What was it with the hair these days, for Christ's sake—the impulse that turned otherwise clean-cut young all-American guys into caricatures of desperadoes?

"Could Barret be your man, do you think?" Billings was asking.

"What?" Sam looked up. "If your people could only solve the computer conundrum, maybe I'll be able to answer that question. I'll want a copy of everything you have in that file, please."

"I'll have it sent up to your office."

"You can copy it now. I'll wait!"

CHAPTER EIGHT

It was a bright, pleasant day on Madison Avenue, and he was in the heart of New York's business district. Sam strode along enjoying the sight of pretty girls out shopping on their lunch breaks. Their vitality was a fleeting reminder of Eleanor. She had been a New York secretary, too, when they had met all those years ago. As quick and as pert as any that graced the sidewalk today, he thought.

They had been the years of wine and roses—the wonderful years when they were first married, long before the insidious, creeping influence of a virulent disease blighted her life—their lives. It had marred her wonderful body and in the end it had killed her.

He arrived at the office building he sought. Shaking himself out of his reverie, he entered to search for the premises of the Digidata Computer Consultancy.

"What business is it of yours?" The aging brassy-haired woman in the seedy office on an upper floor responded to his inquiry.

Sam flashed his ID. "All I want is a simple answer. A yes or no. Is this an accommodation address for the Digidata Computer Consultancy?"

"Well, yes, he was one of my clients. That is, until his time ran out. He gave me no notice, just didn't bother to renew. It often happens that way." She stubbed out her cigarette in an overflowing ashtray and lit another.

"Who is *he?*"

"You've got a warrant?"

Sam sighed. "Look, this is an official inquiry, and it's urgent. If you waste my time now, I'll make sure you waste some of yours when it comes to your license renewal."

"I'm not afraid of you just because you carry that badge.

I run a legitimate operation here. My contact, Postal Inspector Donnelly, carries a badge, too, and if there's any negotiating to do, I go through him."

Fronting for advertising flimflam was a tough way to earn a living, Sam thought. And the woman was accustomed to being defensive. He tried a more gentle approach. "Mrs. Williams," he said quietly, "we both know I can come back with a warrant if necessary. I wasn't aware this outfit was using an accommodation address. Now all I need is to clear up one or two points, and I'll be on my way. Probably I won't have to bother you ever again."

"All I do is answer the phone and take in their mail. Does this have to do with advertising, or anything of that sort?"

"Nothing like that, ma'am. I'm not interested in your end of it. As you saw from my ID, I'm Treasury."

Mrs. Williams thought it over, then said, "Okay, shoot. But if I think I'm going to be incriminating myself, I'll deny every word afterward. You don't have any witnesses."

"Thank you, Mrs. Williams; I appreciate your help. First, I need to know who was behind Digidata."

She flicked deftly through a circular card index before her. "A man by the name of Richard Elegan."

"Just the one?"

"All I ever saw."

"Young?"

"Yeah, fairly young, I guess. Maybe midtwenties, and kind of good-looking in a quiet way."

"Mustache?"

Mrs. Williams's eyebrows met in concentration. "It was a long time ago."

"Is this Richard Elegan?" Sam handed her the photograph of the man called Reginald Barret.

"No, that isn't Elegan. At least, I don't think it is."

"You're not positive?"

She looked again. "I'm positive; it isn't him. What's he done, anyhow?"

"Nothing I'm certain of yet, Mrs. Williams. I'm just eliminating suspects in a case. How tall is Elegan, would you say?"

"Five-eleven," she said promptly.

"You sound sure."

"I remember him reaching up the same height as Inspector Donnelly. Only not so heavily built, if you know what I mean. A woman notices these things." She added, "Funny that I don't remember about the mustache."

"Thanks, Mrs. Williams. This could be a help. Now I'd like as many of Elegan's personal details as you can give me: his home address, phone, bank. . . ."

"It's all on here." Mrs. Williams handed him her record card. "You can see what I earned from him, too. Hardly worth the trouble, is it?"

Sam smiled sympathetically and began writing down the details. "Do you have a record of his calls?"

"Sorry. We don't keep something like that."

"I understand. Well, thanks, Mrs. Williams, for your cooperation."

"I don't want to be wasting my time being any witness in any court." A hint of suspicion had returned.

"That's the last thing on my mind right now, ma'am. Well, I'm obliged, and thanks again." He left, still smiling courteously.

Even before he began the search, he knew the hotel address, the phone number, and the Digidata bank account would yield nothing.

Sam summoned Robert Halpern to his office again. He pointed to the photograph on his desk. "Okay, Robert," he said, "this man calling himself Reginald Barret spent three-and-a-half days in your section when you were working over at the Federal Building. He got into the Treasury by deceit."

"So this is the fellow, huh?" Halpern picked up the photograph and studied it, then dropped it back onto the desk. "Nobody I've ever seen."

"I don't know for certain that he's responsible for the computer thing," Sam said, "but it's the only lead I have for the moment. What I'd like to do is call all the members of your section up here, singly, and ask each one what he or she can tell me about Barret."

"So what's stopping you?"

"It's a clumsy way of handling the problem. I'd rather you talk to some of your people quietly for me and try to find out what you can about Barret. Not his personal behavior—I don't think we're going to learn much there.

What I'm looking for is a professional clue. Someone that good on computers has to be known somewhere, has to have been connected with some style of operation. You will know what to look for, the questions to ask, better than I. . . ."

"I'm not doing your dirty work for you, Mr. Kilmartin. That's out. You'll have to question the staff yourself."

"Well, there's that little matter of confidentiality I told you about. The more fuss I make, the more official the inquiry, the more difficult it's going to be to keep this thing under wraps. Everyone involved here has signed the official secrets document, and it means jail and their jobs if they discuss it outside, but I guess some fool is going to blab sooner or later. Fact is, we're lucky it hasn't got out yet."

"It's not my goddamn problem," Halpern declared angrily.

"I'm afraid it is, Robert. You see, I wasn't entirely frank with you before. As you're the expert in the section, they keep coming back to your name in the absence of someone else to blame. I've told them that, in my opinion, you didn't have anything to do with it, but you know what they're like up there."

"I knew it! I knew all the time you animals were looking for a fall guy. Well, you're not going to lay this on me. You hear that, Mr. Kilmartin? You can go find yourself another turkey." Halpern's voice had risen to a yell, and panic filled his eyes.

"Take it easy, Robert. You have a friend in me. I know you didn't do it, and if it comes to a showdown, I'll be there on your side." Sam spoke soothingly. "Look, if I didn't believe in you, I wouldn't be telling you this, would I? Now just cool it, and leave things to me."

Halpern was fighting down his alarm. "It's damned unfair. . . ."

"I know, Robert. But that's the way things go sometimes. The sooner we can identify the phantom programmer, the sooner you'll be off the hook. Maybe now you can see why you have to give me a little help."

After a silence, Halpern said, more reasonably, "Let me get this straight. All you want me to do is ask around?"

"That's all. But methodically, and using your head. Someone down there must have got a sense of his professional background, his specialties, his preferences, even. You will know the questions to ask better than I do."

"Okay, I'll buy it."

"Good for you."

"It's damned unfair."

"Don't worry, Robert. Just leave yourself in my hands. We'll beat this hotshot yet."

Forty minutes later Halpern was on the phone. He had recovered his confidence and spoke in his normal, reserved tones. "Mr. Kilmartin, I think I have something."

"Yeah?" Sam was surprised at his own intensity. "Go ahead, Robert."

"One of my people here is an IBM specialist. He says he could swear this Barret was steeped in IBM techniques. But really hot, know what I mean? It's the reason he remembers him."

"I don't get the implication."

"If he's an IBM expert of that caliber, it means either he worked for them or he was company-trained to a high standard. Nobody acquires IBM mainframe techniques haphazardly, and certainly no regular programmer. That narrows the field down quite a bit, don't you think?"

"Sure does, Robert. I'm grateful to you. I can't tell you how much this helps."

It was time for action. Sam learned of IBM instructional centers at Chicago, Atlanta, Los Angeles, and New York; he chose the latter, hoping to save time, since the man responsible for vocational programs had his office there.

Malcolm Avery studied the photograph and handed it back. "I don't know the face, Mr. Kilmartin, but that really doesn't mean very much. I don't see many of our trainees personally. You will have to speak with the course instructors. That means visiting the individual plants, I'm afraid."

"Can you tell me if the name Reginald Barret is on your records?"

Avery swiveled his chair to a keyboard at one side of his desk and pressed some buttons. A visual display unit sprang to life. "No, it isn't. Barret is not employed by us at any of our locations, nor has he been. We trained an Angela Barratt as a data entry operator in Chicago some months ago, but that's the nearest."

"Do the names Gregory Whitefish or Richard Elegan appear on your records, Mr. Avery?"

"Richard Elegan and Gregory . . ."

"Whitefish," Sam repeated.

"I'll take a look." Avery pressed buttons. "They're not on any trainee scroll . . ." He pressed again. "Nor on the company payroll."

"Okay, thanks. I wasn't expecting a positive result." Sam was resigned.

Avery touched another button and the screen died. He swiveled back to Sam. "We're highly segmented," he said. "You'll have to be specific about the training this person received, or you may find yourself talking to the wrong instructors."

"Yes, I understand," Sam said. "He's a programmer. A very good one, so I believe. Good enough to function as a systems analyst, too."

"Huh," Avery said.

"Is that significant?"

"It could be. We don't find people like that every day. When we do, we take special care with them."

"How will that fact help me?"

"You'll have fewer people to interview. Just a handful of top instructors who are specialists. If that fails, you can work your way down through the rest."

"Sounds good," Sam said. "Are some of these people here in New York?"

"Just one, at present. She happens to be our best. Her name is Pauline Hennessey. Would you like to meet her? She's working here in the building right now."

"I sure would."

He stared when Pauline Hennessey entered the room, and then he couldn't take his eyes off her. The ash-blond hair, the blue eyes, the pristine correctness took him back sharply to the days when he had first known Eleanor. The proud back, her tall, slim, lithe body—it was a good thing he had never seen Pauline at a distance in the street, he thought. Mistaking her for his wife, he might have died of a heart attack.

When Avery introduced them, she said, "Have we met before, Mr. Kilmartin?"

Sam broke off his gaze. "Forgive me for staring; you remind me of—someone I used to know."

"Lost loves?" She smiled at him sympathetically.

"Yes, in a way," Sam said quietly.

"How can I help you?"

He brought himself back to earth and handed over the photograph. "Do you recognize this person, Miss Hennessey?"

She studied the photo. "No, I can't say that I do."

"Please look very carefully. He may be a student of yours from the past."

She didn't look again. "No, I would remember if he were one of my people."

God, but this woman had confidence, Sam found himself thinking. "He goes by the name of Reginald Barret. Or perhaps Gregory Whitefish . . . or Richard Elegan." He watched her closely for some flicker of recognition after each name. Nothing.

"I've never heard any of those names. What's special about him? Has he robbed the Treasury, or something?" She laughed and went on. "He's a programmer?"

"Yes. A damn good one, by all accounts."

"Oh, he *has* robbed the Treasury." There was amusement in her eyes. "Anyone trained by me should be able to handle that little chore without too much trouble. Of course, whether he'd get away with it is a different matter. . . ." She stopped, seeing Sam's expression. "My God, you're serious."

"I'm serious about getting my hands on this individual, Miss Hennessey," Sam said. He hoped his expression didn't betray that inwardly he was amazed at her perception. "It's very important that I get to know a few things about him."

"Well, if he's as good as you seem to think he is, that shouldn't be too difficult."

"I'm told he gives off signs of having had the best of training."

"Sounds about right. When they leave us our hallmark goes right through to their socks," Avery put in, with a chuckle.

Pauline said pleasantly, "Yes, but it doesn't help us to find who trained him. You will have to ask some of the other instructors, Mr. Kilmartin."

"I guess so. Thanks for trying."

"My pleasure." Pauline walked rapidly to the door. Her

hand on the lever, she hesitated, then turned. "You say this person was more capable than he wanted known?"

"I didn't really say that," Sam responded.

"If he chooses to restrict himself to straightforward programming without any explanation, it speaks for itself. Most can't wait to climb the ladder. Programming is damned hard work, and there are easier jobs in the upper echelons."

She was right. The significance of that had escaped him. "Does that open up any new options?" he asked.

"No, but I was going to say . . . I've had only one student like that."

"Oh?"

"A young fellow from California. At least, he'd been living there and taking a course at UCLA. I think he'd spent a lot of time in Europe, and I got the impression he'd had quite a good general education. . . ."

"Who was that, Pauline?" Avery asked.

"Why, Jordan Freeling. Don't you remember?"

"Oh, yes, of course. Auchterlonie's protégé."

"Jordan was a real microcode wizard," Pauline went on, returning to her chair. "When he chose to, he could run rings around me, and I'm supposed to be one of the best. For some idiotic reason he didn't want me to be aware of it, though." She stopped to think, then continued, "You get to know your students pretty well in an intensive course like ours. I soon realized he was the most capable student I'd ever had, despite the fact that he was trying to fool me."

Sam felt a quickening of the pulse in his throat and a prickling sensation that had started on the back of his neck was now all over his skin. "This young guy, this Jordan Freeling—was he capable of originating something, some entirely new technique? I mean, in your opinion, could he have been responsible for slipping something into a computer program so that all the goddamn experts in the business can't find out how it was done?"

"I don't know," Pauline said seriously. "That's a question nobody can answer. What I can tell you is that we are still using his method of converting hexadecimal systems for data representation—something that he originated. Nothing better has come along."

"I don't know what that means, but it sounds like a yes to me."

"I wonder what happened to Jordan. He never did take up his job in California," Avery said. "Technically, he's in breach of contract, of course."

"Would you please take another look at this photograph?" Sam said. "Could this possibly be your Jordan Freeling?"

"No, it's certainly not Jordan." And then Pauline was looking at it from a couple of angles, and Sam saw new uncertainty in her expression. "At least, I don't think it is. Without the mustache, I guess you could say there is a certain resemblance—"

"Hell, why bother with that?" A photograph landed on the desk, and Avery was closing a drawer. "We have the real McCoy. Here's a photograph of the genuine Jordan Freeling. We always keep a spare on file. We do it right here."

Sam shivered as he reached for the photograph and then sat back to examine it. *Jordan Freeling . . .* he thought. *Strange, but somehow I feel I already know you.*

CHAPTER NINE

Jordan Freeling Elegan Barret Whitefish.

It had to be! The more Sam thought about it, the more certain he became, although there wasn't a shred of evidence. He had backtracked with Jordan's photograph, and none of the people who had met with the phantom programmer were prepared to identify Jordan. But one or two had hesitated and agreed they might see a resemblance, and this was good enough for Sam. He *knew,* and that was all that mattered. Now it was only a question of putting all the pieces together.

The man was an expert on disguise. The role of Professor Plutz over in London began to take on additional meaning. Sam resolved that he would meet with him at the earliest possible time. But even the best of the T-men couldn't cover all bases at once.

In Chuck MacCaskey's office, Sam took a bruised cigar from his breast pocket and lit it. The Freeling file lay on the desk where he had dropped it, and Chuck was studying the photographs of Jordan. "So you think this is him?"

"It's only a hunch, so far. I have nothing positive."

"Can I take this idea upstairs? They're jumping down my throat every day, now."

"No, I can't substantiate it. Wait until I have something more tangible."

"But Sam, I need something to keep them happy! They're asking if we're asleep. If I could just tell them we have this lead—"

"You'd be asking for trouble, Chuck, if it turned out I'm wrong."

"You don't sound too confident, Sam."

"Confidence comes later. What I need now is some proof."

Chuck sighed. "So, what's next?"

"I can find no more leads here in Washington. I've already questioned Freeling's mother—she lives in a boardinghouse over in Arlington. She wants to find out where her son is almost as much as we do. Seems Jordan Freeling hadn't contacted her in quite a long time, when he sent her a cashier's check drawn on a London bank for a large amount of money. She wouldn't say how much. Anyway, Mrs. Freeling wants to use the money to move near her son, when and if she finds him."

"The lady's a fool. All that money just sitting there . . ."

"Well, she's had a rough go of it. So"—Sam stood up—"I'm going out to California. I'm booked on an evening plane."

"If you pin anything down, call me. They're giving me a hard time here."

"Are you sure they've found nothing yet—nothing at all?" Sam asked.

"If they did, they're not telling me. Now listen to this one. I'm told there's a congressman who's chairman of an important committee, and he's got wind of what's up. He wants the whole thing brought into the open, and they've had one hell of a job persuading him otherwise."

"That figures," Sam said laconically. "It can't be kept quiet much longer."

"I'll be glad, in one way, when the bubble bursts. Then we can speed things up and get a team out there looking for accomplices."

"Forget it; there are no accomplices."

"What do you mean?" Chuck stared.

"I'm convinced that Freeling did the whole goddamn thing by himself, bank accounts and all. He's mastered the cutest tricks of disguise—I'm sure of it now. And how do you like this? I sent a query to London about a professor who may just have been his instructor. You know where they found him? In our embassy!"

In the computer science department at UCLA, Sam unearthed little except that Jordan had been avid in his interest. He was still remembered for both his knowledge and his skill, and again Sam heard of Jordan's aptitude outpacing the bounds of the curriculum.

He discovered one thing, though, and it made a major difference: Jordan had a girlfriend, and she, too, left school soon after Jordan melted away. More significant, she later was seen in the area with a baby stroller.

The size and elegance of the Benedict estate, when he found it, was something Sam didn't often see. The maid went off to fetch her mistress, leaving him on the doorstep.

"What can I do for you?" Martha Benedict asked.

"I'm looking for Mr. Jordan Freeling," Sam said. "I was wondering if you could tell me where he is."

The self-possessed, matronly woman merely looked at him.

"I understand that he was friendly with your daughter at one time."

"My daughter has had a number of boyfriends," Martha said.

"I was told this one was special."

"Is that so?" Martha showed no surprise.

"May I come in, ma'am?" Sam asked. "I'd like to ask you one or two questions."

"I'm rather busy right now," Martha told him coolly. "I can answer your questions here."

"What I would really like is to speak with your daughter."

"I've no objection. When you find her, perhaps you will let me know where she is."

"She's not here?"

"Holly has been missing from home for several months."

"Has this been reported to the police?"

"No. She left a note saying she was leaving. I've no reason to assume anything is wrong." Martha showed a momentary flash of fear. "Nothing *is* wrong, is it?"

"Not that I'm aware of, ma'am."

"Thank God. You shouldn't go around frightening people that way."

"I didn't mean to—" Sam stopped and started again. "I understand your daughter has a baby."

Martha hesitated. "Yes, she has."

"Is she married?"

"What damn business is that of yours?"

"I merely want to know if she is married to Jordan Freeling."

"I think you had better come back when my husband is home."

"Where is your husband, Mrs. Benedict."

"He's in San Francisco on business. He'll be back this evening."

Hassling Martha Benedict was getting him nowhere. Perhaps he would be more successful with Paul Benedict. "I'll be back at nine, if that's all right." He turned away, then stopped. "By the way, when did your daughter leave?"

Again Martha hesitated. "It must have been September."

"And the child?"

"She has her daughter with her, of course."

"Thank you, ma'am. I'll be back at nine."

Sam waited near the entrance to the estate for a while, just to see if anyone would emerge. After an hour he decided to put the rest of the day to better use. He visited Jordan's rooming house near the university. He learned that Holly had been a regular visitor. No question—Holly's Mercedes had been highly visible in the street. He checked out the marriage records and found nothing.

He was back at the Beverly Hills house by nine o'clock. Paul and Martha Benedict awaited him with another man. "This is my attorney, James Mannering," Paul told him.

"You don't need an attorney, Mr. Benedict," Sam said. "I just want a few simple answers."

"Why are you bothering us?" Paul demanded stiffly.

"I'm here on government business."

"My wife tells me you were asking questions about our daughter. What is it you want?"

"I'd just like to talk to her," Sam said disarmingly.

"So would we, Mr. Kilmartin."

"You're saying you have no idea where she is or who she's with?"

"My daughter is a grown woman and a mother. She's entitled to lead her own life."

"I understand. But it doesn't answer my question."

"No law says she has to let us know where she is."

"You're being evasive, Mr. Benedict."

Paul looked at his attorney. Mannering cleared his

throat and said, "In the absence of any specific charge, my advice to my client is not to answer any questions on the grounds that he may incriminate himself."

Sam was feeling annoyed. He ignored the attorney. "Look, Mr. Benedict, lawyer or not, I'm going to ask you a question straight out. Is your daughter with Jordan Freeling at this time? But you ought to know that I'm going to catch up with that sonofabitch sooner or later, and it may be that your daughter will be needing my consideration. Now how about answering the goddamn question?"

Sam had almost reached him, he knew. Paul started to answer, but Mannering stepped in with a formal, "My advice remains unchanged, Mr. Benedict."

"Okay, have it your way," Sam said in a resigned voice. He half stood as if to depart. "I'm on my way to Switzerland. If you want to be visiting your daughter and grandchild in a Zurich jail, that's up to you."

Martha, thinking Sam's back was turned, had glanced at Paul in alarm. But Sam's head had swung back sharply, and it was plain that he had observed Martha's distress.

Paul spoke up quickly. "You're wasting your time here, Mr. Kilmartin," he said. "Neither of us has anything to say."

"Oh, no?" A slow grin cracked Sam's features. "Let me correct you, Mr. Benedict. You just said it all."

It was early morning in London when the TWA jumbo touched down on the rain-soaked runway at Heathrow. An hour later Sam entered the American Embassy to interview Hugh Auchterlonie.

Sam's first thought was how Hugh's face was devoid of color—a pallor that reminded him of Robert Halpern's—except that Hugh's eyes were dark, sharp, and aware. "You're waiting to see me, I understand?"

"You are Dr. Auchterlonie?"

"Yes."

"Sam Kilmartin, U.S. Treasury." Sam flipped open his ID from habit.

Hugh didn't glance at it. "Just like the cinema," he muttered. "I've always wanted to see someone do that."

"This is serious, if you don't mind."

"Then how can I help you, Mr. Kilmartin?"

Sam took out the photograph. "Do you recognize this person?"

"Surely. It's Jordan Freeling. What's the blighter been up to?"

"I understand he's about five-eleven in height?"

Hugh sensed Sam's intensity and shed his flippancy. "Is Jordan in some kind of trouble?"

Sam didn't reply directly. Instead he said, "I understand from Mr. Malcolm Avery that Freeling was a protégé of yours."

"I trained him on computers, after a fashion, if that is what you mean."

"It is." He let a rare moment of his own humor slip through. "That was one hell of a job you did there," he added.

"Jordan was one hell of an apprentice," Hugh said.

"First . . . when did you last see him?"

"Oh, a long time ago—several months at least. He called in when he was in London for some reason. We used to correspond, but that fell off."

"Do you have any idea where he is at present?"

"No, I don't. I was aware that Malcolm Avery took Jordan on. It was my recommendation. But a programmer's course—why, that was ridiculous—Jordan could run rings around any programmer."

"This ability of his: Is he really as talented as they say?"

"Quite exceptional, I assure you. Jordan is the best there is. He soon overtook me. Jordan and computers are made for each other. He has a memory like a computer himself, you know, almost infallible. Combine that with an extraordinary propensity for math, and you have a person who, in the days before we used machines to count, would have been considered a genius. That isn't all. His real strength lies in his ingenuity. He's always trying to do things better than the last fellow. Often does, too."

Sam hesitated. "Are you aware of any criminal activity Freeling may have been involved in?"

"Jordan? My God, no. Computer people at our level have no time for that kind of nonsense, Mr. Kilmartin." Looking anxious, he asked, "Has Jordan got himself into some kind of trouble?"

"I'll explain in a moment. I'm going to ask you for an opinion. At the risk of repeating myself, would you say, in your experience with this individual, that he is criminally inclined? I have a reason for asking."

"Mr. Kilmartin, nothing would be farther from Jordan's intentions than criminal behavior, in my view. He comes from a distinguished background. His father was a professional diplomat, and Jordan was a most respectful young man—a pleasant change from attitudes today. He was educated at Wynchgate and Oxford, in addition to his American schooling, and he was accustomed to the company of well-placed people. The epitome of a hardworking, responsible, and capable young man."

"It sounds like you have great regard for him."

"I certainly do, and I'm most concerned. Do you have firm evidence that Jordan is involved in crime, Mr. Kilmartin? Perhaps you're making a mistake."

"I don't think so."

"Look, you haven't told me what it is you think he's done."

Sam sighed loudly. "Has he expressed to you any interest in computer crime specifically?"

"Why, yes, it's one of his pet hobbies." Hugh's eyes suddenly grew round. "Oh, Jesus Christ, he hasn't gone and . . ." His voice trailed off.

"I take it he was knowledgeable in that regard, then?" Sam asked quickly.

Hugh recovered and spoke soberly. "Mr. Kilmartin, if Jordan chose to, I don't doubt that he could arrange some kind of computer theft. So could I, but that doesn't mean I'm a criminal. I trust you will have substantial evidence to back up any allegations. And I want you to know that it's my intention to help Jordan as best I can if he's in trouble. It sounds as if he's in need of a friend."

"When I find him, I'll tell him that."

"Can you tell me exactly what it is he's supposed to have done?"

A small idea was growing in Sam. It was incredible, unbelievable, and he could hardly control his excitement. "Tell me something. If Jordan had worked out a computer scam that was a little obscure to most, is it possible that you might be able to explain how it was done?"

"Most probably. I do know how his mind works, you see."

The excitement had grown into a sensation that threatened to engulf him. "Do you happen to know what he was working on when you saw him last?"

"Yes. That was the time I was speaking to him. We were discussing trapdoors and how they could be used to subvert instructions in program operating systems."

"Are you telling me you know how the sonofabitch did this?" Sam could contain himself no longer.

"Mr. Kilmartin," Hugh responded coolly, "if you would be so kind as to tell me what it is Jordan's supposed to have done, perhaps I'll be able to reply to your question."

"Dr. Auchterlonie, I can't tell you right now what this man has done. But I've got a feeling I'll be talking to him soon. After that I'll come back and we can review the whole thing."

"So you do know where he is?"

"I have an idea," Sam said. "That's all."

"Would you expect that he'll come to London, too?"

"I'm not certain about that. My job is to locate him at this moment, that's all."

"Very well. I'll hope to hear from you, Mr. Kilmartin."

One thing more was on Sam's agenda—one final person to see before he embarked for Switzerland. "Where can I find a man called Professor Plutz?" he asked.

"The floor above. Conference room with a blue door. If he's in the building. He comes and goes very quietly. Not really supposed to be here, you know. Most unofficial."

A few moments later Professor Plutz excused himself to the latest group of agents he was tutoring and met with Sam in the hall outside the lecture room. Sam wondered how this master of disguise could ever look like anything other than a wizened, gray-haired old gentleman. "Do you recall a young fellow named Jordan Freeling?"

"Jordan? Yes, the son of an embassy counselor. I remember him well."

"May I ask"—Sam handed over the authentic photograph of Jordan—"is this his normal appearance?"

"Yes, I would say it is." The professor put on pince-nez to study the picture.

"Can you identify the person in this other photograph?" Sam exhibited the photograph of Reginald Barret.

The professor studied it for a moment. His knowing eyes now were curious. "Is Freeling in some kind of trouble?"

"Please answer the question, Professor."

"It is Jordan Freeling."

"How can you be so sure?"

"How long have you been a detective, Mr. Kilmartin?" the professor said dryly.

"I'm not a detective, sir; I'm Treasury—" Sam stopped and added, "Around twenty-four years."

"Presumably you know your job, after all this time?"

"I guess," Sam agreed.

"I have been a master in the art of disguise for over forty years. That is how I know."

"Yes, I see your point. Okay; thanks, Professor. That's all I need to know."

"It is an unfortunate side to this business that someone can use the ability to change his appearance for both good and bad. I hope Jordan hasn't been making a nuisance of himself."

"There's nothing positive yet, sir."

"You're not stationed here in London, Mr. Kilmartin?"

"No, Professor, I'm from Washington."

"So the United States Treasury sends a man from Washington to London to ask if Jordan Freeling is himself, but there's nothing positive?"

"I can't discuss the matter, I'm afraid. And I'd appreciate it if you would forget this conversation."

Plutz nodded accommodatingly. "Certainly. It's already forgotten."

MacCaskey was on the other end of the line. "Where are you, for Christ's sake, Sam? I've been waiting for your call."

"Heathrow."

"*The* Heathrow? Last I knew, you were in California."

"Listen, I'm shipping out of London right now. I'll be in Zurich tonight, at the International."

"What I want to know is, do you have anything for me?"

Sam hesitated. "It's Jordan Freeling. There's nobody else involved. He did the whole darned thing himself."

"Can you substantiate that?"

"Not yet. I need more time. I need someone in Zurich with savvy, someone who knows his way around. Any suggestions?"

"Not off the top of my head."

"Call me when you find someone. I've got to run now; my flight's boarding."

"Okay, Sam. Good hunting."

CHAPTER TEN

The burgundy-colored Rolls surged luxuriously along the road that snaked beside the Zürichsee. Holly was at the wheel, and Jordan sat beside her with Debbie in between.

"You're a lousy driver, Holly," Jordan was saying. "No finesse. You drive this thing like a truck. You're not on Rodeo Drive now, you know. These narrow roads—when you come to a bend, you have to tuck in."

"Jordan, are you going to stop complaining or aren't you?" She eased off the accelerator, and the rush of air past the car subsided. "Your griping really bugs me!"

"Okay, okay. Just keep going."

The Rolls picked up speed again. "You're in a rotten mood today. Did that lawyer say something to worry you?"

"Friedlander? No, actually he was very reassuring."

"Can't you tell me about it?"

"Well, first, I've already paid him a barrel of dough in advance. But he's worth the money. In his specialty—which is what I need—Friedlander's one of the best lawyers anywhere."

"Jordan . . ." Holly's expression became wistful. "It's really not very pleasant, is it, for all the money? I mean, having to be so apprehensive and insecure all the time?"

"Holly, as I've told you: The first phase is certain to be the most difficult. After that, we should have clear sailing. I'm not certain who 'they' will turn out to be—but once they realize their best recourse is to let me alone, free to walk away with the money, they'll leave us alone. That may take just a little while—no more than days—but we'll have to be flexible during that time. After that, we'll have nothing to be afraid of, anymore."

"Are you sure about that, Jordan? I mean absolutely positive?"

"Absolutely."

"I wish I had your confidence."

"If I lacked confidence, I wouldn't have gotten mixed up in a thing like this."

"Did that package you mailed last week have anything to do with what you're saying now?"

"Yes, it did. It's the key, and it's probably arriving in Washington just about now."

He saw her shudder. "My God, I hope you're right in assuming the danger doesn't really exist. For *all* our sakes. I don't feel like driving anymore, Jordan." The Rolls was slowing again.

"Okay, sweetheart. Stop up ahead at that viewing point by the lake and I'll take over."

When Jordan drove off, Holly sat hugging Debbie in her arms. Her eyes betrayed a hint of fear.

He slowed to turn right into the narrow lane that curled behind the small town of Stäfa and led to their house at the lakeside. The Rapperswil Road, particularly narrow and curving at this point, was lined with warning signs that urged caution. Jordan found out why when he swung the Rolls out to make his turn.

A Cadillac appeared, swooping around the curve from the opposite direction. The driver saw them too late, and his speed did not allow time for pulling away. Before Jordan knew what was happening, the Cadillac had sideswiped the Rolls with a resounding crash, and a shower of body trim and hubcaps was flying in all directions. Its tires screaming, the Cadillac swung broadside across the road past them, halting with its nose buried in a mound of earth.

Jordan was the first to move, and Holly the first to find her voice. "Oh, my God! Are you all right, Jordan?"

"Yeah, sure. You and Debbie?"

"Nothing. We're okay." The shock caught up with Debbie, and she began to bawl. "The damn fool!" Holly said vehemently. "He might have killed us."

Jordan said angrily, "The stupid jerk, coming around a corner at that speed. I'm going to give him a piece of my mind." He was trying to open his door, but it was jammed.

Incensed, he shouldered it, but without effect. "Listen, I'll have to get out on your side. This door is stuck."

Holly was looking past Jordan, annoyance in her expression. "Will you just look at that idiot? He's grinning all over his stupid face."

Jordan's head swung to the other driver, now standing at his window and peering into the Rolls. "Hey, you prick! . . ." He couldn't open the door, but the window responded to his jab at the control button and slid down with a rattle. "Listen, you—" he began.

"Jordan, it is you! I don't believe it."

"Who the hell? . . ." Then Jordan recognized the sallow features, now sporting a full black mustache and smiling broadly. His Royal Highness Prince Hakim El Morro Sa'ud. "You crazy Arab, you! Hey, Hakim, how have you been?" Animosity forgotten in an instant, the two pumped hands through the window.

"Do you know this loony? Do you realize he nearly killed us?" Holly said, aggrieved.

"Aw, he can't help it. He's plain stupid."

"My dear Jordan, I'm so terribly sorry. I lost control of the car, and then there was simply nothing I could do to avoid hitting you. My fault entirely. I'll replace your Rolls, of course, dear boy."

"You bet your ass you will! Hakim, this is my wife, Holly, and Debbie, our daughter."

"Please forgive me, Holly, and a thousand pardons." Hakim bowed his head.

"This is my old buddy, Prince Hakim. You've heard me speak of him. Jeez, what a coincidence! . . ."

"How do you do?" Holly still looked somewhat strained.

The engine was still running. Jordan slipped the Rolls into drive, and it jerked forward. "This seems drivable. Hakim, come around the other side and jump in. We have a house nearby. I'll run Holly and Debbie home; then we can come back and arrange with the local garage to move your car."

"Jordan, ah, I'm not alone," Hakim put in. "Perhaps my companions may join us?"

"Sure. Bring them along."

Hakim ran back to the Cadillac and returned leading three overpainted, brassy-looking girls in short skirts whose high heels made them hobble on the pebbles of the country road. "These are Charlotte, Mimi, and Juliette. None of them speaks English, I'm afraid." He introduced his companions through the driver's window.

"Where are they from, Hakim?"

"Paris, of course."

"You still see Piers?"

"Oh, yes. Regularly."

"His influence, huh?" Jordan grunted. "Okay, ask the girls to come around the car and get in on the other side. Let's get this mess off the highway."

Hakim spoke in French to the girls. At the same time, Holly leaned toward Jordan and said anxiously, in a loud whisper, "Jordan, they look so goddamn cheap!"

"Yeah, the poor guy's got no taste. Never did have."

"But in our house?"

"Come on, Holly, he's my buddy. We can't leave them standing out here on the highway."

"Is he one of those Arab playboys?" By this time the car door had opened on Holly's side, and the party was climbing in.

Later, in the house, Jordan and Hakim sat over coffee. From the direction of the kitchen, they could hear the sounds of Hakim's companions fussing over Debbie and the elegant house and demonstrating their impeccable manners in someone else's home.

"We were worried about you, Jordan, when you went off so suddenly to America. We expected to hear from you. Why did you cut yourself off from us?"

"It wasn't deliberate. Things were happening . . ." Jordan said vaguely.

"Anyhow, I'm glad things turned out well for you in the end. Your wife is gorgeous, and you seem quite happy. How long have you been living here?"

"Not long."

"What other interests do you have?"

"You mean work?" He was silent a moment. "I'm in computers."

"Yes, I thought you would be. Is your business successful?"

"I, ah, I guess you could say it is."

"I'll be returning to Riyadh in a few days. Why don't you bring your wife and child and join me for a vacation? I can promise you a most pleasant stay."

Jordan chuckled. "You were always trying to get me to come to that desert hangout."

"I mean it, Jordan. I would be honored if you would come and stay with me."

"Maybe some other time."

"Nothing would give me greater pleasure than for you to see once and for all that we are not quite the savages you think we are."

"Hey, come on. I never said that."

"No, but you think it!" Jordan started to protest, but Hakim continued, "You forget how well I know you. It has annoyed me since our school days that I earned so little esteem from someone I admire. Perhaps you will change your mind about me when you come to stay in a palace that is equipped with every modern appliance."

Jordan was about to soft-pedal his cynicism. In the past he had put a lot of effort into trying to straighten Hakim out, and now the prince had slipped back into the unreality of his upbringing. "Hakim," he said patiently, "don't go boasting about your gadgets when at the back wall of the palace peasants are squatting in the dust. I won't think more highly of you because you have the latest Jacuzzi."

"But I assure you, Jordan, things aren't like that. Riyadh is a capital city, and—"

"Okay, so the peasants are kept out of sight of the palace gates. Who are you trying to kid?" Perhaps he was being unjustly hard, he thought.

Hakim sighed. "The same old Jordan! You take pleasure in mocking me. You know how much regard I have for you, and you take advantage of it." His lower lip drooped, and he looked more sad than angry.

Jordan changed his mind. They were no longer schoolboys, and Hakim's character was as molded as it was ever going to be. "Hey, we're friends, aren't we? Don't take what I say so seriously. If a guy can't say what he thinks to a buddy, then what the hell?"

Hakim thought it over. "Yes, of course, you are right, as always."

"Hakim, I'd like your opinion—is ten million dollars a lot of money?"

"Certainly."

"I mean *really* a lot of money? Against, say, your family's income from oil, it must be peanuts."

"No, it is a substantial sum. I have an uncle who has just built a palace costing at least ten million dollars, and he is very proud of the fact that it was kept within the allocated budget. Mind you, he has four other palaces."

"Would you say someone with ten million in the bank is rich?"

"Capital? How about disposable income?"

"No disposable income. Just the ten million."

"Why are you asking this peculiar question, Jordan?"

"Because I want the viewpoint of someone who isn't looking up into the sky with his mouth hanging wide open. I'm trying to form a judgment."

Hakim was silent a moment, then said slowly, "It all depends on one's requirements. If one wishes to replace one's fleet of jet planes, one would feel extremely compromised. Does that make sense to you?"

"Yes, that is what I wanted to know." At last he had found something he could learn from Hakim: how to live with the big bucks. It was a different world, and now he had come to realize how small was his own ambition. No matter what happened in the weeks ahead, a visit with Hakim would be beneficial . . . and instructive. "You know," he murmured, "I think I would like to take you up on your invitation to visit your country."

"That is splendid. When may I expect you?"

"Quite soon. I have a little business to attend to first. If I like it in Saudi Arabia, would it be possible for me to live there for a while? A few months? Maybe take a house or something?"

"What for? You are welcome to live with me for as long as you wish. I would consider myself honored. If you desire privacy, I have several suitable houses within the palace grounds. I will have one prepared for you as soon as I return."

CHAPTER ELEVEN

A light tapping came on the door of Sam's hotel room, and he went to open it. The young man who stood there was clean-cut, with short black hair, and expressionless. Sam would have recognized the stance anywhere. "Mr. Kilmartin?" the man inquired.

"That's me."

"I'm Clyde Vigevino. I've been sent along to give you a hand." He flipped open his ID.

Sam recognized the CIA insignia. "Come in, Clyde."

"May I see your identification, please, sir?" He checked Sam's ID and handed it back. "What's the problem?"

"You're the local expert?" Sam asked.

"Not exactly. I'm from the Geneva station," Clyde said. "The local man is in the hospital with appendicitis."

"Shit!" Sam said forcefully. "I need someone who knows this locality well."

"I speak German. Probably that's why I was assigned to you."

"That's important?"

"Around here it is. You know how Switzerland is regionalized. In this section all the terms of reference are German."

"Have you been told anything about this case?"

"Not a thing. I was informed you would brief me."

"Okay. Pull up a chair, Clyde, and I'll tell you what it is we have to do." They sat down at a small table by the window. Sam produced a cigar that he lit before he brought out a photograph of Jordan and slid it across the table. "This is the man we're looking for. He's American, and he's a computer expert." In minutes, Sam briefed Clyde Vigevino on Jordan Freeling.

"That's all you need to know at present," Sam said. "What I want you to do is this: Start checking on all the available information. You can begin with the airlines. He may have come in as Richard Elegan or Reginald Barret or Gregory Whitefish."

"Whitefish?"

"Yeah. Then try Swiss passport control and alien registration. If you smile, maybe they won't make it too tough for you. Tell them it's an emergency. From there run a check on the big hotels in the locality. Don't be afraid to grease a few palms. I'll see the money gets refunded."

"Got you!" Clyde was making notes.

"He may have taken an apartment or a house. If you have no luck with the hotels, follow through with the apartment and real estate people in town."

"Anything else?"

"You have enough to be getting along with."

"Okay, I'll get on it right away."

"Where are you staying, Clyde?"

"Nowhere. I picked up a few things and drove straight here from Geneva as soon as I received my orders. My bag is in the car downstairs."

"Okay, go fetch your bag. You're moving in here with me. Pick up a second room key on your way out. Now get your ass out of here. You're working for the U.S. Treasury. So move it!"

"Yes, sir." Clyde was gone.

Sam decided to place a call to Chuck MacCaskey. He looked at his watch. It was late afternoon on the eastern seaboard. When the dial tone came on, he started the sequence of thirteen digits that would reach MacCaskey's office.

"Sam!" Chuck's voice came on with an unusual excitement. "You'll never guess what's happened. He's written to us!"

"Jordan Freeling?"

"He sent a package to the FBI. Now we have it. I gather that it involves a computer program of some intricate description. He apparently sent a cover letter pointing out its significance, because whoever received it was alert enough to link it with this thing that's been driving us wild. The people upstairs have been bringing in computer wizards from all over the country."

"Could this be another scam?" Sam asked suspiciously.

"I don't think so. I get the impression it must be more important than just another neat fraud. Wesley is looking as grim as you can imagine. But I think it's out of his hands now. I saw two or three national security people in the building. You know what that means. No more games. You can probably expect some company over there before long."

"Try to keep them away, Chuck. I need another day or two."

"I'll try. You're still the front man, so far as I know. What's happening over there?"

"I've got the CIA chap doing routine footwork. He's checking the obvious sources. I'm going to take a run around to the local computer people myself in the morning. Freeling may have bought some equipment or made some inquiries. I've got the feeling I'm near him, Chuck."

"Well, I hope you're right." Chuck was silent for a moment. "How well do you know the Zurich area, Sam?"

"Not too well. I've got a map."

"Then you'd better look on it and find a place called Stäfa."

"What?"

"Stäfa. It's a small town on the east side of the Zurich lake, about a dozen miles out of town."

"Hold the line." Sam flipped open his map. "I've got it. What's so special about this place?"

"It's where Freeling mailed the package."

"He didn't mail it in the city?" Sam felt the adrenaline start pumping. "Maybe this is his first mistake. People in small towns remember strangers with packages."

"That's what I was thinking. He may be clever with computers, but that doesn't mean he's got all the answers. This could be the break we've been looking for."

"Hold it!" Sam's initial excitement was subsiding. "It doesn't gel, Chuck. A man as careful as Freeling isn't going to make a bum move like this. He has no reason to know we even suspect he's in Switzerland. Why tell us the country and the town?" The more he thought about it, the less he liked it. "Could be he's moved on. When was the package mailed?"

"A week ago."

"He could be anywhere by now."

Chuck was silent. Finally he said, "Well, check out this Stäfa place anyhow."

Sam said, "You're not holding out on me, Chuck, are you?"

"What do you mean?"

"That package. Are you *sure* you don't know what's in it?"

"I swear, Sam! As soon as I find out, I'll let you know."

"Okay. Meantime, try to keep the dogs leashed. Tell them I'm hot on the trail—tell them anything you want. I don't want them interfering over here at the last moment. I'll know shortly if I'm wasting my time."

"I'll do my best."

Sam hesitated, then decided to throw Chuck a crumb. "If nothing else works, you can tell them I have found someone who probably can help us bust the computer riddle."

"What? . . ." Chuck almost yelled.

"You'll have it within"—Sam looked at his watch; time was running out fast—"thirty-six hours."

Chuck was too familiar with Sam's stubborn nature to think of arguing. "Can I promise that?" he demanded.

"You have my word."

"Good luck!" The line went silent, the abruptness providing ample testimony to the state of Chuck's nerves.

"Thanks," Sam said into the dead mouthpiece.

A desperate tiredness was creeping over him. He recognized the symptoms; jet lag was catching up, and he would be useless until he had some rest. By the time he had undressed, his eyelids were dropping. He fell asleep with the lights burning brightly.

Sam was awakened by Clyde Vigevino's hand shaking him by the shoulder. "What time is it?" He eased himself up in the bed.

"It's nine o'clock."

"I must have slept right through the night," Sam said almost guiltily.

"Isn't that what people normally do—people who aren't U.S. government agents?" Clyde's voice was strained, his features drawn, his eyes veined. His face bore the sheen of a night's exertions.

"You look as if you've been busy," Sam said.

"I have."

"I'll order some coffee. You can tell me while I—"

"I've already ordered breakfast for us both," Clyde told him. "Bacon and eggs and plenty of coffee. If it's okay with you, I'll shower first. I'm feeling real tacky." He flung his jacket over a chair but stopped short of the bathroom door. "Sorry, sir. Would you, uh, would you like your shower first? I wasn't thinking. . . ."

Sam grunted. "No. Go ahead. I'm fine."

"You're never going to believe what I have to tell you," Clyde called from the bathroom. "Jordan Freeling entered Switzerland under his own name. Quite openly, using his own passport. His wife, Holly, and their child were with him."

"So he *is* married. I knew it." Sam exhaled.

In the bathroom Clyde had begun his shower, and he shouted, "That's not all. He's got spunk; he's gone and registered with the immigration authorities as a temporary resident."

"You mean he's officially on record?" Sam demanded incredulously.

"Correct. He's making no attempt to hide his presence."

"Do you have an address?"

"I have the one he gave the authorities. Whether we'll find him there or not is another matter."

"Is that a town along the Zurich lake called Stäfa?" Sam called.

Clyde's head, dripping, appeared around the doorway. "How in *hell* did you know that?"

"I made a phone call to Washington. Freeling sent a package to the States. It was mailed in Stäfa a week ago."

"He must be supremely confident we can't pull him out of here."

"Yeah, it seems that way." Sam was deep in thought. There was a knock at the door, and he let in a waiter with their breakfast on a trolley. Sam poured himself a cup of coffee and shoveled in sugar. It was hot, but he swallowed it gratefully. They certainly knew how to make coffee, the Swiss.

An important visit was required before they drove out to Stäfa. At 10:15 Sam, with Clyde standing quietly behind, stood impatiently facing a chief inspector at Zurich police headquarters. "It will be my pleasure to cooperate with the United States authorities," the policeman said formally, in good English.

"Thank you, Chief Inspector Bachmann," Sam replied. "We have information that an American citizen wanted by us is living here, just outside Zurich. We're on our way out there now to pick him up. I would like to arrange with you to hold him here in custody while I contact my superiors in Washington for instructions."

"Yes, I see. Is this man the subject of extradition proceedings?"

"No, sir. We haven't had time. I daresay the American authorities will be making the appropriate application."

"You daresay?" Chief Inspector Bachmann's expression became a question mark. "Aren't you sure, Herr Kilmartin?"

"I'm sure he's wanted. That's all I need to know."

"Is this man a known or habitual criminal?"

"No. He is the suspect in an important matter of fraud."

"I see. I take it that an official request for this man's apprehension has been made to INTERPOL?"

"Not yet, Herr Bachmann. It's all happened in a hurry. You know how these things go. We got wind that he might be here in Switzerland, so we came to look for him."

Bachmann looked unconvinced. "May I ask when the crime was committed, Herr Kilmartin?"

Sam hesitated. "About three months ago."

"Don't you think that sufficient time has elapsed to enable you to make the appropriate representations to my government?"

Sam hadn't bargained on obstruction from an authoritarian Swiss policeman. "For Christ's sake! I told you we just learned the guy's hiding out over here."

"Yes, I understand. You say *hiding,* but you also tell me that this man and his family entered the country legally, using an accredited carrier, with his own valid passport and that of his wife and child. Correct me if I am wrong. . . . In addition to which he has been accepted by the government of Switzerland for temporary residence; not so?"

"That is so, sir," Clyde assented.

"So, we cannot establish an attempt at subterfuge, and in fact the man, as a temporary resident, is entitled to the legal protection afforded any other resident of Switzerland."

Sam began to see a red haze before him.

Bachmann went on, "It also means, of course, that this individual is either a person of substantial means, is taking up authorized employment here, or has been granted asylum in our country. That can be easily verified. Of course, he will have signed a declaration that he is not a convicted criminal, and if that statement is false, I will have ample reason to authorize his arrest."

"He has no convictions recorded against him, Herr Bachmann," Sam put in. "Look, what in hell does his past have to do with it? We know he's the man we want, and if he were back in the States, he'd be picked up immediately."

"You miss the point entirely, Herr Kilmartin," the chief inspector said. "What I am seeking is some method of supporting your application to hold this man in custody. I'm not trying to frustrate your efforts. If he were on record at INTERPOL, I would have adequate reason for holding him. But he has committed no crime in Switzerland that I am aware of, and that's the only other reason I could authorize his arrest and detention."

"But this is crazy—" Sam began.

"Herr Kilmartin, we are discussing matters beyond the scope of our jurisdiction. You need only record this man's profile with INTERPOL. Nothing could be simpler, surely." The chief inspector was trying to be helpful. "Until then, I can do nothing."

"Bachmann, I'm running on a tight schedule. I'm going to do exactly what you say, and I'll be back. But if this sucker gets away while I'm filling out forms, I'm going to be raising the roof. You'd better believe it, my friend—"

"Hey, wait a minute, Sam!" It was Clyde's voice. "Why don't you explain to the chief inspector how Freeling could be using computers to damage the image of Swiss banking?"

"Swiss banking?"

"Sure. Didn't I hear how he intended to reveal the details of a lot of secret bank accounts?"

Sam felt the dig in his ribs. "Oh, yes." He spoke more calmly. "That's something else you may wish to know, Herr Bachmann. I didn't mention that this man is a computer expert and he may have gained access to the Swiss banking system. He may be intending to give out information on some private accounts."

"That is a serious crime." Bachmann's eyebrows came together, and his gaze darkened.

"I thought I'd mention it in case you are interested. Of course, if it gets out afterwards that you let him slip through your fingers, I guess you'll be losing some friends among the banks, Chief Inspector." Sam gave Bachmann a supercilious look.

"If what you say is true, I'd be willing to make an exception in this case." Bachmann hesitated, then made a decision. "Very well, when you bring in your man, I will take the responsibility for holding him. I'll keep him twenty-four hours for questioning, on your information. That should give you enough time to record him with INTERPOL."

"Thanks, Chief Inspector."

"As this matter may also concern the Swiss authorities, I will send a police officer and an official vehicle with you to apprehend the suspect. It will not look good for you to make an arrest on Swiss territory, and I would have a lot of explaining to do afterwards."

"Good thinking, Herr Bachmann. Now, can we get out there before he takes it on the lam?"

CHAPTER TWELVE

It was an opulent, distinctive house, standing alone on the edge of a small bluff, and the side that jutted out over the Zürichsee was almost entirely glass. Sam thought it an intriguing place, clearly an indulgence by someone determined to satisfy a whim. He cautioned Clyde and the Swiss policeman to remain in the car and trudged along the pebbled drive toward an imposing front door. A burgundy Rolls, damaged on one side, stood nearby.

Sam pressed a bell by the door and heard an answering gong deep inside the house. He had to press again before the door opened and a young woman dressed in denims, her skin still golden with a California tan, fair hair tied back with a gay scarf, peered out. She held a toddler by the hand. "Yes?"

Sam took his time in answering, savoring the moment. "Holly Benedict?" he inquired softly.

Holly drew herself up and her grip tightened on the child's hand. "My name is Freeling."

"Yes, of course." Sam smiled and looked down. "Debbie is a beautiful child, Mrs. Freeling. May I see your husband, please?"

"Who are you?"

"I'm Sam Kilmartin, U.S. Treasury." He flipped open his ID, but Holly didn't even look at it. "I think he is expecting me."

"Come in." At the pace of the toddling child, Holly led the way into the dramatic interior. Holly indicated a staircase that stretched across the entire width of the entrance hall. "He's up there. The room overlooking the lake." She held down the button of a wall-mounted intercom long enough to say, "There's a man from Washington here to see you, Jordan. He's coming up."

Sam mounted the stairs almost leisurely, relishing every step. He was approaching the end of a rocky road, the best moment in any investigation. When he entered the large room above, he was immediately struck by the panorama of the lake beyond the glass. He thought he was alone until he heard a sound from the overstuffed cushions of a big davenport.

Jordan unfolded himself and stood up. "I've been wondering which department would be handling my case," he said. "It doesn't seem to fall into the sphere of the CIA, so I sent my material in care of the FBI."

"I'm Sam Kilmartin, U.S. Treasury." He didn't bother with his ID.

Jordan smiled as he shook Sam's hand. "Treasury. I guess it figures." Sam refrained from saying what sprang to his mind instantly: *After all, you stole from the Treasury; what would you expect?*

Sam studied the spare, serious young man. A face one wouldn't pick out in a crowd, except perhaps for the pallor of the skin, he thought. Were all computer experts allergic to the sun? "You're one hell of a hard man to find, Freeling," Sam said, "but here we are." He felt a slight disappointment at the young computer wizard's unexceptional appearance. But then, what had he been expecting, he asked himself—an overpowering presence? Penetrating eyes, maybe?

"I thought I had made it easy for you," Jordan was saying.

"What?"

"I left my name and address all over the place."

"Well, yes, you did in the end. I have to admit I don't know why," Sam said with a rueful smile. "You had a good head start."

"Haven't you been in touch with your home office?"

"Yes, I spoke to my people last night."

"Did they receive a package from me?"

"Yes, I understand they did. They're looking at it now, apparently. I don't know what it contains."

"Oh, I see. You're a little early. You should have waited until they had investigated the contents. Perhaps you would like to come back later."

Sam was amused. "So that you can move on to your next hideout?"

"You're not making sense, Mr. Kilmartin. I let you know I was here, didn't I?"

Sam didn't know the answer, and it wasn't his problem. His mission had been to find Freeling, and that part of the job was done. "I'd like you to come along with me, please."

"You don't seem to understand. You can't arrest me."

"It's true I'm outside U.S. jurisdiction, but I have a Swiss police officer waiting outside to make it official."

"I'm not talking about that. I mean I don't want the indignity. It surely would be most upsetting to my wife. In any case, you're spoiling my arrangements."

"Oh. I'm sorry if I'm inconveniencing you." Sam was astounded at Jordan's gall. His voice hardened. "Okay, we've played games long enough. Get your hat and let's hit the road."

"Just a moment. Perhaps I'd better explain. You will be told, after your people have completely investigated that package—so that they comprehend its full significance—that I am not to be arrested. You don't want to make a fool of yourself and your department, do you, Mr. Kilmartin? Actually, it would be much worse than that."

Sam had acquired enough respect for Jordan to be cautious. On the other hand, his instructions were clear. He had no authority to delay now. More important, the time limit was getting uncomfortably tight. "I've got my orders, and they don't include letting you go free. Until I hear otherwise, I'm taking you into custody."

"Oh, my God!" Jordan's tone was exasperated. "You're going to spoil everything. Look, Mr. Kilmartin, why don't you call your home office from here? You can use my telephone. They must have analyzed the material I sent them by now."

"Well . . . all right." Sam was irked by Jordan's youthful impudence but simultaneously intrigued by what he knew to be an unusual intellect.

"Good." Jordan sounded relieved. "Go ahead. The telephone's over there."

"Except for one thing." Sam was enjoying his small moment of triumph. "It's in the early hours of the morning in Washington, and nobody is in the office." Now he was being deliberately awkward. He had Chuck's home number, but he was damned if he was going to use it to oblige this arrogant youngster, genius or not. Jordan's righteous self-possession in the face of the humiliation he had caused the U.S. authorities was proving too much for Sam's instincts.

"Oh, I see. Provided nothing goes wrong outside of nine to five, Washington time, the interests of the United States are well protected. Is that it, Mr. Kilmartin? And let me assure you the genuine interests of our country are involved."

Jordan's sardonic note annoyed Sam even more. "There's no emergency here. All that's happening is that a thief who stole other people's money is being apprehended. Thieves are arrested every day of the week, you know, Freeling. You're not that important." As soon as he had said it, he wished he had not become riled.

"I'm not?"

Sam was amazed to see that Jordan appeared genuinely hurt. "Perhaps you are right. Perhaps it's unimportant to show how the entire nation's computer operations are based on fallacy and are totally insecure. How one person, using his own ingenuity, can bust the most sophisticated industry in the world wide open. You may be right . . . maybe that's unimportant."

Sam's words were bugging Jordan, and he had more to say. "You call me a thief, Mr. Kilmartin, and technically, I suppose, that's correct. But it does tend to disregard the fact that I'm a person of principle. Let me give you an example. I suppose you're aware of how much money I took?"

"Ten million plus," Sam responded.

"Yes. A drop in the bucket, of course, compared to the amount spent on computer research annually. Faulty computers—computers that don't provide the security they're supposed to but in which the nation's institutions put their total faith. Am I getting through to you, Mr. Kilmartin? Have you thought of how much I might have taken if I'd wanted to?"

"No, certainly I haven't."

"Perhaps a hundred million—even more," Jordan said nonchalantly. "Effectively, that means I elected *not* to steal ninety million. I took enough for my purpose and no more. Doesn't that make me a person of principle?"

"I only have your word for that," Sam said. "I think you

took what you knew you could get away with." He didn't mean what he was saying. Privately he had to believe Jordan.

"Clearly you haven't studied the subject, Mr. Kilmartin."

"I've studied human nature, and greed. You're not so different from the rest, Freeling."

"No. No, I hope I'm not," Jordan said enigmatically, gazing out over the lake.

"Despite your magnanimity, I'm going to suggest that you now accompany me to the Zurich police station." Sam had regained his self-control.

"And I was going to suggest that we both save ourselves trouble and wait here until your Washington office opens."

"I can't do that," Sam said. "I'm pushed for time."

"Too bad," Jordan murmured.

Sam wondered to whom the remark was directed, but he had decided that the time for discussion was past.

It had taken hours to book Jordan. The Swiss procedures were unfamiliar to Sam and strictly formal in the case of a foreign national. Chief Inspector Bachmann hovered in the background all the while to ensure that no regulation was infringed, no piece of paper went unsigned. Finally, when it was all over and Jordan was on his way to the cells beneath the police station, a Swiss lawyer named Friedlander came storming in to demand Jordan's release. Only that Sam shouted louder than the lawyer persuaded Bachmann to honor his commitment to hold Jordan for twenty-four hours.

It was midafternoon by the time Sam and Clyde were in the car on the way back to the International. Clyde said, "Well, I'll be getting back to Geneva."

"Thanks for your help."

"Quite a character, that Freeling. A person would never guess to look at him that he stole ten million."

"Yeah. He could have made it a hundred million if he'd wanted, you know."

Clyde whistled. "Is that a fact? A man has to have real character to walk away from that kind of money."

It was almost an echo of his conversation with Jordan that morning. "I'd appreciate it if you would keep that information under your hat for a while, Clyde," he said. "It's still classified."

Sam was annoyed that the Zurich police had insisted on full details of Jordan's crime and had also required an exact figure for the amount stolen. He knew better than to enter false information on official documents. The trouble was the whole story was now on the Zurich police blotter, and he could see little hope of maintaining secrecy. And then the small matter of arranging for Jordan's INTERPOL registration. That could be done from Washington, and the quicker he organized things through MacCaskey, the better, Sam thought.

In the hotel room a red message light on the telephone was showing. "Washington called three times this morning, Mr. Kilmartin. You are to call back immediately, please. It is urgent."

"Okay, can you give me a line?"

"Also, a cablegram has arrived for you. Do you wish it sent up to your room?"

"Yes, please."

"A bellman will be on his way, sir."

"Thanks. I'll make the Washington call when I've seen the cablegram." He turned to Clyde. "Something's happened. Something's gone goddamn wrong. I can smell it."

A few moments later the bellman tapped on the door. Sam exchanged a couple of francs for a brightly colored envelope and tore it open as he closed the door.

The dateline was Washington, midday. It was signed *Wesley,* and it read:

> URGENT FOR IMMEDIATE ACTION. DROP CASE AGAINST SUSPECT AND ENSURE NO HARASSMENT. IMPERATIVE YOU ENSURE UTMOST SECRECY. CALL WASHINGTON SOONEST.

Sam threw the cablegram to Clyde and flopped into a chair. "What did I tell you?"

"Jesus! What do we do now?"

"We go back and get Freeling out."

"You going to be in trouble over this, Sam?"

"I'm never really in trouble, am I?" Sam passed a hand over his forehead. "Call down for some coffee, will you, Clyde?"

"Hadn't you better call Washington?" Sam sat looking like thunder, and Clyde didn't say it a second time. He ordered coffee from room service.

When he had regained his calm, he put through the call. "Where have you been, Sam?" MacCaskey's voice was chilly. "We've been waiting all day for you to have the courtesy to call. And if you don't already know, I sent a cablegram in case you were having trouble getting through."

"Yeah, I know. You're too late."

"What do you mean, we're too late?" Chuck's tone grew frigid.

"I've just come back from slapping Freeling into a Zurich jail."

"Oh, no. Oh, my God . . ." Chuck sounded stricken.

"What's wrong with you people? It's okay—he knows there was a mix-up of sorts. He told me. I'll go back there and get him out, dammit, if that's what you want."

"Do it right away, Sam. When Wesley learns of this, there's going to be hell to pay."

"You can tell Wesley from me to go take a running—" Sam checked himself. "Now listen: Details of Freeling's computer scam are on the Zurich police blotter."

"*Jesus!* You've *got* to find some way of getting that information out of there. It's absolutely vital."

"Yeah, yeah, I know. I'll talk to them when I go back—tell them it was all a mistake. Make a fool of myself. Maybe offer to contribute to their police benevolent fund if they have one—ah, how's the department kitty?"

"For God's sake, Sam, why are you worrying over a few lousy bucks at a time like this?" Chuck's voice rose.

"Ho, I've heard that before," Sam said doggedly. "Remember when I had to pay for that fiasco in Mexico City out of my own pocket?"

"That was at least ten years ago." A tinge of desperation entered Chuck's tone. "You have a memory like an elephant's, you know that?"

"Just so we understand each other. Now tell me, why are we turning Freeling loose?"

Chuck calmed. "I don't know, Sam. I wish I did."

"I want to know what was in that package he sent."

"I told you all I know about it. It's my guess it's another

computer mystery, like the first one. It seems Freeling is using it as a lever to buy his freedom."

"Yes, it seems that way," Sam said soberly. "But we're wasting time now. I'd better get back to the jail before something else goes wrong."

"Right. Let me know right away what happens, Sam."

"Don't I always?"

"Like hell!"

Sam signaled for Clyde to accompany him and made for the door.

CHAPTER THIRTEEN

Beneath the Zurich police building, Sam followed a square-jawed jailer along the corridor that led to Jordan Freeling's cell. Down here the walls were windowless and brilliantly lit by fluorescent lights. The place was antiseptically clean.

Jordan rose from the scrubbed wooden bench supported by chains to the wall and stood calmly. Sam stepped into the cell and motioned for the jailer to leave them. The man went off, leaving the cell door open. Jordan's gaze flicked to the open door and back to Sam.

"You're not surprised," Sam said. It was more a statement than a question. "You knew you would be sprung."

"Yes, if everything went according to plan," Jordan said.

After a moment's silence, Sam asked, "What is this great plan of yours, anyhow?"

"You don't know?" Jordan's eyebrows rose.

"No, as a matter of fact, I don't." He took a used cigar from his top pocket, put it in his mouth, and started to light it.

"I'd rather you didn't smoke, Mr. Kilmartin."

"What's that?" Sam's eyes swiveled up.

"It's so confined in here. Can't you wait until we get outside?"

Sam stopped, suppressing the irritation he felt when someone objected to his smoking. The match was burning his fingers. He blew it out. "I suppose you think you're clever, making a monkey out of me?"

"Don't take it personally. If you had listened to me we could have avoided this embarrassing situation."

Suddenly reaching a conclusion, Sam said, "You owe me an explanation."

"Oh?"

"I think I'm entitled to know the reason you're being released."

"What you think is irrelevant," Jordan said in a matter-of-fact voice. "Can we get out of this dump now?"

Sam ignored him. "They didn't tell me what was in the package you sent. I'd like you to tell me."

"You're a fool for wanting to know, Mr. Kilmartin."

"Is that so?" Sam controlled his voice. "Well, let me tell you something, wise guy. We're all fools at some time. Maybe you'll find that out one day. I still want to know why they've decided to let you walk away free as a bird with ten million dollars."

"If they want you to know, I'm sure they'll tell you." He was a little too flip, and it annoyed Sam, who had no chance to reply before Jordan added, "Your orders are to release me, are they not? I'm waiting to go."

"That is correct. I'm ordered to let you go." What he intended doing was on his own head. He had been relying on his own judgment for a long time, and he could hope it wouldn't let him down now. "The thing is, it could take some time for me to obtain your release."

"What do you mean?" Jordan asked suspiciously.

"Just that." Jordan was unaware of Bachmann's twenty-four-hour limit, and they had managed to keep the lawyer out. "These Swiss, they do everything slowly. It is not the United States here, you know, Freeling. As you saw, there's a lot of documentation when a foreign national is accused of something, and some formalities. It takes time to reverse the procedure."

"How much time?"

"I don't know exactly. Could be a couple of weeks, maybe, before you walk out of here. A couple of months, even, if I don't hurry things along. I guess it's up to me." Sam stuck his tongue in his cheek provocatively. He waited, but Jordan said nothing, just stood glaring angrily. It tickled Sam that with the door standing open and the jailer gone, a person with more street sense than Jordan would have known that he was free to walk out any time he chose. Jordan, in his orderly way, was awaiting an invitation to depart. It was a small edge for Sam, and he decided to make the most of it. "Holly's going to be awfully worried, all alone in that big house, don't you think?"

"You keep away from Holly. You're a bastard, Kilmartin!"

"Ah." It was the first break in Jordan's composure Sam had seen. He was human after all. "You're in my ballpark now, sonny," he said wryly.

Jordan stood looking sullen, and Sam could sense the wheels going around in his head. It took him less than a minute to decide. His reproving look faded, and he appeared to have regained his equilibrium. "There's something I would like you to consider seriously, Mr. Kilmartin," he said in careful tones. "Your superiors and I, completely independently, have decided it's not in the general interest for you to be aware of the contents of that package. Don't you think that is reason enough for you to accept the fact and let it go?"

It was persuasive but not persuasive enough. He was darned if he'd let go now, Sam thought. "I want to know what it is you're holding over the head of the American government."

"Very well, if you're that determined . . ." Then Jordan was silent for so long Sam suspected he'd changed his mind. "I want your sworn word, as an agent of the American government," he said quietly, "that you'll immediately forget what I tell you. Is that understood?"

"It is," Sam responded through his teeth.

"After all, neither of us wants to see the U.S. get hurt." Jordan had casually dropped that comment in, and it flashed through Sam's mind that perhaps he had overstepped the bounds of propriety. The suspicion began in him that he might be better off not knowing what Jordan was about to reveal. But it was too late now, and he was carried along on a wave of his own creation. Jordan continued, "The package contained details of a second, highly sophisticated method of operating system subversion—"

Sam interrupted. "I take it you're talking about computer programs?"

"Of course, what else? It's something totally original, I assure you. The thing is, though the method is complex and difficult to identify, it's relatively easy to use, once a person has the hang of it. What is more, anyone with a fundamental understanding of microcode and assembly language procedures can penetrate standard computer modes if he has access. I'm aware of no defense against it."

"I'm not sure I understand fully what's implied here," Sam said stiffly. He didn't understand at all.

"I'll spell it out for you," Jordan said patiently. "Among other things, the system of electronic money transfers would be wide open to abuse. The ten million dollars I took will look like chicken feed next to the losses there *could* be. Computer security as we know it would be ineffective. Altogether, it would cause havoc in a computer-oriented society. Get the picture?"

"Yes, but what I don't get is why you sent them the details. You did say you told them how it could be done?"

"That's correct." In answer to Sam's baffled look, Jordan added, "Obviously I have no intention of using this method myself."

"Then why go to the trouble of devising it?"

"Not much use being a math whiz unless one puts the talent to use, right?" Jordan said it lightly, with a shrug that was almost apologetic.

"I can think of better ways to employ your talents," Sam came back. "I take it you're blackmailing them with the threat of exposing your method?"

"I don't like the word blackmail. And it's really not applicable here. You see, Mr. Kilmartin, I've been working *for* the companies involved, as well as the government. True, no one hired me to do this work. . . . I took it upon myself. But once the implications of what I've done are understood, I'm certain I will be thanked."

"And the ten million bucks?"

"I've earned it. I consider it my fee for services rendered. Computer people will have to work their butts off to catch up with me. But it will mean a better product for the user."

"It's still blackmail in my opinion."

Two white spots had appeared high on Jordan's cheeks, and he glared at Sam. "You're beginning to annoy me, Mr. Kilmartin. I haven't told you everything because I wasn't sure you could be trusted. But if someone in your position hasn't learned to keep his mouth shut by now, then God help American security. So, I'm going to tell you the rest. . . ."

Sam felt a sudden chill move upward on his spine. He stood waiting in silence for Jordan to continue. "Other ramifications are evident," Jordan went on. "The method provides keys that can be used to break down almost any computer security code. I don't have to remind you, Mr. Kilmartin, that satellites, missiles, and communications are almost entirely controlled by computer functions. If you would exercise your mind, you would see that in the wrong hands this method could render the United States virtually defenseless or, worse, turn any offensive capability back on itself."

Talking with Jordan Freeling was a little like having a conversation with an unstable atom bomb, Sam decided. The ten million dollars was indeed beginning to look like small potatoes.

"And what happens if terrorists or some other enemies of the U.S. get hold of you and squeeze the information out of you?" he asked.

"That depends on how good American security is, doesn't it? Any enemies need never know."

Sam thought again of the information in the Zurich police files. He'd have to take care of that right away.

A long silence prevailed in the too-bright, claustrophobic cell. "Am I free to go now?" His voice was hardly audible.

"What?" Sam's thoughts, too, had drifted. "Oh, I guess so. Just walk upstairs. The jailer has instructions to release you."

"Thanks." Jordan stepped toward the door.

"Oh, Jordan . . ." It was the first time Sam had used his name.

"Yes?" He stopped.

"If you happen to think of—that is, devise—some means of preventing computer subversion—I'd appreciate it if you would let us know. Contact me—I'll take care of the details. Here's my card. You have my word there will be no harassment. Uncle Sam comes first. . . ." He stopped. Somehow he couldn't put into words what he wanted to say.

"Are you appealing to my patriotism?"

"Yes, I guess I am." Sam's voice became firmer.

"You don't have to, you know." A smile was playing around Jordan's mouth. "Good-bye, Mr. Kilmartin." And he was gone.

For a while Sam stood unmoving, alone in the sterile

cell. He took out a match and lit the damp stogie. He had to suck hard to get it going and blew out thick, satisfying clouds of smoke. When the cell stank, really stank, he dropped the butt on the polished floor and ground it out with his heel.

He turned. It was time to head for home.